THE LAST HOUSE GUEST

ALSO BY MEGAN MIRANDA

The Perfect Stranger
All the Missing Girls

THE LAST HOUSE GUEST

MEGAN MIRANDA

CORVUS

First published in the United States in 2019 by Simon & Schuster, New York.

First published in trade paperback in Great Britain in 2019 by Corvus, an imprint of Atlantic Books Ltd.

This paperback edition published in 2020.

10 9 8 7 6 5 4 3 2 1

A CIP catalogue record for this book is available from the British Library.

Paperback ISBN: 978 1 78649 293 7
E-book ISBN: 978 1 78649 292 0
OME ISBN: 978 1 83895 066 8

Corvus
An imprint of Atlantic Books Ltd
Ormond House
26–27 Boswell Street
London
WC1N 3JZ

www.corvus-books.co.uk

For Rachel

SUMMER

2017

The Plus-One Party

I almost went back for her. When she didn't show. When she didn't answer her phone. When she didn't reply to my text.

But there were the drinks, and the cars blocking me in, and the responsibility—I was supposed to be keeping an eye on things. I was expected to keep the night running smoothly.

Anyway, she would laugh at me for coming back. Roll her eyes. Say, *I already have one mother, Avery.*

These are excuses, I know.

———

I HAD ARRIVED AT the overlook first.

The party was at the rental on the cul-de-sac this year, a three-bedroom house at the end of a long tree-lined road, barely enough room for two cars to maneuver at the same time. The Lomans had named it Blue Robin, for the pale blue clapboard siding and the way the squared roof looked like the top of a bird feeder.

Though I thought it was more fitting for the way it was set back in the trees, a flash of color as you stepped to the side, something you couldn't really see until you were already upon it.

It wasn't the nicest location or the one with the best view—too far to see the ocean, just close enough to hear—but it was the farthest from the bed-and-breakfast down the road, and the patio was surrounded by tightly packed evergreens, so hopefully, no one would notice or complain.

The Lomans' summer rentals all looked the same on the inside, anyway, so that sometimes I'd leave a walk-through completely disoriented: a porch swing in place of the stone steps; the ocean instead of the mountains. Each home had the same tiled floor, the same shade of granite, the same style of rustic-meets-upscale. And the walls throughout, decorated with scenes of Littleport: the lighthouse, the white masts dancing in the harbor, the foam-crested waves colliding with the sea cliffs on either side. A drowned coast, it was called—fingers of land rising from the ocean, the rocky coastline trying to stand its ground against the surf, islands appearing and vanishing in the distance with the tide.

I got it, I did. Why the long weekend drives from the cities or the temporary relocation for the summer season; why the exclusivity of a place that seemed so small and unassuming. It was a town carved out of the untouched wild, mountains on one side, ocean on the other, accessible only by a single coastal road and patience. It existed through pure stubbornness, pushing back against nature from both sides.

Growing up here made you feel as if you were forged from this same character.

I emptied the box of leftover liquor from the main house onto the granite island, hid away the fragile decorations, turned on the pool lights. Then I poured myself a drink and sat on the back patio, listening to the sounds of the ocean. A chill of autumn wind moved through the trees, and I shivered, pulling my jacket tighter.

This annual party always teetered on the edge of something— one last fight against the turning of the season. Winter settled in the bones here, dark and endless. It was coming, just as soon as the visitors were leaving.

But first there would be this.

Another wave crashed in the distance. I closed my eyes, counting the seconds. Waiting.

We were here tonight to ring out the summer season, but it had already swept out to sea without our permission.

———

LUCIANA ARRIVED JUST AS the party was hitting its momentum. I didn't see her come in, but she stood alone in the kitchen, unsure of herself. She stood out, tall and unmoving in the hub of activity, taking it all in. Her first Plus-One party. So different, I knew, from the parties she'd been attending all summer, her welcome to the world of Summers in Littleport, Maine.

I touched her elbow, still cold somehow. She flinched as she turned my way, then exhaled like she was glad to see me. "This is not exactly what I expected," she said.

She was too done up for the occasion. Hair curled just so, tailored pants, heels. Like she was attending a brunch.

I smiled. "Is Sadie with you?" I looked around the room for the familiar dark blond hair parted down the middle, the thin braids woven from her temples and clipped together at the back, a child from another era. I stood on my toes, trying to tune in to the sound of her laughter.

Luce shook her head, the dark waves slipping over her shoulders. "No, I think she was still packing. Parker dropped me off. Said he wanted to leave the car at the bed-and-breakfast so we could get out easier after." She gestured in the general direction of the Point Bed-and-Breakfast, a converted Victorian eight-bedroom home at the tip of the overlook, complete with multiple turrets and a widow's walk. There, you could almost make out the entirety of Littleport—all the parts that mattered, anyway—from the harbor to the sandy strip of Breaker Beach, its bluffs jutting out into the sea, where the Lomans lived at the northern edge of town.

"He shouldn't park there," I said, phone already in my hand. So much for the owners of the B&B not noticing if people were going to start leaving cars in their lot.

Luce shrugged. Parker Loman did what Parker Loman wanted to do, never worrying about the repercussions.

I held the phone to my ear. I could barely hear the ringing over the music and cupped a hand over the other side.

Hi, you've reached Sadie Loman—

I pressed end, slid the phone back into my pocket, then handed Luce a red plastic cup. "Here," I said. What I really wanted to say was, *My God, take a breath, relax,* but this was already exceeding the typical limits of my conversations with Luciana Suarez. She held the cup tentatively as I moved the half-empty bottles around, looking for the whiskey I knew she preferred. It was one thing I really liked about her.

After I poured, she frowned and said, "Thanks."

"No problem."

A full season together and she still didn't know what to make of me, the woman living in the guesthouse beside her boyfriend's summer home. Friend or foe. Ally or antagonist.

Then she seemed to decide on something, because she leaned a little closer, as if getting ready to share a secret. "I still don't really get it."

I grinned. "You'll see." She'd been questioning the Plus-One party since Parker and Sadie told her about it; told her they wouldn't be leaving with their parents on Labor Day weekend but would be staying until the week after the end of the season for this. One last night for the people who stayed from Memorial Day to Labor Day, the weeks making up the summer season, plus one. Spilling over into the lives of the folks who lived here year-round.

Unlike the parties the Lomans had taken her to all summer, this party would have no caterers, no hostesses, no bartenders. In their place would be an assortment of leftovers from the visitors emptying the liquor cabinets, the fridges, the pantries. Nothing matched. Nothing had a place. It was a night of excess, a long goodbye, nine months to forget and to hope that others had, too.

The Plus-One party was both exclusive and not. There was no guest list. If you heard about it, you were in. The adults with real responsibilities had all gone back to their normal lives by now. The younger kids had returned to school, and their parents had left along with them. So this fell to the midgap. College age and up, before the responsibilities of life kept you back. Until things like this wore you thin.

Tonight circumstances leveled us out, and you couldn't tell just from looking who was a resident and who was a visitor. We pretended that: Strip us down and we're all the same.

Luce checked her fine gold watch twice in as many minutes, twisting it back and forth over the bone of her wrist each time. "God," she said, "he's taking forever."

———

PARKER ARRIVED LAST, HIS gaze seeking us out easily from the doorway. All heads turned his way, as often happened when Parker Loman entered the room. It was the way he carried himself, an aloofness he'd perfected, designed to keep everyone on their toes.

"They're going to notice the car," I said when he joined us.

He leaned down and slipped an arm around Luce. "You worry too much, Avery."

I did, but it was only because he'd never considered how he appeared to the other side—the residents who lived here, who both needed and resented people like him.

"Where's Sadie?" I asked over the music.

"I thought she was getting a ride with you." He shrugged, then looked somewhere over my shoulder. "She told me not to wait for her earlier. Guess that was Sadie-speak for *not coming.*"

I shook my head. Sadie hadn't missed a Plus-One since the first one we'd attended together, the summer we were eighteen.

Earlier in the day, she'd thrown open the door to the guesthouse without knocking, called my name from the front room, then again even as she entered my bedroom, where I sat with the laptop open on the white comforter, in my pajama shorts and long-sleeve thermal with my hair in a bun on top of my head.

She was already dressed for the day, whereas I was catching up on my responsibilities for Grant Loman's property management company, one thread of his massive real estate development firm. Sadie, wearing a blue slip dress and gold strappy sandals, had leaned on her hip so I could see the jut of her bone, and said, *What do we think of this?* The dress clung to every line and curve.

I'd reclined against my pillows, bent my knees, thinking she was going to stay. *You know you'll freeze, right?* I'd said. The temperature had plummeted the last few evenings—a precursor to the abandoning, as the locals called it. In a week, the restaurants and shops along Harbor Drive would change hours, while the landscapers became school maintenance and bus drivers, and the kids who worked as waitresses and deckhands took off for the slopes in New Hampshire to work as ski instructors. The rest of us were accustomed to sucking the summer dry, as if stockpiling water before a drought.

Sadie had rolled her eyes. *I already have one mother,* she'd said, but she'd pieced through my closet and shrugged on a chocolate brown sweater, which had been hers anyway. It turned her outfit the perfect blend of dressy and casual. Effortless. She'd spun toward the door, her fingers restless in the ends of her hair, her energy spilling over.

What else could she have been getting ready for if not this?

Through the open patio doors, I noticed Connor sitting at the edge of the pool, his jeans rolled up and his bare feet dangling in the water, glowing blue from the light below. I almost walked up to him and asked if he'd seen her, but that was only because drinking opened up a sense of nostalgia in me. Even then, I thought better of it. He caught me staring, and I turned away. I hadn't expected to see him here, was all.

I pulled out my phone, sent her a text: *Where are you?*

I was still watching the screen when I saw the dots indicating she was writing a response. Then they stopped, but no message came through.

I sent one more: *???*

No response. I stared at the screen for another minute before slipping the phone away again, assuming she was on her way, despite Parker's claim.

Someone in the kitchen was dancing. Parker tipped his head back and laughed. The magic was happening.

There was a hand on my back, and I closed my eyes, leaning in to it, becoming someone else.

It's how these things go.

———

BY MIDNIGHT, EVERYTHING HAD turned fragmented and hazy, the room thick with heat and laughter despite the open patio doors. Parker caught my gaze over the crowd from just inside the patio exit, tipped his head slightly toward the front door. Warning me.

I followed his eyes. There were two police officers standing in the open doorway, the cold air sobering us as the gust funneled from the entrance out the back doors. Neither man had a hat on, as if they were trying to blend in. I already knew this would fall to me.

The house was in the Lomans' name, but I was listed as the property manager. More important, I was the one expected to navigate the two worlds here, like I belonged to both, when really I was a member of neither.

I recognized the two men but not well enough to pull their names from memory. Without the summer visitors, Littleport had a population of just under three thousand. It was clear they recognized me, too. I'd spent the year between ages eighteen and nineteen in and out of trouble, and the officers were old enough to remember that time.

I didn't wait to hear their complaint. "I'm sorry," I said, making sure my voice was steady and firm. "I'll make sure we keep the noise level down." Already, I was gesturing to no one in particular to lower the volume.

But the officers didn't acknowledge my apology. "We're looking for Parker Loman," the shorter of the two said, scanning the crowd. I turned toward Parker, who had already begun pushing through the crowd in our direction.

"Parker Loman?" the taller officer said when he was within earshot. Of course they knew it was him.

Parker nodded, his back straight. "What can I do for you gentlemen," he said, becoming business Parker even as a piece of dark hair fell into his eyes; the sheen of sweat made his face glow brighter.

"We need to speak with you outside," the taller man said, and Parker, ever the appeaser, knew the line to walk.

"Of course," he said, not moving any closer. "Can you tell me what this is about first?" He also knew when to talk and when to demand a lawyer. He already had his phone in his hand.

"Your sister," the officer said, and the shorter man's gaze slipped to the side. "Sadie." He gestured Parker closer, lowering his voice so I couldn't make out what they were saying, but everything shifted. The way Parker was standing, his expression, the phone hanging limply at his side. I stepped closer, something fluttering in my chest. I caught the end of the exchange. "What was she wearing, last time you saw her?" the officer asked.

Parker narrowed his eyes. "I don't . . ." He looked at the room behind him, seeming to expect that she'd slipped inside without either of us noticing.

I didn't understand the question, but I knew the answer. "A blue dress," I said. "Brown sweater. Gold sandals."

The men in uniform shared a quick look, then stepped aside, allowing me into their group. "Any identifying marks?"

Parker pressed his eyes shut. "Wait," he said, like he could redirect the conversation, alter the inevitable course of events to follow.

"Yes, she does, right?" Luce said. I hadn't noticed her standing there; she was just beyond Parker's shoulder. Her hair was pulled back and her makeup had started to run, faint circles under her eyes. Luce stepped forward, her gaze darting between Parker and me. She nodded, more sure of herself. "A tattoo," she said. "Right here." She pointed to the spot on her own body, just on the inside of her left hip bone. Her finger traced the shape of a figure eight turned on its side—the symbol of infinity.

The cop's jaw tensed, and that was when the bottom fell away in a rush.

We had become temporarily unmoored, small boats in the ocean, and I sensed that seasick feeling I could never quite overcome out on the water at night, despite growing up so close to the coast. A disorienting darkness with no frame of reference.

The taller cop had a hand on Parker's arm. "Your sister was found on Breaker Beach . . ."

The room buzzed, and Luce's hands went to her mouth, but I still wasn't sure what they were saying. What Sadie was doing on Breaker Beach. I pictured her dancing, barefoot. Skinny-dipping in the ice-cold water on a dare. Her face lit up from the glow of a bonfire we'd made from driftwood.

Behind us, half the party continued, but the noise was dropping. The music, cut.

"Call your parents," the officer continued. "We need you to come down to the station."

"No," I said, "she's . . ." *Packing. Getting ready. On her way.* The cop's eyes widened, and he looked down at my hands. They were gripping the edge of his sleeve, my fingertips blanched white.

I released him, backed up a step, bumped into another body. The dots on my phone—she had been writing to me. The cops had to be wrong. I pulled out my phone to check. But my question marks to Sadie remained unacknowledged.

Parker pushed past the men, charging out the front door, disappearing around the back of the house, headed down the path toward the B&B. In the commotion, you couldn't contain us. Luce and I sprinted after him through the trees, eventually catching up in the gravel parking lot, pushing into his car.

The only noise as we drove past the dark storefronts lining Harbor Drive was the periodic hitch in Luce's breath. I leaned closer to the window when we reached the curve leading to Breaker Beach, the lights flashing ahead, the police cars blocking the entrance to the lot. But an officer stood guard behind the dunes, gesturing with a glowing stick for us to drive on by.

Parker didn't even slow down. He took the car up the incline of Landing Lane to the house at the end of the street, standing dark behind the stone-edged drive.

Parker stopped the car and went straight inside—either to check for Sadie, also disbelieving, or to call his parents in privacy. Luce followed him slowly up the front steps, but she looked over her shoulder first, at me.

I stumbled around the corner of the house, my hand on the siding to steady myself, passing the black gate surrounding the pool, heading straight for the cliff path beyond. The path traced the edge of the bluffs until they ended abruptly at the northern tip of Breaker Beach. But there was a set of steps cut into the rock from there, leading down to the sand.

I wanted to see the beach for myself, to believe. See what the police were doing down below. See if Sadie was arguing with them. If we had misunderstood. Even though I knew better by then. This place, it took people from me. And I had grown complacent in forgetting that.

I could hear the crash of the waves colliding with the cliffs to my left, could picture the way the force of the water foamed in the daylight. But everything was dark, and I moved by sound alone. In the distance, the lighthouse beyond the Point flashed periodically as the light circled, and I headed toward it in a daze.

There was movement just ahead in the dark, farther down the cliff path. A flashlight shining in my direction so I had to raise an arm to block my eyes. The shadow of a man walked toward me, his walkie-talkie crackling. "Ma'am, you can't be out here," he said.

The flashlight swung back, and that was when I saw them, a glint caught in the beam of light. I felt the earth tilting.

A familiar pair of gold strappy sandals, kicked off just before the edge of the rocks.

SUMMER

2018

CHAPTER 1

There was a storm offshore at dusk. I could see it coming in the shelf of darker clouds looming near the horizon. Feel it in the wind blowing in from the north, colder than the evening air. I hadn't heard anything in the forecast, but that meant nothing for a summer night in Littleport.

I stepped back from the bluffs, imagined Sadie standing here instead, as I often did. Her blue dress trailing behind her in the wind, her blond hair blowing across her face, her eyes drifting shut. Her toes curled on the edge, a slow shift in weight. The moment—the fulcrum on which her life balanced.

I often imagined the last thing she was writing to me, standing on the edge: *There are things even you don't know.*

I can't do this anymore.

Remember me.

But in the end, the silence was perfectly, tragically Sadie Loman, leaving everyone wanting more.

———

THE LOMANS' SPRAWLING ESTATE had once felt like home, warm and comforting—the stone base, the blue-gray clapboard siding, doors and glass panes trimmed in white, and every window lit up on summer nights, like the house was alive. Reduced now to a dark and hollow shell.

In the winter, it had been easier to pretend: handling the maintenance of the properties around town, coordinating the future bookings, overseeing the new construction. I was accustomed to the stillness of the off-season, the lingering quiet. But the summer bustle, the visitors, the way I was always on call, smile in place, voice accommodating—the house was a stark contrast. An absence you could feel; ghosts in the corner of your vision.

Now each evening I'd walk by on my way to the guest cottage and catch sight of something that made me look twice—a blur of movement. Thinking for an awful, beautiful moment: *Sadie.* But the only thing I ever saw in the darkened windows was my distorted reflection watching back. My own personal haunting.

———

IN THE DAYS AFTER Sadie's death, I remained on the outskirts, coming only when summoned, speaking only when called upon. Everything mattered, and nothing did.

I gave my stilted statement about that night to the two men who knocked on my door the next morning. The detective in charge was the same man who'd found me on the cliffs the night before. His name was Detective Collins, and every pointed question came from him. He wanted to know when I'd last seen Sadie (here in the guesthouse, around noon), whether she'd told me her plans for that night (she hadn't), how she'd been acting that day (like Sadie).

But my answers lagged unnaturally behind, as if some connection had been severed. I could hear myself from a remove as the interview was happening.

You, Luciana, and Parker each arrived at the party separately. How did that go again?

I was there first. Luciana arrived next. Parker arrived last.

Here, a pause. *And Connor Harlow? We heard he was at the party.*

A nod. A gap. *Connor was there, too.*

I told them about the message, showed them my phone, promised she'd been writing to me when all of us were already at the party together. *How many drinks had you had by then?* Detective Collins had asked. And I'd said two, meaning three.

He tore a sheet of lined paper off his notepad, wrote out a list of our names, asked me to fill in the arrival times as well as I could. I estimated Luce's arrival based on the time I'd called Sadie and Parker's on the time I'd sent the text, asking where she was.

Avery Greer—6:40 p.m.

Luciana Suarez—8 p.m.

Parker Loman—8:30 p.m.

Connor Harlow—?

I hadn't seen Connor come in, and I'd frowned at the page. *Connor got there before Parker. I'm not sure when,* I'd said.

Detective Collins had twisted the paper back his way, eyes skimming the list. *That's a big gap between you and the next person.*

I told him I was setting up. Told him the first-timers always came early.

The investigation that followed was tight and to the point, which the Lomans must've appreciated, all things considered. The house had remained dark, since Grant and Bianca were called back in the middle of the night with word of Sadie's death. When the cleaning company and the pool van showed up before Memorial Day—dusting out the cobwebs, shining the counters, opening up the pool—I'd watched from behind the curtains of the guesthouse, thinking maybe the Lomans would be back. They were not ones to linger in sentimentality or uncertainty. They were the type who favored commitment and facts, regardless of which way they bent.

So, the facts, then: There were no signs of foul play. No drugs or alcohol in her system. No inconsistencies in the interviews. It seemed no one had motive to hurt Sadie Loman, nor opportunity. Anyone who had a relationship with her was accounted for at the Plus-One party.

It was hard to simultaneously grieve and reconstruct your own alibi. It was tempting to accuse someone else just to give yourself some space. It would have been so easy. But none of us had done it, and I thought that was a testament to Sadie herself. That none of us could imagine wanting her dead.

The official cause of death was drowning, but there would have been no surviving the fall—the rocks and the current, the force and the cold.

She could've slipped, I told the detectives. This, I had wanted so badly to believe. That there wasn't something I had missed. Some sign that I could trace back, some moment when I could've intervened. But it was the shoes at first that made them think otherwise. A deliberate move. The gold sandals left behind. Like she'd stopped to unstrap them on her way to the edge. A moment of pause before she continued on.

I fought it even as her family accepted it. Sadie was my anchor, my coconspirator, the force that had grounded my life for so many years. If I imagined her jumping, then everything tilted precariously, just as it had that night.

But later that evening, after the interviews, they found the note inside the kitchen garbage can. Possibly swept up in the mess of an emptied pantry, everything laid out on the counters—the result of Luce trying to clean, to bring some order, before Grant and Bianca arrived in the middle of the night. But knowing Sadie, more likely a draft that she had decided against; a commitment to the fact that no words would do.

I hadn't seen the warnings. The cause and effect that had brought Sadie to this moment. But I knew how fast a spiral could grab you, how far the surface could seem from below.

I knew exactly what Littleport could do.

———

I WAS ALONE UP here now.

Still living and working out of the guesthouse.

The inside of the one-bedroom apartment was decorated like a dollhouse version of the main residence, with the same wainscoting and dark wood floors. But the walls were tighter, the ceilings lower, the windows thin enough that you could hear the wind rattle the edges at night. The ocean view was partially obstructed through the trees.

I sat at the desk in the living room, finishing up the last of the paperwork before bed. There had been damage at one of the rentals earlier in the week—a broken flat-screen television, the surface fractured, the whole thing hanging crookedly from the wall; and one shattered ceramic vase below the television. The renters swore it hadn't been them, claiming an intruder while they were out, though nothing was taken, and there was no sign of forced entry.

I'd driven straight over after they called in a panic. Surveyed the scene as they pointed out the damage with trembling hands. A narrow weatherworn house we called Trail's End located on the fringes of downtown, its faded siding and overgrown path to the coastline only adding to its charm. Now the renters pointed to the unlit path and the distance from the neighbors as a lapse in security, the potential for danger.

They promised they had locked up before leaving for the day.

They were sure, implying that the fault lay on my end somehow. The way they kept mentioning this fact—*We locked the doors, we always do*—was enough to keep me from believing them. Or wonder whether they were trying to cover up for something more sinister: an argument, someone throwing the vase, end over end, until it connected with the television.

Well, damage done, either way. It wasn't enough for the company to pursue, especially from a family who'd been coming for the entire month of August the last three years, despite what might be happening within those walls.

I stretched out on the couch, reaching for the remote before heading to my bedroom. I'd gotten into the habit of falling asleep with the television on. The low hum of voices in the next room, beneath the sound of the gently rattling window frame.

I've known enough of loss to accept that grief may lose its sharpness with time, but memory only tightens. Moments replay.

In the silence, all I could hear was Sadie's voice, calling my name as she walked inside. The last time I saw her.

Sometimes, in my memory, she lingers there, in the entrance of my room, like she's waiting for me to notice something.

———

I WOKE TO SILENCE.

It was still dark, but the noise from the television was gone. Nothing but the window rattling as a strong gust blew in from somewhere offshore. I flipped the switch on the bedside table lamp, but nothing happened. The electricity was out again.

It'd been happening more often, always at night, always when I'd have to find a flashlight to reset the fuse in the box beside the garage. It was a concession for living in a town like this. Exclusive, yes. But too far from the city and too susceptible to the surroundings. The infrastructure out on the coast hadn't caught up to the demand, money or not. Most places had backup generators for the winter, just in case; a good storm could knock us off the grid for a week or more. Summer blackouts were the other extreme—too many people, the population tripled in size. Everything stretched too thin. Grid overload.

But as far as I could tell, this was localized—just me. Something an electrician should take a look at, probably.

The sound of the wind outside almost made me decide to wait it out until morning, except the charge on my cell was in the red, and I didn't like the idea of being up here alone, with no power and no phone.

The night was colder than I'd expected as I raced down the path toward the garage, flashlight in hand. The metal door to the fuse box was cold to the touch and slightly ajar. There was a keyhole at the base, but I'd wedged it open myself earlier this month, the first time this happened.

I flipped the master switch and slammed the metal door closed again, making sure it latched this time.

Another gust of wind blew as I turned back, and the sound of a door slamming shut cut through the night, made me freeze. The noise had come from the main residence, on the other side of the garage.

I cycled through the possibilities: a pool chair caught in the wind, a piece of debris colliding with the side of the house. Or something I forgot to secure myself—the back doors left unlatched, maybe.

The lockbox for the spare key was hidden just under the stone overhang of the porch, and my fingers fumbled the code in the dark twice before the lid popped open.

Another gust of wind, another noise, closer this time—the hinges of a gate echoing through the night as I jogged up the steps of the front porch.

I knew something was wrong as soon as I slid the key into the lock—it was already unlocked. The door creaked open, and my hand brushed the wall just inside, connecting with the foyer switch, illuminating the empty space from the chandelier above.

It was then that I saw it. Through the foyer, down the hall at the back of the house. The shadow of a man standing before the glass patio doors, silhouetted in the moonlight.

"Oh," I said, taking a step back just as he took a step closer.

I would know the shape of him anywhere. Parker Loman.

CHAPTER 2

Jesus Christ," I said, my hand fumbling for the rest of the light switches. "You scared me to death. What are you doing here?"

"It's my house," Parker answered. "What are *you* doing here?"

Everything was light then. The open expanse of the downstairs, the vaulted ceilings, the hallway spanning the distance between me and him.

"I heard something." I held up the flashlight as evidence.

He tipped his head to the side, a familiar move, like he was conceding something. His hair had grown in, or else he was styling it differently. But it softened his edges, smoothing out the cheekbones, and for a second, when he turned, I could see the shadow of Sadie in him.

He shifted and she was gone. "I'm surprised you're still here," he said. As if their local business had continued to operate for the past year on momentum alone. I almost answered: *Where else would*

I go? But then he grinned, and I imagined I must've shaken him pretty good, walking in his front door unannounced.

The truth was, I had thought about leaving multiple times. Not just here but the town itself. I'd come to believe there was some toxicity hidden at its core that no one else seemed to notice. But more than the business, more than the job, I had made a life for myself here. I was too tied up in this place.

Still, sometimes I felt that staying was nothing more than a test of endurance bordering on masochism. I wasn't sure what I was trying to prove anymore.

I could feel my heartbeat slowing. "I didn't notice a car," I said, taking in the downstairs, categorizing the changes: two leather bags at the base of the wide staircase, a key ring thrown on the entryway table; an open bottle on the granite island, a mug beside it; and Parker, sleeves of his button-down rolled up and collar loosened like he'd just arrived from work, not sometime in the middle of the night.

"It's in the garage. Just drove up this evening."

I cleared my throat, nodded to his bags. "Is Luce here?" I hadn't heard her name in a while, but Grant kept our conversations focused on the business, and Sadie was no longer here to fill me in on the personal details of the Lomans' lives. There'd been rumors, but that meant nothing. I'd been the subject of plenty of unfounded rumors myself.

Parker stopped at the island, a whole expanse between us, and picked up the mug, taking a long drink. "Just me. We're taking a break," he said.

A break. It was something Sadie would've said, inconsequential and vaguely optimistic. But his grip on the mug, his glance to the side, told me otherwise.

"Well, come on in. Join me for a drink, Avery."

"I have to be at a property early tomorrow," I said. But my

words trailed off with his returning look. He smirked, pulled a second mug out, and poured.

Parker's expression said he knew exactly who I was, and there was no point in pretending. Didn't matter that I was currently overseeing all of the family's properties in Littleport—six summers, and you get to know a person's habits pretty well.

I'd known him longer than that. It was the way of things, if you'd grown up here: the Randolphs, on Hawks Ridge; the Shores, who'd remodeled an old inn at the corner of the town green, then proceeded to have a series of affairs and now shared their massive plot like a child of divorce, never seen at the same time; and the Lomans, who lived up on the bluffs, overlooking all of Littleport, and then expanded, their tendrils spreading out around town until their name was synonymous with summer. The rentals, the family, the parties. The promise of something.

The locals referred to the Lomans' main residence as the Breakers, a subtle jab that once bonded the rest of us together. It was partly a nod to the home's proximity to Breaker Beach and partly an allusion to the Vanderbilt mansion in Newport, a level of wealth even the Lomans couldn't aspire to. Always whispered in jest, a joke everyone was in on but them.

Parker slid the second mug across the surface, liquid sloshing out the side. He was this haphazard only when he was well on his way to drunk. I twisted the mug back and forth on the countertop.

He sighed and turned around, taking in the living room. "God, this place," he said, and then I picked up the drink. Because I hadn't seen him in eleven months, because I knew what he meant: this place. Now. Without Sadie. Their enlarged family photo from years earlier still hung behind the couch. The four of them smiling, all dressed in beige and white, the dunes of Breaker Beach out of focus in the background. I could see the before and after, same as Parker.

He raised his mug, clanked it against mine with enough force to convey this wasn't his first drink, just in case I hadn't been able to tell.

"Hear, hear," he said, frowning. It was what Sadie always said when we were getting ready to go out. Shot glasses in a row, a messy pour—*hear, hear.* Fortifying herself while I was going in the other direction. Glasses tipped back and the burn in my throat, my lips on fire.

I closed my eyes at the first sip, felt the loosening, the warmth. "There, there," I answered quietly, out of habit.

"Well," Parker said, pouring himself half a glass more. "Here we are."

I sat on the stool beside him, nursing my mug. "How long are you staying?" I wondered if this was because of Luce, if they'd been living together and now he needed somewhere to escape.

"Just until the dedication ceremony."

I took another sip, deeper than intended. I'd been avoiding the tribute to Sadie. The memorial was to be a brass bell that didn't work, that would sit at the entrance of Breaker Beach. *For all souls to find their way home,* it would say, the words hand-chiseled. It had been put to a vote.

Littleport was full of memorials, and I'd long since had my fill of them. From the benches that lined the footpaths to the statues of the fishermen in front of the town hall, we were becoming a place in service not only to the visitors but to the dead. My dad had a classroom in the elementary school. My mom, a wall at the gallery on Harbor Drive. A gold plaque for your loss.

I shifted in my seat. "Your parents coming up?"

He shook his head. "Dad's busy. Very busy. And Bee, well, it probably wouldn't be best for her." I'd forgotten this, how Parker and Sadie referred to Bianca as Bee—never to her face, never in her presence. Always in a removed affect, like there was some great distance between them. I thought it an eccentricity of the wealthy. Lord knows, I'd discovered enough of them over the years.

"How are you doing, Parker?"

He twisted in the stool to face me. Like he'd just realized I was there, who I was. His eyes traced the contours of my face.

"Not great," he said, relaxing in his seat. It was the alcohol, I knew, that made him this honest.

Sadie had been my best friend since the summer we met. Her parents had practically taken me in—funding my courses, promising work if I proved myself worthy. I'd been living and working out of their guesthouse for years, ever since Grant Loman had purchased my grandmother's home. And after all this time when we'd occupied the same plane of existence, Parker had rarely made a comment of any depth.

His fingers reached for a section of my hair, tugging gently before letting it drop again. "Your hair is different."

"Oh." I ran my palm down the side, smoothing it back. It had been less an active change and more the path of least resistance. I'd let the highlights grow out over the year, the color back to a deeper brown, and then I'd cut it to my shoulders, keeping the side part. But that was one of the things about seeing people only in the summer—there was nothing gradual about a change. We grew in jolts. We shifted abruptly.

"You look older," he added. And then, "It's not a bad thing."

I could feel my cheeks heating up, and I tipped the mug back to hide it. It was the alcohol, and the nostalgia, and this house. Like everything was always just a moment from bursting. *Summer strung,* Connor used to call it. And it stuck, with or without him.

"We *are* older," I said, which made Parker smile.

"Should we retire to the sitting room, then?" he said, but I couldn't tell whether he was making fun of himself or me.

"Gonna use the bathroom," I said. I needed the time. Parker

had a way of looking at you like you were the only thing in the world worth knowing. Before Luce, I'd seen him use it a dozen times on a dozen different girls. Didn't mean I'd never thought about it.

I walked down the hall to the mudroom and the side door to the outside. The bathroom here had a window over the toilet, uncovered, facing the sea. All of the windows facing the water were left uncovered to the view. As if you could ever forget the ocean's presence. The sand and the salt that seemed to permeate everything here—lodged in the gap between the curb and the street, rusting the cars, the relentless assault on the wooden storefronts along Harbor Drive. I could smell the salt air as I ran my fingers through my hair.

I splashed water on my face, thought I caught a shadow passing underneath the door. I turned off the faucet and stared at the knob, holding my breath, but nothing happened.

Just a figment of my imagination. The hope of a long-ago memory.

It was a quirk of the Loman house that none of the interior doors had locks. I never knew whether this was a design flaw—a trade-off for the smooth antique-style knobs—or whether it was meant to signify an elite status. That you always paused at a closed door to knock. If it inspired in people some sort of restraint; that there would be no secrets here.

Either way, it was the reason I'd met Sadie Loman. Here, in this very room.

———

IT WAS NOT THE first time I'd seen her. This was the summer after graduation, nearly six months after the death of my grandmother. A slick of ice, a concussion followed by a stroke that left me as the last Greer in Littleport.

I had ricocheted through the winter, untethered and dangerous. Graduated through the generosity of makeup assignments and special circumstances. Become equally unpredictable and unreliable in turn. And still there were people like Evelyn, my grandmother's neighbor, hiring me for odd jobs, trying to make sure I got by.

All it did was bring me closer to more of the things I didn't have.

That was the problem with a place like this: Everything was right out in the open, including the life you could never have.

Keep everything in balance, in check, and you could open a storefront selling homemade soap, or run a catering company from the kitchen of the inn. You could make a living, or close to it, out on the sea, if you loved it enough. You could sell ice cream or coffee from a shop that functioned primarily four months of the year, that carried you through. You could have a dream as long as you were willing to give something up for it.

Just as long as you remained invisible, as was intended.

———

EVELYN HAD HIRED ME for the Lomans' Welcome to Summer party. I wore the uniform—black pants, white shirt, hair back — that was meant to make you blend in, become unnoticeable. I was sitting on the closed lid of the toilet, wrapping the base of my hand in toilet paper, silently cursing to myself and trying to stop the blood, when the door swung open and then quietly latched again. Sadie Loman stood there, facing away, with her palms pressed to the door, her head tipped down.

Meet someone alone in a bathroom, hiding, and you know something about her right away.

I cleared my throat, standing abruptly. "Sorry, I'm just . . ." I tried to edge by her, keeping close to the wall as I moved, trying to remain invisible, forgettable.

She made no effort to hide her assessing eyes. "I didn't know anyone was in here," she said. No apology, because Sadie Loman didn't have to apologize to anyone. This was her house.

The pink crept up her neck then, in the way I'd come to know so well. Like I'd been the one to catch her instead. *The curse of the fair-skinned,* she'd explained later. That and the faint freckles across the bridge of her nose made her look younger than her age, which she compensated for in other ways.

"Are you okay?" she asked, frowning at the blood seeping through the toilet paper wrapped around my hand.

"Yeah, I just cut myself." I pressed down harder, but it didn't help. "You?"

"Oh, you know," she said, waving her hand airily around. But I didn't. Not then. I'd come to know it better, the airy wave of her hand: *All this,* the Lomans.

She reached her hand out for mine, gesturing me closer, and there was nothing to do but acquiesce. She unwound the paper, leaning closer, then pressed her lips together. "I hope you have a tetanus shot," she said. "First sign is lockjaw." She clicked her teeth together, like the sound of a bone popping. "Fever. Headaches. Muscle spasms. Until finally you can't swallow or breathe. It's not a quick way to die, is what I'm saying." She raised her hazel eyes to mine. She was so close I could see the line of makeup under her eyes, the slight imperfection where her finger had slipped.

"It was a knife," I said, "in the kitchen." Not a dirty nail. I assumed that was what tetanus was from.

"Oh, well, still. Be careful. Any infection that gets to your bloodstream can lead to sepsis. Also not a good way to go, if we're making a list."

I couldn't tell whether she was serious. But I cracked a smile, and she did the same.

"Studying medicine?" I asked.

She let out a single bite of laughter. "Finance. At least that's the plan. Fascinating, right? The path to death is just a personal interest."

This was before she knew about my parents and the speed at which they did or did not die. Before she could've known it was a thing I often wondered, and so I could forgive her the flippancy with which she discussed death. But the truth was, there was something almost alluring about it—this person who did not know me, who could toss a joke about death my way without flinching after.

"I'm kidding," she said as she ran my hand under the cold water of the sink, the sting numbing. My stomach twisted with a memory I couldn't grasp—a sudden pang of yearning. "This is my favorite place in the world. Nothing bad is allowed to happen here. I forbid it." Then she rummaged through the lower cabinet and pulled out a bandage. Underneath the sink was an assortment of ointments, bandages, sewing kits, and bathroom products.

"Wow, you're prepared for anything here," I said.

"Except voyeurs." She looked up at the uncovered window and briefly smiled. "You're lucky," she said, smoothing out the bandage. "You just missed the vein."

"Oh, there's blood on your sweater," I said, appalled that some part of me had stained her. The perfect sweater over the perfect dress on this perfect summer night. She shrugged off the sweater, balled it up, threw it in the porcelain pail. Something that cost more than what I was getting paid for the entire day, I was sure.

She sneaked out as quietly as she had entered, leaving me there. A chance encounter, I assumed.

But it was just the start. A world had opened up to me from the slip of a blade. A world of untouchable things.

———

NOW, CATCHING SIGHT OF myself in that same mirror, splashing water on my face to cool my cheeks, I could almost hear her low laughter. The look she would give me, knowing her brother and I were alone in a house, drinking, in the middle of the night. I stared at my reflection, the hollows under my eyes, remembering. "Don't do it." I whispered it out loud, to be sure of myself. The act of speaking held me accountable, contained something else within me.

Sometimes it helped to imagine Sadie saying it. Like a bell rattling in my chest, guiding me back.

———

PARKER WAS SPRAWLED ON the couch under the old family portrait, staring out the uncovered windows into the darkness, his gaze unfocused. I didn't know if it was such a good idea to leave him. I was more careful now. Looking for what was hidden under the surface of a word or a gesture.

"You're not going to finish that drink, are you," he said, still staring out the window.

A drop of rain hit the glass, then another—a fork of lightning in the distance, offshore. "I should get back before the storm hits," I said, but he waved me off.

"I can't believe they're having the party again," he said, like it had just occurred to him. "A dedication ceremony and then the Plus-One." He took a drink. "It's just like this place." Then he turned to me. "Are you going?"

"No," I said, as if it had been my own decision. I couldn't tell him that I didn't know anything about any Plus-One party this year, whether it was happening again or where it would be. There were a handful of weeks left in the season, and I hadn't heard a word about it. But he'd been here a matter of hours and already knew.

He nodded once. In the Loman family, there was always a right answer. I had learned quickly that they were not asking questions in order to gather your thoughts but to assess you.

I rinsed out my mug, keeping my distance. "I'll call the cleaners if you're going to be staying."

"Avery, hold up," he said, but I didn't wait to hear what he was going to say.

"Sleep it off, Parker."

He sighed. "Come with me tomorrow."

I froze, my hand on the granite counter. "Come with you where?"

"This meeting with the dedication committee," he said, frowning. "For Sadie. Lunch at Bay Street. I could use a friend there."

A friend. As if that's what we were.

Still. "All right," I said, feeling, for the first time in almost a year, the familiar stirrings of summer. Bay Street sounded like a location selected by Parker, not by the committee. The Lomans had a table there, though technically, Bay Street did not have a reservation system. It sounded like something he would do to make them remember his place, and theirs.

I thought there was a fifty-fifty shot he wouldn't remember this conversation in the morning. Or would regret the invitation, pretend it didn't exist.

But if I'd learned nothing else from the Lomans, I'd at least learned this: Promises made without clarity of thought still counted. A careless *yes* and you were bound.

———

OUTSIDE, IN THE DARK, I could hear the steady patter of rain picking up on the gutters. I ducked my head, ready to make a run for it. But in the beam of the flashlight, I saw what had drawn me here in the first place. The garbage can tucked into the alcove outside the mudroom entrance, tipped over, contents exposed. The gate of the tall white lattice fencing that kept it enclosed now swinging ajar.

I froze, flashlight scanning the trees, the edge of the garage. Another gust blew in with the rain, and the gate creaked once more, knocking against the side of the house.

The wind, then.

I'd fix it in the morning. The sky opened up. The storm was here.

CHAPTER 3

I *was surfacing from a* dream when the phone rang the next morning. It was an old dream: the feel of the rocking of the sea, everything unsteady, like I was inside one of my mother's paintings—stranded in the chaos of the waves outside the harbor, looking in.

The room was spinning when I opened my eyes, my stomach plummeting. It was the liquor in the middle of the night, the lack of sleep. I fumbled for my phone as I glanced at the clock—eight a.m. on the nose. I didn't recognize the number.

"Hello?" I tried to sound like I hadn't been sleeping, but I was still staring up at the ceiling, trying to recover my bearings.

"Ms. Greer?"

I sat upright before responding. *Ms. Greer* meant business, meant the Lomans, meant the type of people who would expect me to be sitting at a desk by this hour instead of cross-legged in bed, tasting stale whiskey. "Yes. Who's speaking?" I replied.

"Kevin Donaldson," he answered, "staying at the Blue Robin. Something happened. Someone's been in here."

"Pardon? Who was there?" I said. I tried to think when I had scheduled the cleaners, whether I'd screwed up the Donaldsons' checkout date. People like this didn't like someone coming and going unannounced when they were away, even me. It was why they stayed in one of our properties instead of a bed-and-breakfast or a hotel suite. I was already heading for my desk tucked away in the living room, opening the folders in a stack beside my laptop until I found the right house.

I had his rental agreement in my hand even as he responded: "We got home late, around midnight. Someone had obviously gone through our things. Nothing was taken, though."

I was running through a list of who had a key. Whether there were any new hires at any of the vendors we used. Whom to call next, which one I'd bet my money on. "I'm so sorry to hear this," I said.

My next question would be: *Did you leave any doors or windows open?* But I didn't want to seem like I was blaming the Donaldsons, especially if nothing had been taken. Still, it would help to know.

"Did you call the police?" I asked.

"Of course. Last night. We tried calling you first, but you didn't answer." *Of course.* They must've tried me when I was at the main house with Parker last night. "Someone came and took our statement, took a quick look around."

I closed my eyes, drawing in a slow breath. Protocol was always to call Grant Loman before involving the cops. A police report at a rental property wasn't good for business.

"Look," he continued, "it doesn't matter that nothing was taken. This is obviously unsettling. We'll be leaving this morning and would like a refund for the rest of our stay. Three days."

"Yes, I understand," I said, fingers to my temple. Even though there were only two days remaining on their contract. Not worth the fight in the service industry, I knew from experience. "I can get that in the mail by this afternoon."

"No, we'd like to pick it up before we go," he said. His tone of voice told me this was not up for debate. I had dealt with his type before. Half my job involved biting my tongue. "We'll be staying at the Point Bed-and-Breakfast for the remainder of the week," he continued. "Where's your office located?"

My office was wherever I happened to be, and I didn't want anyone showing up on the Loman property with a business concern. We handled agreements and finances online, primarily, and I used my P.O. box for anything else. "I will personally deliver it to the Point later this afternoon. The check will be at the front desk before the end of the business day."

———

I TEXTED PARKER SO I could plan my day's schedule, but my message bounced back as undeliverable.

Despite the fact that I'd overslept, the walk-through wasn't scheduled until ten. I had time for a morning run if I kept it short. I could check in with Parker on the way back.

———

THE ONLY EVIDENCE OF the storm last night was the soft give of the earth beneath my feet. The morning was crisp and sunny, the way of Littleport postcards in the downtown shops. These were the days that catered to the tourists, that kept us in business: picturesque, quaint, protected and surrounded in turn by untamable nature.

In truth, the place was wild and brutal and swung to extremes. From the nor'easters that could quickly drop an easy foot of snow and ice, downing half the power lines, to the summer calm with the birds calling, the buoy bell tolling in a rhythm out at sea. From the high-crested waves that could tear a boat from its mooring, to the gentle lapping of the tide against your toes in the beach sand. The quaint bustle to the barren loneliness. A powder keg to a ghost town.

As I passed the garage, I noticed that the garbage can had been fixed, the gate secured. Parker was apparently up and out, unfazed by the late night and the liquor.

I had just set my foot on the first step of their porch when the front door swung open. Parker stopped abruptly, doing a double take.

It was the same look he'd given me the first time he saw me. I'd been sitting in Sadie's room, cross-legged on her ivory bedspread, while she painted our nails a shimmering purple, the vial balanced precariously on her knee between us, nothing but sea and sky behind her through the glass doors of her balcony, blue on blue to the curve of the horizon.

Her hand had hovered in midair at the sound of footsteps coming down the hall, and she'd looked up just as Parker walked by. He was nineteen then, one year older than we were, just finished with his first year of college. But something had stopped him midstride. He'd looked at me, then back at Sadie, and the corner of her mouth had twitched.

"Dad's looking for you," he'd said.

"He's not looking very hard, then." She'd gone back to painting her nails, but he hadn't left the doorway. His eyes flicked to me again, then away, like he didn't want to get caught staring.

Sadie had audibly sighed. "This is Avery. Avery, my brother, Parker."

He was barefoot, in worn jeans, a free advertisement T-shirt. So different than he looked in the carefully staged portrait downstairs. A faint scar bisected the edge of his left eyebrow. I'd waved my hand, and he did the same. Then he took a step back into the hall and continued on.

I'd been looking at the empty hallway when her voice cut through the silence. "Don't," she'd said.

"What?"

She shook her head. "Just don't."

"I won't."

She'd capped the bottle, blowing lightly on her nails. "Seriously. It won't end well."

As if everything that promised to follow would be contingent on this. Her attention, her friendship, this world.

"I said I wouldn't." I was not accustomed to being bossed around, to taking orders. It had been just me and my grandmother since I was fourteen, and she'd been dead six months by then.

Sadie had blinked slowly. "They all say that."

———

PARKER LOMAN HAD GROWN broader in the years since then, more put together, self-assured. He would not falter in the hallway. But I raised my hand, just like I did back then, and he did the same. "Hi. I tried texting you first."

He nodded, continued on down the steps. "Changed my number. Here." He held out his hand for my phone and updated his contact info. I wondered if he'd changed his number because of Luce. Or Sadie. If people called him, friends with condolences, journalists looking for a story, old acquaintances coming out of the woodwork in a tragedy. Whether he needed to cull his list, his world shrinking back to the core and rebuilding—like I had once done.

"What time is the lunch?" I asked.

"It's scheduled for one-thirty. I already added you to the reservation. Want to drive over together?"

I was taken aback, not only that he remembered but that he

was following through. "I've got a few errands to run after, better drive myself."

"All right, see you then." He walked backward a few steps in the direction of the garage. "Off to pick up some groceries. There's nothing in the house. I mean, other than the whiskey." He smirked. "Should I get anything else?"

I'd forgotten how charming he could be, how disarming. "No," I said. "We're good."

"Well," he called, still smiling, "guess I'll let you get to that early appointment."

———

I KEPT TO A familiar path. Taking the incline down Landing Lane, stretching my legs in the process. Reaching the edge of downtown before looping back and ending at Breaker Beach.

August used to be my favorite time of year in Littleport, from both sides of the divide. There was something in the air, a thrumming, the town in perpetual motion. This place was named for the Little family, but everyone here—residents and visitors alike—had adopted the moniker like a mission. Everything must remain minuscule in the town center. Small wooden signs with hand-painted letters, low awnings, narrowed planks. The visitors during the summer sat at small bistro tables with ocean views, and they drank from small flute glasses, speaking in small voices. There were little lights strung from rafters, as if we were all saying to one another: *It's always a holiday here.*

It was an act, and we were all playing.

Step outside the town center, and the act was gone. The summer homes towered two, three stories above the perfectly landscaped yards, perched even higher on cliffsides. Long stone-lined drives, sprawling wraparound porches, portrait-style windows reflecting the sky and the sea. Beautiful, magnificent monstrosities.

I'd grown up closer to the inland edge of town, in a three-bedroom ranch with one room converted to my mother's studio. She'd ripped out the carpeting and pulled off the closet doors, lining the shelves with row after row of paints and dyes. Every room had been painted a bright color except that one, as if she needed a blank and neutral palette just to imagine something more.

Our only view then was of the trees and, beyond that, the boat in the Harlows' driveway. Connor and I used to race the trail behind our homes, startling the hikers as we wove around them, slowing down for nothing.

My grandmother's bungalow, where I'd spent my teenage years, was in an older waterfront community. The scent of turpentine and paint I'd grown accustomed to had been replaced with the sweet sea roses that lined the perimeter of her backyard, mixed with the salt air. Families had lived in the Stone Hollow neighborhood generations gone back, staking their claim before the rising prices and holding it.

I'd known every facet of this place, lived a life in each different quarter. Had believed at one time, wholeheartedly, in its magic.

I stopped running when I hit the sandy strip of Breaker Beach. Hands on knees, catching my breath, sneakers sinking into the sand. Later in the day, the tourists would gather here, soaking up the sun. Kids building sandcastles or running from the tide—the water was too cold, even in the heat of summer.

But for now, I was the only one here.

The sand was damp from the storm last night, and I could see one other set of footprints crossing the beach, ending here, just before the parking lot. I walked across the sand, toward the edge of the cliffs and the rocky steps built in to the side of the bluffs. Here, the footsteps stopped abruptly, as if someone had headed down this path in the other direction, leaving from the house.

I stopped, hand on the cold rocks, a chill rising. Looking at the dunes behind me and imagining someone else there. These prints were recent, not yet washed away by the encroaching tide. That feeling, once more, that I was not alone here.

The power outage last night, the noises in the dark, the footprints this morning.

I shook it off—I always did this, went three steps too far, trying to map things forward and back, so I could see something coming this time. A habit from a time when I could trust only myself and the things I knew to be true.

It was probably Parker out for a run earlier. The call about the second break-in shaking me. The unsteady dream of the sea lingering—the memory of my mother's words in my ear as she worked, telling me to *look again,* to tell her what I saw, even though it always looked exactly the same to me.

It was this place and everything that had happened here— always making me look for something that didn't exist.

This was where Sadie had been found. A call to the police around 10:45 p.m. from a man walking his dog that night. A local who knew the shape of the place. Who saw something in the shadows, a shimmer of blue in the moonlight.

Her leg, caught on the rocks at low tide. The ocean forgetting her in its retreat.

CHAPTER 4

Bay Street meant trying hard without looking like you were trying at all. I pieced through my closet, a collection of my own items and Sadie's hand-me-downs, imagining Sadie taking out an outfit at random, holding it up to my shoulders, the feel of her fingers at my collarbone as she twisted me back and forth, deciding.

At the end of each season, she'd leave me some dresses, or shirts, or bags. Everything thrown on my bed in a heap. Most of it wound up being either too tight or too short, which she declared perfect but also kept me from truly blending in to her circle. Their world was old money that said you didn't have to show it to prove it. The clothes didn't matter; it was the details, the way you carried it, and I could never get it just right.

Even when she dressed like me, she commanded attention.

———

THE WEEKEND AFTER SHE'D found me hiding out in her bathroom, she remembered me. A bonfire and a couple of cars hidden behind the dunes of Breaker Beach at night, the rest of us arriving on foot. Boat coolers repurposed for cheap beer. Matches taken to a pile of rotting driftwood.

It was the silence that made me turn around and see her. A presence I could feel rather than hear. "Hi there," she said, like she'd been waiting for me to notice her. There was a group of us gathered around the fire, but she was speaking just to me. She was shorter than I remembered, or maybe it was because she was barefoot. Her flip-flops hung from her left hand; she wore loose jean shorts fraying at the hem, a hooded sweatshirt zipped up against the night chill. "No tetanus, I see? Or sepsis? Man, I'm good."

I held up my hand to her. "Apparently, I'll live."

She smiled her face-splitting smile, all straight white teeth shining in the moonlight. The light from the flames moved like shadows over her face. "Sadie Loman," she said, holding out her hand.

I half laughed. "I know. I'm Avery."

She looked around, lowered her voice. "I saw the smoke from my backyard and got curious. I'm never invited to these things."

"You're really not missing anything," I said, but that was kind of a lie. These nights on the beach were a freedom for us. A way to claim something. I'd shown up out of habit but immediately regretted it. Everyone was celebrating—graduation, a new life— and for the first time, I had started to wonder what I was doing here. What had brought me here and now what was keeping me here. Beyond the boundaries of this town, there was a directionless, limitless wild, but *anywhere* might as well have been nowhere to someone like me.

My dad had grown up in Littleport—after attending a local college, he'd come back with his teaching degree, as he'd always known he would. My mother had found herself here by accident. She'd driven through on her way up the coast, the backseat of her secondhand car stuffed full of luggage and supplies, everything she owned in the world.

She said there was something about this place that had stopped her. That she was drawn in by something she couldn't let go, something she was chasing. Something I later saw in draft after draft in her studio, hidden away in stacks. I could see it in her face as she was working, shifting her angle, her perspective, and looking again. Like there was some intangible element she couldn't quite grasp.

The beauty of her finished pieces was that you could see not only the image but her intention. This feeling that something was missing, and it pulled you closer, thinking you might be the one to uncover it.

But that was the trick of the place—it lured you in under false pretenses, and then it took everything from you.

Sadie wrinkled her nose at the scene around the bonfire. "It's going to rain, you know?"

I could feel it in the air, the humidity. But the weather had held, and that was half the fun. Like we were daring nature to do something. "Maybe," I said.

"No, it is." And as if she had control over the weather, too, I felt the first drop on my cheek, heavy and chilled. "Want to come back? We can make it if we run."

I looked at the group of kids I'd gone to school with. Everyone casting glances my way. Connor sitting on a nearby log, doing his best to pretend I didn't exist. I wanted to scream—my world shrinking as I watched. And this feeling I couldn't shake recently, that all along I had just been passing through.

"You know, there's a shortcut." I pointed to the steps cut into the rocks, though from where we stood, you couldn't make them out.

She raised an eyebrow, and I never figured out whether she'd known about the steps from the start or I'd opened up something new for her that night. But when I walked over to the steps, she followed, her hands gripping the rock holds after me. The rain started falling when we were on top of the bluffs, and I could see the commotion below in the glow of the bonfire—the shadows of people picking up coolers, running for the cars.

Sadie had a hand at my elbow as she took a step back. "Don't hurt yourself," she said.

"What?"

In the moonlight, I could only see her eyes clearly—large and unblinking. "We're close to the edge," she said. She peered to the side, and I followed her gaze, though it was only darkness below.

We weren't that close—not close enough where a misstep could be fatal—but I stepped back anyway. She gripped my wrist as we ran for the shelter of her backyard, laughing. We collapsed onto the couch just under the overhang of the patio, the pool lit up before us, the ocean beyond. The windows were dark behind us, and she slipped inside briefly, returning with a bottle of some expensive-looking liquor. I didn't even know what kind.

The perimeter of their yard was lit up in an amber glow, hidden lights around the black pool gate, so we could see the rain falling in a curtain, like it was separating here from there. "Welcome to the Breakers," she said, placing her sandy feet up on the woven table in front of us. As if she had forgotten that I'd been working a party here just the week earlier.

I stared at the side of her face, so I could see the corner of her lip curled up in a knowing smile. "What?" she said, facing me. "Isn't that what you call this place?"

I blinked slowly. I thought maybe this was the key to success: eternal optimism. Taking an insult and repurposing it for your own benefit. Taking everything, even this, and owning it. Looking again and seeing something new. And I felt, in that moment, completely sure of one single truth: My mother would love her.

"Yes," I said, "it's just—I've already been here before."

Her smile grew until it reached her eyes, and her head tipped back slightly, almost like she was laughing. I felt her looking me over closely. If she recognized the sweater I was wearing, she didn't say.

She raised the bottle toward me, then toward the ocean. "Hear, hear," she said, tipping the bottle back, wiping her hand across her lips after.

I thought of Connor down at the beach, ignoring me. My grandmother's empty house waiting for me. The silence, the silence.

I took a long drink, my mouth on the cool glass, the edges of my nerves on fire. "There, there," I said, and she laughed.

We drank it straight, watching the lightning offshore, close enough to spark something in the atmosphere. I felt like a live wire. Her fingers closed over mine as she reached for the bottle, and then I was grounded.

———

I IGNORED SADIE'S CLOTHES hanging in my closet, settling for my own business attire—dress pants and a white sleeveless blouse—because I couldn't stomach the thought of Parker seeing me in his sister's clothes.

I arrived at Bay Street first, because I was always early. A vestigial fear ever since I started working for Grant Loman, that he could fire me for any reason and all of this would be over.

When her parents first met me, I'd arrived as a series of failures: something Sadie had found on the beach and would hopefully get over just as quickly. They all must've thought I was a phase Sadie would outgrow. A finely tuned, controlled rebellion.

She'd sprung the meeting on me with no time to either prepare or back out. "I told them I was bringing a friend to dinner," she said as we walked up the front steps later that first week.

"Oh, no, I don't—"

"Please. They'll love you." She paused, cracked a smile. "They'll *like* you," she amended.

"Or vaguely tolerate me for your benefit?"

"Oh, it wouldn't be for my benefit. Come on, it's just dinner. Please, save me from the monotony." That airy wave of her hand again. *All this. My life.*

"I don't know anything about them," I said, even though that wasn't true.

She stopped just before the front door. "All you really need to know is that my dad is the brains of the operation, and my mom is the brawn." I'd laughed, thinking she was joking. Bianca was petite, slight, with a childlike pitch to her voice. But Sadie just raised an eyebrow. "My dad said it wasn't safe to build up here. And yet," she said, gesturing as she pushed open the front door, "here we are. *And* she runs the family charitable foundation." Her voice had dropped to a whisper then, while I was desperately trying to take everything in. "All must worship at the shrine of Bianca Loman."

"Sadie?" A woman's voice echoed from somewhere out of sight. "Is that you?"

"Here we go," Sadie mumbled, nudging my hip with hers.

I came to understand that this was what the flourish of her hand always meant—the mother, Bianca. Grant had only one mood, stable and unrelenting, but at least it was predictable. From him, I learned what power truly was. Bianca could lull you into complacency with her praise, only to strike when your guard was down. But anyone could take someone down; even I could do that. To hoist someone out of one world and into another—that was true power.

That first dinner, I copied Sadie's every movement, sitting

quietly, hoping to slide in. But I noticed their jaws tensing as the list of offenses mounted: no college on the horizon; no career plan; no future.

Sadie won them over for me, in small doses, in her way. I was a project. By the end of that summer, her father had offered me a stipend to take some business courses nearby, an investment in the future, he said. The next, they purchased my grandmother's house, letting me stay at their guesthouse as part of the trade. A taste of what it meant to be Sadie Loman.

———

EVENTUALLY, I WAS WORKING full-time for Loman Properties, managing and overseeing all of their assets in Littleport while they were away. I had worked my way up, had proved myself.

But it was hard to shake the sort of paranoia that comes from the doorbell ringing twice in the middle of the night, long after my parents should've been home, when I expected to open the door to my mother rifling through her purse, laughing, pushing the dark hair from her eyes—*I lost the keys again*—and my dad's sly smile as he watched her, shaking his head. Only to reveal police officers on the front porch instead.

So I was always early—for a meeting, a walk-through, a phone call. Falsely believing I was in a position to see something coming head-on this time.

"Reservation for Parker Loman," I told the hostess. There was always a thrill in giving the Loman name, watching the subtle shift in an expression, the quick accommodation. She smiled as she led me to the table, in service to something greater than me.

I sat with my back to the wall, facing the open room and the windows overlooking the dock and the harbor beyond, from one story above ground level. But I froze a few moments later when Detective Collins was led by the same hostess in my direction.

A flip of her hair as she gestured to my table, and my stomach dropped. His smile fractured for just a second when he saw me, but I had composed my face by the time he sat down. "Hi, Avery, I didn't realize you'd be joining us," he said.

The napkin was bunched together in my lap, and I slowly released my grip. "Didn't realize you were a member of this committee, either, Detective." But it made sense; had I given it much thought at all, I probably would have landed on his name.

"Ben, please," he said.

Along with Justine McCann, the town commissioner, Detective Ben Collins organized and hosted most public relations events in town, from the kids' parade on July Fourth to the Founder's Day festivities on Harbor Drive. He was the man whom I'd seen on the cliffs that night. Who had shone his flashlight in my face, blinding me with the light. And he was the man who had interviewed me, after. Who wanted to know everything about the party and why I'd been back at the edge of the cliffs.

He was considered traditionally handsome—broad-shouldered, strong-jawed, bright-eyed, just beginning to show the signs of age, which somehow seemed to heighten his appeal with others, but I could only ever see him in negative space. Always, as on that night, with a beam of light cutting him into horrific angles.

"Well," he said, taking a sip of his water, "it's good to see you. Been a while. Where've you been staying these days?"

I didn't answer, pretending to look over the menu. "Good to see you, too," I said.

It was hard to know where small talk ended and interrogation began. Before they'd found Sadie's note, he'd sat across from me at my kitchen table and picked through my story of that night over and over. As if he'd heard something in my initial statement that had struck him as off.

Who were you with? Why did you call her? Text her? And here, he would always stop: *But you didn't go back for her?*

It was rapid-fire and brutal, so that sometimes I couldn't tell whether I was pulling a memory of that night or just of what I'd told him last.

Who else was there? Did you know she was seeing Connor Harlow?

"I'm glad you're here," he said. "Truth is, I was getting ready to call you this afternoon."

I held my breath, waiting. That list of names he'd given me, I'd realized, was a way to find a hole in someone's story. To shake out the truth. So when he'd stood to take a call during the interview, and his partner had turned away, I'd snapped a photo of that list with my phone, trying to see what they saw. It was all for nothing, though. They found Sadie's note the same day, and none of it mattered anymore. But sitting across from him now, I half expected him to pick at a detail again, searching for a discrepancy.

"Heard there was some trouble at one of the properties last night," he said.

"Oh, yes." I shook my head. "Nothing was taken."

He smoothed the tablecloth in front of him. "The tenants were spooked pretty good."

My head darted up. "You were there?"

He nodded. "I took the call. Walked in, looked around, made them feel safe."

"Why didn't you call me last night?" My only missed call had been from the Donaldsons.

"Wasn't worth waking anyone up over," he said. "Honestly, I couldn't see any evidence that someone else had been there."

"Well," I said, my shoulders relaxing, "we're not going to be filing a claim either way. The tenants decided to leave. No need to write up a report."

He watched me carefully for a long beat of silence. "I know how to do my job, Avery."

I looked away, that same feeling taking root again. Like there was something he was searching for, hidden underneath my words.

"Oh, there's Parker," I said, watching him enter the room with Justine McCann and another woman. When they got closer, I recognized the third person but couldn't put a name to the face. She looked about my age, light brown hair in a French braid, red-rimmed glasses that perfectly matched her lipstick.

Parker leaned down and air-kissed my cheek, which was surprising. "Sorry if you've been waiting long," he said.

"Not at all."

He shook the detective's hand and finished up introductions. "Justine, you know Avery Greer?"

"Of course," Justine answered, polite smile. She was the oldest person in our group by at least two decades, and she commanded attention with that fact alone. "Glad you could join us, Avery. This is my assistant, Erica Hopkins."

"Actually, we've met before," Erica said, her hands curled on the back of a chair. "You and your grandmother used to live next door to my aunt. Evelyn?"

"Right. Yes. Hi." That was how I recognized her. Erica Hopkins hadn't gone to school with us, but she'd visited her aunt in the summers. I hadn't seen her in years, though.

She smiled tightly. "Nice to see you again."

"How are your parents, Parker?" Detective Collins asked as they took their seats around the circular table.

"All right." Parker ran a hand through his hair, his thumb down the side of his face. A nervous habit, scratching the faint shadow of a beard. "They'll make it up for the dedication after all."

"That's wonderful," Justine said, hands clasped together. As if we could pull a positive out of this. A tribute to a dead girl. A visit from her grieving parents, who had wanted to blame this whole thing on the people in town. I didn't even realize I was shaking my head until I noticed the detective looking at me curiously.

"A few requests, though," Parker added, rubbing his hands against his pants under the table. I watched as he became business Parker. Readjusting the sleeves of his button-down, a warning of what was to come. It would be easy to attribute his position to nepotism alone, but I had to concede that he was startlingly effective, making us all believe we were on the same side, wanting the same thing—and he knew just what we needed.

Eventually, I zoned out as they discussed the press for the Lomans' new foundation. A suicide-prevention community outreach program, dedicated to providing mental health services and screenings. I knew all about it already, had read the pieces, the public interest stories. Sadie's death had somehow only made the Lomans more interesting, more worthy. As if they had been humanized by tragedy. Leveled by Sadie's death and slowly emerging once more, re-formed from the ashes of their lives. The whole thing was nauseating.

I focused on the lobster salad that had been served to the entire table, light and satisfying, trying to recall the last time I'd joined the Lomans here.

I remembered in a sudden jolt: Sadie's birthday. Late July of last year. Her parents and Parker and Luce and me. She'd been unfocused. Jumpy. She'd recently changed roles at her job. I'd thought she was preoccupied. *Distant and detached,* was how the police described it after. As if this was the first sign we had missed.

"Avery?" Parker was looking at me like he'd just asked me a question. "Will you handle the newspaper piece? Find the right photo?"

"Of course," I said. And then I understood my role. Justine had brought her assistant, and Parker had brought his. I was an employee of the Lomans, a set piece, a show of clout. I'd even dressed the part.

"I'll be in touch soon," Erica said as we stepped outside, handing me her card. She walked down the wooden steps before the rest of us. When she reached the car, she stared back up, but I couldn't read her expression.

I could only imagine what Evelyn had told her.

———

PARKER STOOD BESIDE ME as the others drove away. He touched my shoulder, and I flinched.

"Are you upset? Avery, I'm sorry. My parents sent me here, thinking I could handle this. But I can't. I really need your help with this."

I crossed the street to my car, wedged between two expensive SUVs, and he matched me stride for stride. "Jesus, Parker. A little heads-up next time? Also, I didn't realize Detective Collins would be part of this. God."

He put a hand on the roof of my car, leaning over me. "I know. I know it isn't easy."

I was guessing he didn't. By the time Parker had given his statement, the family lawyer was with him. His father was probably in the room as well, overseeing everything. Parker was the victim's brother and was treated accordingly. I was a product of Littleport, a piece severely out of place, and Detective Collins didn't trust me from the start.

Can anyone vouch for you the entire time, Avery?

Parker, Luce, there was a houseful of people. They saw me. I was there.

You could've left. They can't account for every single moment.

But I didn't. And I told you, she was messaging me. She was fine.

What about Connor Harlow?

What about him?

Would you know his state of mind last night?

I wouldn't know anything. Me and Connor don't speak anymore.

"It would mean a lot," Parker said, "if you would help me here." Changing tactics to get me on his side.

"I thought you said your parents weren't coming up for the dedication," I said, unable to hide the accusation in my voice.

He looked down at his phone, sending a message. "Well, it's not definite. They probably won't." Half paying attention. Half caring. "But better if the others think that. It'll make everything easier." Parker always told people what they wanted to hear, and I couldn't tell which of us he was playing right then.

His lies, either then or now, so effortless.

As, I had believed, their entire lives had been.

CHAPTER 5

When *I stepped inside* the Point Bed-and-Breakfast, Mr. Sylva smiled politely. In the summer, we kept our faces calm and predictable, a mask, part of the endless charade. Mr. Sylva gave no indication that when we were kids, Faith and I once raced these hallways, our bare feet stomping in time to our laughter, while he called after us, *Girls! Be careful!* Or that years later, he'd had to call the police to remove me from the premises.

"Good afternoon," he said. Faith's father had the look of a fisherman, with a weathered tan and hands gnarled not from hauling in lobster crates but from carpentry, not that anyone could tell the difference. The Sylvas all looked like they were one with the Maine coast, part of the product. Though Mrs. Sylva's hair had gone gray at her temples last I'd seen, the rest was still a fiery red. And the lines around her face were deeply grooved, like she'd spent years on the balcony, watching the ocean, facing the wind. Faith's hair was closer to auburn, but it was curly and wild and she never bothered to tame it—perfectly Faith. Whatever they were advertising, people were buying, judging from the looks of the place.

I walked straight to the large oak reception desk in the two-story foyer, placing the envelope on the surface, my scrawling script on the front: *Kevin Donaldson*. "Hi, Mr. Sylva. I believe the Donaldson family was scheduled to check in sometime today? Would you mind passing this along?"

The doors opened from the kitchen entrance behind the desk, and Faith froze in her steps, the doors swaying behind her. "Oh. I didn't know anyone was out here." She cleared her throat, obvious that by *anyone,* she meant me.

"Hi, Faith. Welcome back." Her loose T-shirt hung from one shoulder, so I could see the jut of her collarbone. Black leggings and black slip-ons and her hair in a ponytail. At a quick glance, she could still be that girl sneaking into the kitchen for a midnight snack during weekend sleepovers, who roamed the property bare-foot both inside and out with a literal spring to her step—like she was waiting for the starting gun. But she'd gotten skinnier since I'd seen her last. From the way she was looking me over, she was probably assessing the changes in me, too.

"Thanks." She quickly pivoted toward the front desk. "Mom needs the numbers for lunch when you get a chance."

Mr. Sylva nodded, and Faith disappeared behind the swinging doors once more. I'd heard she'd finished her graduate program, moved back, and was poised to take over the bed-and-breakfast as soon as her parents retired.

"Must be nice to have her home again," I said.

"It is. You'll have to stop by to visit and catch up sometime when she's not so busy."

"Definitely." Pleasantries. He didn't mean them, and neither did I.

Footsteps echoed from the hall above, and I looked up on instinct, catching nothing but shadows at the top of the curved double staircase.

The main house was enormous and had expanded steadily with time; I used to think it was a castle. There were arched doorways, hidden window seats, closets within closets. A wooden rail along the cliffs out back made of raw lumber. Balconies looming dangerously close to the edge of the overlook, saltwater mist perpetually coating the railings. Faith had lived there, too, up on the top floor, a converted attic space where we all passed around a bottle for the first time in middle school.

For a second I remembered Connor as he was back then, how he could never seem to stand still. How he could disappear while you were turned away, only to walk in the door just when you noticed he was gone. This feeling that he was living an entire second life in the pause, while the rest of us were stuck in slow motion.

Mr. Sylva's gaze followed mine to the staircase landing, and as the footsteps retreated, he leaned closer, lowering his voice. "The Donaldsons have already settled in. Seemed a bit shaken, to be honest. What happened up there, Avery?" He jutted his chin to the side, in the direction of the rentals on the overlook. They were within walking distance, though not plainly in sight.

"Don't know," I said, peering up at the empty, shadowed hall once more. "I'm off to take a look."

————

THE DONALDSON FAMILY HAD been staying at the Blue Robin, the location of the last Plus-One party. This wasn't the first time I'd been back since then, but I never lingered for long. I kept my walk-throughs brief and efficient between visitors. There was too much, otherwise, to remind me.

This wasn't the scene of Sadie's demise, so the police had left it well enough alone. But it would always be the place I'd been the last time I could imagine her alive. Where I was waiting for her final message, the last thing she wanted to tell me:

No one understands.

I'll miss you.

Forgive me.

I would never know exactly what she had wanted to say. Though the police had tried to find her phone, the GPS had been deactivated for as long as I'd known her—a leftover suspicion from her teen years that her parents were tracking her, watching her every move. The phone had been offline when the police tried to reach it, most likely lost to the sea when she jumped.

There was a path that wove through the trees from the B&B to the overlook, passing right behind the Blue Robin. I could take my car just as easily, looping back down the drive to the next turnoff, but I didn't want to alert anyone that I was coming; I didn't want anyone to notice my car and ask what was going on.

I walked the same path I'd raced down nearly a year earlier, following Parker and Luce. Racing toward something we had no ability to stop. In hindsight, I knew that Parker shouldn't have been driving. None of us should have. The night had blurred edges, as parties often did for me. Bits and pieces came back to me in surprising flashes during the questioning, morphing into a stilted time line of things I had said or done, seen or heard.

Standing on the front porch now, I could almost feel the people on the other side—the heat, the laughter—before everything had turned.

The Donaldsons had followed protocol, leaving the house key in an envelope inside the mail drop beside the front door. Not the most secure method, I knew, but it was all part of the act. Part of the story we told about this place. There were a lot of obvious dangers in Littleport, despite the claims we made to the contrary for the tourists. *A safe place,* we told them, and technically, if you looked at the crime statistics, that was true.

But there were other dangers. A car on a dark, winding road. A slick of ice on the sidewalk. The edge of the cliffs, the current, the rocks.

The mountains and the water; the cold in the winter; the complacency of the summer.

The near-misses that were never reported: the hikers who went missing (found two days later), the woman who fell into a gorge (she managed to call for help, but she was lucky she had her phone), the kayakers who got pulled in by the lobstermen, one after the other, all season long, misjudging the current and panicking.

And there were more, the ones we pretended didn't exist.

The house still smelled of breakfast when I stepped inside. They'd left their dishes in the sink, soaking in the water, even though they were supposed to load up the dishwasher before the cleaning company came in.

I couldn't see it at first, the signs of someone else, like Detective Collins had said. The chairs off center in the dining room, probably from the Donaldson family. Same with the dirty fingerprints on the surfaces and the corner of the living room rug, flipped up and inverted.

But then the smaller details came into focus: The upside-down cushion on a couch, like someone had removed the cushions and replaced this one the wrong way. The legs of the dining room table no longer lining up with the indentations on the throw rug beneath. I didn't think the Donaldsons would've had any cause to rearrange the furniture.

I circled the house, running my fingers along the windowsills, the door frames, checking the locks. Everything seemed secure. I stopped at the second window facing the back, a little sleeker than all the others. It had been replaced sometime after the Plus-One party, because there was a spiderweb of cracks running through it. An accident the night of the party, the risks of inviting a cross section of the population into your home.

I had ordered the replacement window myself. Now I ran my fingers around the edges, slightly thinner, with a sleeker lock. It was in the locked position. But it was a newer model than the other windows, the latch so narrow I wasn't sure it fit properly. I lifted from the base, and the glass slid up with no resistance, lock or not. I cursed to myself. At least I didn't have to worry about someone with a key.

In the meantime, I needed to confirm that nothing of ours had been taken; we didn't use much of value to decorate the rentals, but best to do a quick check anyway. With the way the cushions were turned up, it seemed like whoever had been in here was looking for hidden valuables. In a place without a safe, that's what the guests are known to do: Put laptops between the mattress and box spring. Leave jewelry in the bottom of drawers, stowed under clothes.

The door to the master bedroom at the end of the hall was closed, but I figured that was where anything of value would've been hidden—where someone would've gone looking.

As soon as I opened the door, I got a whiff of sea salt and lavender. A candle left burning on the white wooden dresser. Forgotten when the Donaldsons checked out. There weren't any rules expressly forbidding it, but it made me second-guess having candles in the house. I blew out the flame, the wisp of black smoke curling in front of the mirror before disappearing.

The drawers had each been emptied of any clothes inside, and there was nothing left behind on the bathroom surfaces. The queen-size bed was unmade, with just the white quilt crumpled at the base. I opened the chest at the foot of the bed, where we kept extra blankets, and the scent reminded me of my grandmother's old attic, stale and earthy. A spider scurried across the top blanket, and I jumped back, goose bumps forming on my arms. These blankets had probably remained untouched all season. They needed to be run through the wash, the entire chest cleaned out with furniture polish and a vacuum—there was one last family scheduled for next week.

I scooped out the stack of blankets and quilts, holding my breath, and something caught my eye in the bottom corner.

It was a phone. At first I assumed it had been left behind by the Donaldsons, hidden away just like I would've done. But the front screen was cracked in the upper-left corner, and it appeared dead, probably lost and forgotten by a family who'd been here earlier in the season. I went to slip it into my pocket, but a streak of red on the corner of the simple black case caught my eye. Nail polish, I knew. From the beginning of last summer, when she'd been texting before her nails were dry.

Attempting to wipe it off had only made it worse. *Gives it character,* she said.

I sat on the edge of the bed, my hand shaking.

I knew I was holding Sadie Loman's phone in my hand.

SUMMER

2017

The Plus-One Party

9:00 p.m.

This was a mistake.

I stood on the front porch of the Blue Robin, watching as people emerged from the surrounding trees in groups of two and three, carrying drinks, laughing. Traipsing through the wooded lots from their cars, some not bothering with the front door, coming in through the patio instead. I hoped the sound of us would get swallowed up by the sea.

The party was supposed to be at the Lomans' house this year, but Sadie was dead set against it. She and Parker had been arguing about it, Parker saying it was only fair, as if he were accustomed to playing by the rules, and Sadie appealing to his sense of control: *You really want them in our house? Going through our things? In our* rooms. *Come on, you know how it can get.*

Parker had tried to address each point, which was how he worked, in business and in life: *So, Avery can help keep an eye on things. So, we'll make the bedrooms off-limits.*

Oh? she had said, her eyes wide and mocking. *There are no locks, so how are you planning to enforce that, exactly? With a barricade of furniture? Are you going to* fight *them if they disobey?*

You're being ridiculous, Parker had said, turning away, which was the wrong move.

I felt my shoulders tensing as Sadie sucked in a breath, leaned toward him. *Fine. You* go ahead and tell Dad his desk was defaced by a drunken local. *You* can tell Bee someone vomited in her kitchen.

He laughed. *Jesus, no one's going to deface a fucking desk, Sadie. Stop acting like everyone's trash. And really,* he said, eyes leveling on her, *nothing worse than you've already done.*

It was then that I stepped in. *We could have it at one of the rentals,* I said. *Both of the homes on the overlook will be vacant that week.*

Sadie nodded, her face visibly relaxing, fists unclenching. I could see the idea taking hold in Parker, his jaw shifting around as he mulled it over. *Sunset Retreat,* he said, *it has more space.*

But I shook my head. No one knew these properties better than I did. *No,* I said, *the Blue Robin has more privacy. No one will notice us there.*

———

BUT NOW, STANDING ON the front porch while the party hit full swing, I wasn't so sure about that. Cars lined the street in both directions, which was probably some fire code violation with the lack of street space left behind. I craned my neck to see my car, which I'd parked at the edge of the short driveway of Sunset Retreat across the way, facing out, to keep other cars off the property. Someone had already blocked me in, parking on an angle directly in front of the entrance to the drive.

Between the trees and the dark, I couldn't even see how far the line of cars stretched. There were no streetlights up here yet—just the porch light above me and the occasional headlight shining down the stretch of pavement whenever a car turned in.

"Everything okay?" Parker stood behind me in the open doorway. He frowned, peering over my shoulder into the darkness.

"Yes, everything's fine." There was a list of things I could worry about: the number of people who were still arriving, the amount of liquor, the fact that, though I'd removed the fragile decorations, I had not thought to pull out the throw rugs from under the furniture, and those would be harder to replace.

But tonight I did not have to be myself. Tonight was for forgetting.

———

I FOLLOWED PARKER INSIDE, lost him in the mass of bodies in the kitchen. Found myself in the middle of a familiar game.

The music had turned, something frenetic, and no one was dancing or swaying to the beat. But there was a group hovering around the island, a cluster of shot glasses on the surface between them.

I wedged my way into the group. "Hear, hear," I said, picking one up, smiling.

"Just in time," the man beside me said. I recognized him vaguely, but he was a little younger, and I'd long since given up memorizing the names of the newer visitors. "I was just about to tell everyone about Greg and Carys Fontaine," he continued.

Greg slammed his glass down, mouth agape.

"Don't try to deny it," the other man said, wide smile. "I saw you. Down at the Fold."

Greg shook his head and smiled then, before downing the next shot. Moving on.

It was a purging of secrets, of trysts and regrets. A game with no rules and no exit strategy but to drink some more. A secret told or one exposed, and you would drink. And then later, you would make some new ones.

Round and round they went. I barely recognized the bulk of the names by now.

Six years earlier, Sadie and I had stood side by side at a table much like this one, at my very first Plus-One party. We had slipped into an easy comfort after that day at the beach, spent the months that followed in a way that felt both inevitable and unsustainable, and the Plus-One was the perfect way to see it out.

One of Parker's friends had leveled his finger at Sadie's face and announced, *You've been at my house. With my brother.* The red had crept up her neck, but instead of pulling back, she leaned in to it. *You're right, I have. Can you blame me? I mean, look, I'm blushing right now, just thinking about it.*

It made her bolder, the way she wore her embarrassment on her skin. She said there was no use hiding from herself when her face already gave everything away.

I watched the friend's eyes trail after her the rest of the night. The thing about her back then was she was skinny in a childish way. Easy to overlook in a group photo. But even then she could have you in her thrall, quick as that.

Looking back, this was the thing I was most taken with—the idea that you didn't have to apologize. Not for what you'd done and not for who you were. Of all the promises that had been opened up to me that first summer, this was the most intoxicating of all.

"Hey," Greg said, looking around the room, his slack expression landing back on me. "Where's Sadie?"

Greg Randolph, I knew from six years circling this world. From the secrets Sadie would share, the way she could sum everyone up in a sentence fragment. His home, in a mountain enclave called Hawks Ridge, was almost as stunning as the Lomans'. But the thing I remembered most clearly about her assessment of Greg

Randolph was the first thing she'd ever said of him: *A mean drunk, like his father.* He used to be broad and muscular but was currently sliding toward soft, the edges of his face losing definition; dark slicked-back hair, a tan across the bridge of his nose that bordered on a burn. Over the years, he had not been quiet in his pursuit of Sadie, and she had not been quiet in her resounding rejection.

Since we were purging the truth here, I didn't hold back. "On her way," I said, "but still not interested in seeing you."

There was muffled laughter around the island, but no one drank, and Greg's dark eyebrows shot up—a quick burst of anger that he couldn't hide. But he recovered quickly, his lips stretching into a knowing smile. "Oh, I'm fully aware. Last I saw your friend Sadie, she was getting off a boat with that local guy I just saw." He jutted his chin toward the patio, but I didn't see whom he meant. "It was just the two of them at sunset. Never thought she'd go for that sort of thing, but what do I know. Figured it was my turn to share. A shame for her to miss it."

I frowned, and the man beside Greg said, "The one from the yacht club?"

Greg laughed. "No, no, nothing like that. The guy who runs the fishing charters, you know?"

Connor. He had to be talking about Connor. In truth, Connor did a lot more than that. He practically ran the day-to-day of his parents' distribution company. Handled the books, took shipments from the docks, made sure the day's catch made it to every restaurant in town, big or small. Brought the visitors out on charters during his downtime, after. But that wasn't his main job.

"I'm surprised you didn't know," Greg said, and I hated that he could read it in my face. He smiled, but my head was spinning. Connor. Sadie and Connor. It didn't make sense, but that must've been why he was here tonight. Greg gestured to the next shot glass. "You gonna take this one for her?"

I pushed the glass closer to him. "Pass," I said, going for indifference, channeling the way Sadie would shake him off.

"While we're chatting," Greg said, leaning an elbow on the island, sticky with alcohol, "I was wondering. Well, we were *all* sort of wondering. What is it that you do for the Lomans, exactly?"

He was so close, I could feel his breath on the exhale, sharp and sour. I recoiled on impulse from the stench, though he smiled wider, wrongly assuming he'd struck a nerve. I'd heard the rumors. That I was Grant's mistress. Or Bianca's. That I was in service to something dark and secret, something they tried to cover up by planting me right out in the open. As if the idea of generosity, of friendship, of a family that extended beyond the circumstances of your birth, was something too hard to fathom.

Jealousy, Sadie would say. *An ugly, ugly thing.* And then: *Don't worry, we're the Breakers. They have to hate us.*

"This isn't how the game goes," I said. Because I knew that defense only redoubled their curiosity.

Greg leaned toward me, almost losing his balance. Barely two hours into the party, and already he was sloppy drunk. "The game goes however I want it to go, friend."

It occurred to me then that he never used my name. I wondered if he even knew it, or if this was all part of some power play to him. I backed away, spinning directly into Luce, her brown eyes unnaturally wide. She had a hand on my arm, colder than expected. "I've been looking for you," she said. "Something happened."

"What? What happened?" But I was stuck in the previous conversation, my mind playing catch-up.

"The window."

She dragged me through the kitchen to the corner of the living room. One of the windows facing the backyard beside the patio had been broken. No, it had been *almost* broken. The glass was in one piece, but it would have to be replaced. It looked like someone had taken a bat to it. I lowered my face so I was eye level with the point of impact, ran my fingers over the spiderweb of grooves radiating out from the center.

Through the glass, Connor was arguing with someone in the shadows. I shifted my perspective, trying to see, but his image through the window fractured into a dozen pieces against the night sky.

He looked in my direction, and then he stepped away, out of frame. I closed my eyes, breathing in slowly. "We should cover it up," I said, "so no one gets hurt."

I knew we kept a first-aid kit in the master bathroom down the hall, along with athletic tape. The tape seemed the best option, both as a deterrent and a stopgap until tomorrow.

But the door to the master bedroom was already locked. "Dammit," I said, slamming my hand into the wood, the noise echoing through the narrow hallway. I hoped it made them jump.

"Guess Sadie was right not to have the party at their house," Luce said.

I sighed. "It's fine," I said. Even though I had felt the glass under my fingers ready to give way. It was one push from shattering, from really injuring someone. I had been prepared for someone to end up in the pool before the night was out. Expected a couple spills, a stain that would have to be professionally treated, maybe. But I had not been expecting any real damage.

A woman raised a red cup in the air. "To summer!" she said.

Luce raised hers in response, then spotted someone across the room—Parker, I assumed. She left me standing there alone, at the entrance to the dark hallway.

No one seemed to notice when I slipped out the front. When I circled to the side of the house, breathing in the solitude. Nothing but trees and the muffled sound of people inside.

I wasn't the only one out here. A twig cracking, a brittle leaf crunching, the rustle of fabric coming closer. "Hello?" I called. And then: "Sadie?"

She moved like that. Light on her feet. Sure of herself. Not likely to pause for the sake of anybody else.

But the woods fell silent after that, and when I pulled up the flashlight on my phone, I saw nothing but shadows crisscrossing the darkness.

SUMMER

2018

CHAPTER 6

I *sat there on the* edge of the bed as the seconds ticked by, staring at the phone in my hand.

Sadie's phone, which the police never found. Sadie's phone, presumably lost to the sea, torn from her hand when she jumped, or tossed into the abyss in the moments before.

If Sadie was alone that night, how did her phone end up *here*?

Now I pictured the dots lighting up the message window, imagined her final text:

Help me—

There was a creak from outside the bedroom, and I stood quickly, my heart pounding.

"Avery? You in here?"

I slid the phone into my back pocket as I walked out of the room, down the short hall. Connor was standing in the middle of the front foyer, looking up the staircase instead. "Oh," he said.

"Hey, hi." I couldn't orient myself. Not with the phone in my back pocket and Connor before me, in the house where we'd all been when she died.

I was caught half a step behind, because Connor and I no longer had the type of relationship where we spoke to each other or sought each other out. And now that he was standing in the room with me, it seemed he didn't know what he was doing here, either.

He was dressed for work, in jeans and a red polo with the Harlow family logo on the upper-left corner. Even so, Connor always reminded me of the ocean. His blue eyes had a sheen to them, like he'd been squinting at the sun for too long. The saltwater grit left behind on his palms. His skin twice as tan as anyone else's, from out on the sea, where the sun gets you double: once from above and once from the reflection off the surface. And brown hair streaked through from the summer months, escaping out the bottom of his hat. He'd always been thin, more wiry than strong, but he'd grown into the sharper angles of his face by the time we were in high school.

"What are you doing here?" I asked.

He didn't speak at first, just stood between me and the front door, looking me over. I knew what he was seeing: the slacks, the dress shoes, the sleeveless blouse that transformed me into a different person with a different role. Or maybe it was just the way I was standing, frozen in place, unsure how to move—like I had something to hide. And for a moment, I could only hear the detective's questions: *What about Connor Harlow? Would you know his state of mind last night?*

Connor frowned, like he could tell what I was thinking. "Sorry," he said. "The door was open. I saw your car at the B&B when I was making my delivery. Mr. Sylva told me what happened. Everything okay here?" He looked around, taking in the downstairs.

"Nothing's missing," I said.

"Kids?"

I nodded slowly, but I wasn't sure; I thought we were talking ourselves into something. If not for the presence of the phone I'd just found, it was the most logical explanation. Something we were all too familiar with here. In the off-season, we had a youth problem. We had a drug problem. We had a boredom problem. An inescapable, existential problem. We would do anything to pass the winter here. It was a bigger problem if it was bleeding over into the summer.

We had all peered inside the homes in the off-season. Curiosity, boredom, a tempting of fate. Seeing how far we could get and how much we could get away with.

Connor and I knew as well as anyone. He and Faith and I had stood at the base of the Lomans' house one winter long ago, me on his shoulders, climbing onto a second-story balcony, shimmying through a window of the master bedroom that had been left open. We didn't take anything. We were only curious. Faith had opened the freezer, the fridge, the bathroom cabinets, the desk drawers—all empty—her fingers trailing every surface as she moved. Connor had walked the rooms of the unoccupied home, not touching anything, as if committing them to memory.

But I had stopped in the living room, stood before the picture hanging on the wall behind the sofa. Staring back at the family there. The mother and daughter, blond and slight; father and son, darker hair, matching eyes. A hand on the shoulder of each child. Four pieces of a set, smiling, with the dunes of Breaker Beach behind them. The closest I'd been to Sadie Loman. I'd stepped closer, seen the finer details: the crooked eyetooth that had yet to be fixed. I pictured her mother holding the curling iron to her otherwise pin-straight hair. The photographer smoothing out any imperfections so that her freckles faded away, into her skin.

Eventually, Connor had circled back, found me standing in

front of that family portrait in their living room. He'd nudged my shoulder, whispered into my ear, *Let's get out of here. This place gives me the creeps.*

———

NOW HE STOOD ON the other side of the room, and I still didn't know what he was doing here. Why he was so interested in a break-in at a rental where nothing had been taken.

"Whoever it is, they came in through that window," I said, shaking off the chill. "The lock doesn't latch."

His eyes met mine for a brief moment, like he was remembering, too. "You need the number for a window repair?"

"No, I got it." I stared out the glass, picturing Connor's face as it appeared that night, fractured in my memory. "Do you remember how it broke, the night Sadie died?"

He flinched at her name, then rubbed the scruff of his jaw to hide it. "Not sure. Just saw that girl standing on the other side, checking it out. Parker Loman's girlfriend."

"Luce," I said. Every move I made that summer, it seemed that she was watching.

He shrugged with one shoulder. "She seemed upset, so I figured she did it, honestly. Why?"

"No reason. Just thinking about it." Because Sadie's phone was in my pocket and nothing made sense anymore. I was holding my breath, willing him to leave before he noticed my hands. How I had to press them to the sides of my legs to keep them from shaking. But Connor paced the room slowly, eyes roaming over the windows, the furniture, the walls.

"I remember that picture," he said, pointing at the painting that hung from the wall.

It was my mother's print, taken from Connor's dad's boat one evening, in the autumn before the car crash. We were in middle school, thirteen, maybe. Outside the harbor, she'd taken photo after photo of the coastline as evening turned to dusk turned to dark. The homes along the coast were no longer lit up and welcoming but appeared monstrous, darker shadows standing guard in the night. She kept taking pictures every time the light shifted, until the dark had settled, complete, and I couldn't make out the shadows anymore, couldn't tell sea from land from sky, and I lost all sense of orientation and vomited over the edge of the boat.

"I think the kids have had enough, Lena," Mr. Harlow said with a laugh.

She'd tried to capture it in this painting, after endless drafts in her studio. The final product existed in shades of blue and gray, something between dusk and night. The gray of the water fading into the dark of the cliffs, disappearing into the blue of the night. As if you could take the image in your hand and shake it back into focus.

Years later, I'd had it reprinted, and I'd hung it from the living room wall of every home I oversaw. A piece of her in all the Loman homes, and nobody knew it but me.

Staring at her painting, I was overcome with the impulse to do it—to reach out and grab it. I wanted to take this moment and shake it into focus. Stretch a hand through time and grasp on to Sadie's arm.

Until Sadie's note was found, Detective Collins's questions kept circling back to Connor Harlow, even though his alibi panned out. He'd been at the party; no one ever saw him leave. Still. He had been spotted with Sadie earlier that week. Sadie had told no one about it. As far as I knew, neither had Connor.

"Did you see her that night, Connor?" I asked as he was still facing away.

He froze, his back stiffening. "No," he said, knowing exactly what I was referring to. "I didn't see her that night, and I wasn't seeing her at all. Which I told the police. Over and over."

When Connor was angry, his voice dropped. His breathing slowed. Like his body was going into some sort of primitive state, conserving energy before a strike.

"People saw you two." I remembered what Greg Randolph had said about Sadie and Connor on his boat. "Don't lie for my benefit." As if there was something remaining, seven years later, that he needed to handle with care.

He turned back around slowly. "I wouldn't dare. What would be the point of that?"

I could see the tension in his shoulders, the way his teeth were clenched together. But all I could remember was the list Detective Collins had put in front of me. The names. The times. And the fact that I couldn't answer for Connor. "When did you get to the party that night?"

He shifted on his feet. "Why are you doing this?"

I shook my head. "It's not a hard question. I'm assuming you told the police already."

He stared back, eyes blazing. "Sometime after eight," he said, monotone. "You were in the kitchen, with that girl—with Luce." His gaze drifted to the side, to the kitchen. "You were on the phone. I walked right by you."

I closed my eyes, trying to feel him there in my memory. The phone held to my ear, the sound of endless ringing. I had made only one call that night—the call to Sadie when she didn't pick up.

"You know," he continued, eyes narrowing, "I expected these questions from the police. Even from the Lomans. But *this* . . ." He trailed off. "She killed herself, Avery."

Maybe the silence between us was better after all. Because the things we had to say were going to slide to places neither of us wanted to go.

He shook his head as if he realized the same thing. "Well, it's been fun catching up."

82

My arms were crossed over my chest as he made his way back outside to the delivery van in the drive. From the front door, I saw the sheer white curtains in the house across the street—Sunset Retreat—fall back into place. I could see the outline of a shadow there. A single figure, unmoving, watching as I locked the front door and made my way around the house toward the wooded path, disappearing into the trees.

The biggest danger of all in Littleport was assuming that you were invisible. That no one else saw you.

CHAPTER 7

I couldn't tell if Parker was back home, but I didn't want him seeing me, stopping me, following me. I practically ran from my car into the guesthouse, locking the front door behind me. My hands were still shaking with misplaced adrenaline.

Sadie and I had the same model phone. My charger should work. I connected her phone to the wire on my desk and stared at the black screen, waiting. Pacing in front of the living room windows. Hearing her words again, the last thing she said to me: *What do we think of this?*

This time the scene shifted until I saw a different possibility: She'd been planning to meet someone. The pale skin of her shoulders, the nervous energy that I had mistaken for anticipation, a thrumming excitement for the party that night.

Now I was walking through another potential version of events.

Somewhere in my phone, I had a copy of that list, the one

Detective Collins had written out for me last summer. I scrolled back in time until I found it, slightly blurred, my hand already pulling away as I took the photo just when the detective turned back. I had to zoom in to see it, twist it to the side, but there we were. The list of names: *Avery Greer, Luciana Suarez, Parker Loman, Connor Harlow*. Our arrival times written in my handwriting.

There was something the police had been looking for in here. A story that didn't add up. I tore a blank sheet of paper from the notepad on my desk, copying the list—now complete with the information Connor had given me:

Me—6:40 p.m.

Luce—8 p.m.

Connor—8:10 p.m.

Parker—8:30 p.m.

I tapped the back of my pen against my desk until the rhythm made me anxious. Maybe Sadie and Connor had plans to meet up. Maybe when she told Parker not to wait for her, it was because Connor was supposed to give her a ride to the party.

I had no idea what she'd been up to earlier in the day while I was working. She was dressed and ready by the early afternoon, while I had been reconciling the rental property finances all day, caught up in the end-of-season work. Luce said she thought Sadie was packing. Parker said Sadie told him not to wait for her.

But somehow her phone had ended up at the rental house across town while her body was washing up on the shore of Breaker Beach. Was it possible that someone had hidden it inside the chest recently? Or had it been there ever since the night she died?

As soon as the display of her phone lit up, prompting the passcode screen, I pressed my thumb to the pad. The screen flashed a message to *try again,* and my stomach dropped.

Sadie and I had just come out of a rough spot in the weeks before she died. Until then, we'd had access to each other's phones for years. So we could check a text, see the weather, take a picture. It was a show of trust. It was a promise.

It had never occurred to me that she might've locked me out when things turned cold.

I wiped my hand against my shirt and tried to hold perfectly still but could feel my pulse all the way to the tips of my fingers. I held my breath as I tried once more.

The passcode grid disappeared—I was in.

The background of her home screen was a picture of the water. I hadn't seen it before, but it looked as if it had been taken from the edge of the bluffs at sunrise—the sky two shades of blue and the sun glowing amber just over the horizon. As if she'd stood out there before, contemplating the moment that would follow.

Last I'd seen her phone, the backdrop had been a gradient in shades of purple.

The first thing I did was open her messages to see if she'd sent me something that never came through. But the only things in her inbox were the messages from me. The first, asking where she was. The second, a string of three question marks.

I was listed as *Avie* in her phone. It was the name she called me whenever we were out in a crowd, a press of bodies, the blur of alcohol—*Where are you, Avie?*—as if she were telling people that I belonged to her.

There was nothing else in there. No messages from anyone else, and none of our previous correspondence. I wasn't sure whether the police could access her old messages, either with or without the phone, but there was nothing here for me. Her call log was empty as well. No calls or messages had come through after the ones I had sent. I had presumed that her phone had been lost to the sea, and that was the reason it had been offline when the police tried to ping it. But I looked at the crack in the upper corner again, wondering if her phone had been dropped or thrown—if the same event that had cracked the screen had knocked the power out, too.

Had she been afraid as she stood at the entrance to my room? Had her face faltered, like she was waiting for me to come with her? To ask her what was wrong?

I clicked on the email icon, but her work account had been deactivated in the year since her death. She had a second, personal account that was overstuffed with nothing of relevance—spam, sale alerts, recurrent appointment reminders that she'd never gotten the chance to cancel. Anything prior to her death was no longer accessible. I tried not to do anything permanent or traceable on her phone, like clicking any of the unread emails open. But there was no harm in looking.

I checked her photos next, a page of thumbnails that had not been deleted. I sat on my desk chair, scrolling through them while the phone was still gaining charge. Scenic pictures taken around Littleport: a winding mountain road in a tunnel of trees, the docks, the bluffs, Breaker Beach at dusk. I'd never gotten the sense that she'd been interested in photography, but Littleport had a way of doing that to people. Inspiring you to see more, to crack open your soul and look again.

Scrolling back further, I saw more pictures of a personal variety: Sadie with the ocean behind her; Sadie and Luce at the pool; Parker and Luce across the table from her, out to dinner somewhere. Clinking glasses. Laughing.

I stopped scrolling. An image of a man, familiar in a way that stopped my heart.

Sunglasses on, hands behind his head, lying back, shirtless and tan. Connor, on his boat. Sadie, standing above him to get the shot.

Maybe these photos had been accessible from elsewhere by the police. Maybe this was why the police kept asking about Connor.

About the two of them together. He could deny it all he wanted, but here he was.

———

SADIE HAD KNOWN CONNOR'S name almost as long as she'd known mine. But as far as I was aware, they had never spoken before. That first summer, while Sadie's world was opening up to me, she was looking at mine with a sort of unrestrained curiosity.

Her eyes lit up at my stories—the more outrageous, the better. It became addictive, taking these pieces of that dark, lonely winter and re-forming them for her benefit.

How I spent the winter in a stupor, like time had frozen. How I drank like I was searching for something, so sure I would find it, the deeper I sank. How I fought my friends, pushing them away, the stupid, reckless things I did. Trusting no one and losing everyone's trust in return.

For a long time, I was forgiven my transgressions—it was grief, and wasn't I a tragic cliché, stuck in a loop of anger and bitterness? But people must've realized what I too soon understood: that grief did not create anything that had not existed before. It only heightened what was already there. Removing the binds that once shielded me.

Here, then, was the true Avery Greer.

But Sadie didn't see it that way. Or she did, but she didn't mind it. Didn't think I was something to shy away from.

We'd spend late afternoons sitting on the patio of Harbor Club, overlooking the docks and the streets of downtown, ordering lemonade and watching the people meandering the grid of shops below. Sadie always added extra packets of sugar as she drank, even though I could already see the granules floating, impossible to dissolve.

She'd point someone out below whenever they caught her eye: *Stella Bryant. Our parents are friends, so she's over all the time. Insufferable, truly.* And another: *Olsen, one of Parker's friends. Kissed him when I was fourteen, and he's been scared to talk to me ever since. Come to think of it, I still have no idea what his first name is.*

Once she pointed her straw over the edge of the railing, toward the dock. *Who's that?*

Who?

She rolled her eyes. *The guy you keep looking at.*

She didn't blink, and neither did I, until I sighed, leaning back in my chair. *Connor Harlow. Friend turned fling turned terrible idea.*

Oh, she said, her face lighting up as she leaned closer, chin in hands. *Come on, don't stop there. Tell me everything.*

I skipped the worst part, about who I became over the past winter. The things about myself I'd rather not know. I skipped how he had been my oldest friend, my best friend, the role she was currently replacing. *Typical story. Slept with him once, before I knew it was a bad idea.* I cringed. *And then once more, after I already knew it.* She laughed, loud and surprising. *And then,* I continued, *because self-destruction knows no bounds, he found me on the beach with his friend the next week.*

She blinked twice, her eyes sparkling. *Well, hello there. Nice to meet you. I'm Sadie.*

I laughed. *And then,* I told her, fueled by her response, *I showed up drunk at our friends' house. The Point B&B, you know it? I mean out-of-my-mind drunk, looking for him. Convinced he and my friend Faith were bonding over my current state. And when Faith tried to get me to calm down, I made such a scene, her parents called the police.*

Sadie's mouth formed a perfect *O.* She was delighted.

One more part, the punch line of my life: *The police arrived just in time to see me push Faith. She tripped backward on one of those pool hoses, you know? Broke her arm. The whole thing was a mess.*

The confession was worth it just to see Sadie's face. *Were you arrested?* she asked, her eyes unnaturally wide.

No. Small town, and Faith didn't press charges. A warning. An accident. I added air quotes to *accident,* even though it was. I hadn't meant to hurt Faith, not that I could remember the details that well. Still, it turned out the general population was much less forgiving when physical assault was involved.

She sipped her lemonade once more, never breaking eye contact. *Your life is so much more interesting than mine, Avery.*

I really doubt that, I said. Later, Faith had said I was *crazy, fucked up, in need of some serious help.* When even your closest friends give up on you, you're as good as done. But I loved Sadie's reaction. So I kept sharing the stories of that winter—the recklessness, the wildness—owning all of it. Feeling the weightless quality that comes with turning over parts of your life to someone else. When we finally stood, she put a hand down on the table, catching herself. *Head rush,* she said. *I think I'm high on your life.*

I curtseyed. *I feel it's only fair to prepare you.*

All these things that had pushed people away, they only pulled her in closer, and I wanted to find even more. To make her laugh and shake her head. To watch, while I kept sliding toward some undefinable edge. To become everything I had been trying to forget, until the season turned two months later and she was gone. A quick stop back home in Connecticut before returning to college in Boston.

We texted. We called.

The following May, when she finally returned, I was waiting for her on the bluffs, and she said, *Do you trust me,* and I did—there was no thought to it, no other choice. She drove us straight to the tattoo parlor two towns up the coast and said, *Close your eyes.*

———

CONNOR WAS MINE. HE was my story, my past. But over the years, Sadie's and my lives started to blur. Her house became my house.

Her clothes in my closet. Car keys on each other's key rings. Shared memories. I admired Grant because she did; resented Bianca because she felt the same. We hated and loved in pairs. I watched the world through her eyes. I thought I was seeing something new.

But she hadn't told me about Connor, and I hadn't noticed. I'd been too distracted by the money that had gone missing at work and the resulting fallout. The way I'd been avoided and ignored after—a feeling I could not tolerate yet again.

Now I scrolled through her contacts in alphabetical order. *Bee, Dad, Junior.* I knew the last referred to Parker, had been a joke, a name she started to call him, to bother him, when he cast aside the expected rebellion of his youth.

He'll take over the company one day, she'd explained when I questioned it. *A little star protégé. A junior asshole.*

What about you? I knew she was studying finance, interning with her father, learning the ropes of the company herself. It could've just as easily been rightfully hers.

Never me. I'm not tall enough.

I had scrolled through both the *C*'s and *H*'s without stumbling upon anything related to Connor, when, at the end of the list, there he was. Listed as *'Connor,* so his name fell to the bottom of the alphabet.

I never knew what Sadie's suicide note said. I knew only that it existed, and that it closed the case in a way that made sense.

But before they found the note, there was a reason the police kept asking me about Connor Harlow, and it must've been this— the hint of a secret relationship, something worth hiding.

And now: his image in her phone, his name with an asterisk, as if she were guiding the way back to him.

Well, he always was a terrible liar.

———

I PLUGGED SADIE'S PHONE into my laptop, copying her photos.

The images were still transferring when a car pulled slowly up the drive. I peered through the window beside my front door in time to see Parker stepping out of his idling car to slide open the garage door. I folded the list of names and times I'd just copied down, slid it carefully into my purse.

I needed to talk to him. There had been two confirmed break-ins at their rental properties. Noises in the night, footsteps in the sand.

And now I was thinking of someone else with Sadie after I had sent her that message. Someone out there on the bluffs with her. Arguing. Pushing her, maybe. The phone falling on the rocks in the process, shattering. The other person picking it up, coming to the party, hiding her phone when the police arrived. Someone who had been at the party after all. Someone who could've slipped out and come back with no one knowing.

CHAPTER 8

The garage door was open, but Parker stood with his back to
me, rifling through the trunk of his black car.

"Do you have a minute?" I asked, making him jump.

He closed the trunk and turned around, hand to heart, then
shook his head. "Now you're the one giving me a heart attack."

The garage here was as exclusive as the main house: a sliding
door like that of a barn, with the same slanted-ceiling architecture.
And it was immaculately organized inside—red containers of gasoline for the generator, in the corners; tools hung along the walls,
probably touched only by the landscaping company; cans of paint
on the shelves, left behind when the painters came through two
years earlier.

But there was a layer of dust over everything here, and it
smelled faintly of exhaust and chemicals. A forgotten extension of
the Lomans' property.

I shifted on my feet. "Have you noticed anything off since you've been back?"

He frowned, lines forming around his mouth where there'd been none, last I'd noticed. "What do you mean by *off*?"

"The power went out in the guesthouse last night. It's happened a couple times. You saw the garbage can, right?" I shook my head, trying to show him that I didn't think it was serious, either.

The familiar line formed between his eyes. "Probably the wind. I could feel it even when I was driving in last night."

"No, you're right. I was just wondering. The main house, everything seems fine?"

"I guess so. Not like we left much behind. Come on," he said, gesturing me out of the garage. "I want to lock up." As if something worrisome had worked its way inside his head regardless of his words. His hand trembled faintly as he slid the garage door closed, engaging the lock. The Parker I once knew was unflappable, but loss can manifest in other ways. Signs of age, of illness, of pain. A tremor in the fingers, nervous system on overdrive. A wound slow to heal.

The summer after my parents died, a heavy ache would settle in my legs every night, even though, by all accounts, I was too old for growing pains. Still, every night, my grandmother would rub my calves, the backs of my heels, the bend of my knees, while I braced myself on the bed until the tension released. If I closed my eyes, I could still imagine the feel of her dry fingertips, her singular focus on this one thing she could fix. So that by the time it passed, months later, I believed I had earned my place in the world, in this body.

Maybe Sadie's death would make Parker more than he had previously been. Give him some depth, some compassion. A perspective he'd always been lacking.

He walked toward the house, and I fell into stride beside him.

He stopped on the porch steps, the key ring looped on his finger. "That all, Avery? I'm working remotely this week. Have a couple calls I need to jump on soon."

"No, that's not all." I cleared my throat, wished we were back in the night before, sitting on the couch inside, when he was loose with liquor, more vulnerable and open. "I was wondering about the investigation. About the note."

Parker rocked back on his heels, the wood creaking underneath us.

"I was wondering, who was it for?" I couldn't help it, wanting to know. Sadie had left her text to me unfinished. Who had she left her last words for instead?

The frown lines around Parker's face were deepening again. "I don't know. I mean, it wasn't addressed to anyone in particular. We found it in the *trash*."

"You don't think she meant to leave it for you?"

He rubbed a hand down his face, then put the keys back in his pocket and sat on the porch step. "I don't know. I don't know why Sadie did half the things she did, most of the time."

In all the years I'd known them, Sadie and Parker had never seemed close. Even though they shared the same circle, both professionally and personally, neither seemed that interested in the other's life beyond the surface of things.

I frowned, sitting beside him, choosing my words carefully, quietly, so as not to disturb the balance of the moment. "What did it say?"

"What does it matter now? I don't know, she was making peace or whatever. I guess it was for Dad and Bee."

"Making peace for what?" I was already losing him. He'd put his hands on the porch step, pushing himself upright, but I grabbed his wrist, surprising us both. "Please, Parker. What did she say, exactly? It's important."

He stared at my hand on his wrist, and I slowly uncurled my fingers. "No, Avery, it's not important. It's done with. I don't remember."

And that was how I knew he was lying. How could he not be? Her last words, the ones I'd been trying to conjure into being, picturing the dots on my phone, given to him. But maybe he really didn't care. Didn't see her as I did. Didn't store her words every time she spoke them, keeping them all, filing them away to revisit later.

"Do you still have it?"

He shrugged and then sighed. "My guess, it's still with the police." We were so close, I could see the muscle in his jaw tensing.

"But if it was really that vague, *making peace or whatever,* that shouldn't be enough, right? The police can't know for sure she jumped. Not one hundred percent."

He looked at me out of the corner of his eye. "She was obsessed with death, Avery. Come on, you knew that, too."

I blinked slowly, remembering. It was true that she was quick to mention the things that might harm us, but I never took it seriously. It was how we met—a warning of tetanus, sepsis. And it continued on, poking through the surface at random times. A warning, a joke, the dark, dark humor. An elaborate play. But sometimes I wasn't sure. Whether it was an act or not. Whether I was in on the game or an unsuspecting bystander.

I flashed to sleeping on the lounge chairs on her pool deck, the afternoon sun warming my skin. How I'd felt her hand resting on my neck, her fingers just under my jaw. My eyes had shot open at her touch.

I thought maybe you were dead, she'd said, not moving away.

I was sleeping.

It can happen, you know—the brain fails to send a message to your lungs, to breathe. Usually you wake up, gasping for air. But sometimes you don't.

I'd pushed myself to sitting, and only then did her hand slip away. I placed my own hand there, on instinct, until I could feel the flutter of my pulse. *You seem really broken up about it,* I joked.

Well, I'm a little upset that I won't be able to practice my recently acquired CPR skills and save your life and have you forever in my debt.

I smiled then, my face mirroring hers.

She never saw the threat of death in the things that could truly harm us: drinking to excess so close to the water, the cars we got into, the people we barely knew. The way we pushed each other to more and more until something had to give, and the thing that finally gave was the season, and she was gone, and the winter cool slowed everything: my heart rate, my breathing, time. Until it grew unbearable in the other extreme, and every day was waiting for the spark of spring, the promise of summer on the horizon once more.

Parker called it obsession, but it wasn't.

I saw obsession in the stacks of paintings in my mother's studio; in the boats setting out on the ocean before dawn, day after day. Obsession was the gravity that kept you in orbit, a force you were continually spiraling toward, even when you were looking away.

"Just because you talk about it doesn't mean you want to *do* it," I finally replied. The other possibility was too painful: that she had been crying out for help, and we had merely stood back and watched.

Parker took a deep breath. "She would stare at her veins sometimes . . ." He cringed, and I could feel my own blood pulsing there. "You didn't know what was going on under the surface." He shook his head. "When you take everything together, it's the thing that makes the most sense."

"But how are they sure the note was even hers?"

"They matched her handwriting." He pushed himself off the porch step, pulling out his house keys.

I was wrong about the phone signifying something danger-ous, then. The phone was not where it should've been, but there were other ways it could've gotten to the house in the last eleven months. Maybe Sadie had dropped it on her way to the edge or left it behind, beside her gold shoes. Maybe someone had gone back for her that night when I had not. Who found the phone and took it in an impulsive move. Something worth protecting inside, to keep hidden.

Knowing what I knew now about Connor's photo, his name in her phone, I wondered if it had been him all along. If he'd somehow ended up with her phone and panicked, knowing what might lay in-side. Losing or leaving it in the chaos of that night, when the police arrived. If that was why he had shown up at the Blue Robin after I was there today. If he'd heard about the break-in and been worried.

There were ways, after all, to capture someone without putting them in jail. A civil case for wrongful death. I'd heard about that on the news before—the people who pushed someone to suicide, convinced them to do it, or pressed them to see no other option, taken for all they were worth by the family left behind.

There were many forms to justice. Something more satisfying than an immobile brass bell with a melancholy phrase—everything about it so far from the person Sadie had been.

I pictured her hastily writing a note. Balling it up. Staring out the window. Her jaw hardening.

Sadie didn't handwrite many things. She kept notes on her phone, sent texts and emails. Always had her laptop open on her desk.

"Parker," I said as the key slid into the lock. "What did they match it to?"

His hand froze. "Her diary."

But I shook my head again. Nothing made sense. "Sadie didn't keep a diary."

The door creaked open, and he stepped inside, turning around. "Obviously, she did. Obviously, there's plenty you didn't know. Is it such a surprise that she wouldn't reveal the contents of her diary to you? She didn't tell you everything, Avery. And if you think she did, you sure do have a high opinion of yourself."

He shut the door, made a show of turning the lock after, so I could hear the thunk echo inside the wooden frame.

And to think I'd almost shown him Sadie's phone.

———

PARKER NEVER WANTED ME here. He made that clear, both verbally and not, after the decision had already been made. Grant had wanted my grandmother's property, which I was in danger of losing anyway. The mortgage had been paid down with my parents' small life insurance payout—not enough to live on but enough to gift me the security of a place to call my own. So the remaining monthly payments weren't the primary problem. It was all the accompanying costs—the insurance, the taxes, the appliances. It was the last of my grandmother's medical bills and every responsibility suddenly falling in my lap. But still, it was home. And I had nowhere else to go. The visitors had priced us all out of our own homes, so the best I could hope for would be an apartment, alone, miles from the coast.

Others had also offered to buy the home—the other residents of Stone Hollow didn't want the land to go to rentals—but the Lomans were offering me something else. To step into their world, live on their property, become a part of their circle. So I sold my house, and therefore my soul, to the Lomans.

When Grant offered to let me use their guesthouse, I said I'd need that part in writing—experience had turned me wary of taking anyone at their word, despite their best intentions—and he tipped his head back and laughed, just like Sadie would do. *You're going to be okay, kid,* was what he said to me. It was the smallest sort of compliment, but I remembered the warmth that swept through me then. This belief that I would, that he could see it in me, too.

But I could hear them arguing about it later, after Grant drew up the papers. Parker's voice was too low to hear clearly, but I heard Sadie calling him selfish, and Grant's steady voice explaining what was to happen, no room for questions. *It is fair, and it's the right thing to do. The house is never used. Grow up, Parker.*

Parker didn't argue any more after that, but he was the only one who hadn't helped me move.

Bianca had handled the practicalities—having me set up a P.O. box and list her address as the physical location so that, officially, I existed in relation to them: Avery Greer, c/o 1 Landing Lane.

Grant himself had helped at my grandmother's house, hiring a few men to transport the boxes as he surveyed the lot, the frame of the house, the rooms. Assessing everything, assigning it a value, deciding whether it was worth more standing or demolished.

Sadie came, too, saying no one should have to deal with Grant Loman on their own, but I appreciated his efficiency in all its unsentimental brutality.

I felt myself becoming something in his grip. A slice here, a piece deemed unnecessary and tossed aside. Until you were left with only the things worth keeping. A brutal efficiency he applied to projects and people alike.

At the end, I had just a stack of boxes, all labeled by Sadie's red Sharpie. The looping *S* for *Sell,* the slanting *K* for *Keep.* My life, restructured in her capable hands.

There were four boxes of my own things worth keeping. And one more that was stacked full of my parents' things, my grandparents' things. Wedding albums and mementos. Family pictures and a recipe book from my grandmother's kitchen, a shoebox of letters from and to my grandfather when he was overseas. The file of paperwork shifting everything that once was theirs into my possession. Like I was moving not only me but my entire history. All the people who had brought me to this moment in time.

Now I pictured Sadie with the marker in her hand, the cap between her teeth.

The moment when she sat back and gazed around my empty, empty house. The lonely existence I was leaving behind for something new. Grant stood beyond the window, facing away, one hand on his hip, the other with a phone to his ear. Inside was only silence. Sadie looked momentarily stunned, her lips pressed together, as if the emotion might spill over at any second. It was like she was seeing me as someone else for the first time. *This is going to be good, Avery.*

And right then—with the house I'd been in danger of losing stripped down to its roots, feeling like I had finally fought my way out of something—I believed her.

———

IT HAD SEEMED SO generous of them at the time. But I'd spent the last year alone up here, with nothing but the ghosts for company. Sadie, lingering in my doorway the last time I saw her. My mother, whispering in my ear, asking what I see.

And so I've kept looking back, trying to find the place where everything veered off track. I start, every time, at the beginning:

I see Grant and Bianca, watching as Sadie brought me home. I imagine them asking around town, mentioning my name, hearing the stories, knowing everything there was to know. Witnessing the thread connecting me and Sadie becoming taut and strong. I wondered if they feared their daughter being dragged down into my world, just as I felt myself being pulled up into theirs. They must have understood that the only way to keep their daughter on track, under control, was to get me there, too.

That was what everyone missed when they wondered what I was doing in the Loman home. Their rumors were wrong, but so was my defense. I had seen it first as a generosity of spirit but then started to see it as an act of control. A true taste of what it was like to be Sadie Loman. A beautiful puppet on a string. Something that could've pushed her to the brink.

Buy your house and keep you here. Fund your education, direct you in kind. Employ you, monitor you, mold your path.

My home is your home. Your life is my life.

There will be no locks or secrets here.

CHAPTER 9

There was only one change I made to Sadie's phone before leaving. Only one thing removed, which I didn't think anyone would notice.

In the settings, I deleted the extra thumbprint before shutting it down.

———

THE DRIVE TO THE police station was almost the same as the drive to the harbor. The fight against the gridlock of cars and pedestrians in the downtown section. The rubbernecking at the sight of the ocean and the village green. I had to pass straight through it all to reach the building on the rise of hill at the edge of the harbor.

I pulled into the parking lot overlooking the harbor below, all glass windows and smooth white stone.

I asked for Detective Collins at the curved front desk of the lobby, which was more fitting for a hotel than a police station. The woman behind the desk picked up the phone, gave my name, and asked me to wait, gesturing to the grid of chairs by the window. It was deceptive, the openness, the buzzing bright lights of the place—made you think you had nothing to hide.

I'd just sunk into the stiff cushioning when I realized she knew who I was without asking. Not that I should be surprised. My name had been known around here since I was fourteen, in one way or another.

There was an accident.

Such a simple, benign phrase for the upheaval of everything I'd ever known.

A dark road, a mountain curve, and my entire life had been changed in an instant while I slept. I'd been driven to the hospital, placed in a small waiting room. Given food I couldn't touch, soda that fizzed against the back of my throat until I gagged. I'd sat there then, only half believing, trying desperately to remember the last interaction I'd had with my parents:

My dad calling down the hall, *There's leftover pizza in the fridge,* my mom ducking into my room, one shoe on, the other in her hand, *Don't stay up too late.* I'd given her a thumbs-up without removing the phone from my ear. Faith had been on the other end, and my mom, noticing, had mouthed, *Bye.* It was the last thing I could remember from either of them. They were heading for a gallery show a few towns away, bringing my grandmother as well.

I'd fallen asleep watching television. I hadn't even noticed something was wrong.

A policewoman placed a hand on my shoulder while I sat at the hospital, staring at the fizzing soda—*Is there someone else we can call?*

They'd tried the Harlows first, but it was Mrs. Sylva who came to pick me up. I'd stayed in a vacant room at the B&B until my grandmother was released the next night. She didn't have a scratch on her, but her neck was in a brace from the impact of the tree, the front of the car crushed like an accordion. They'd thought she was dead at first. That was what the first officer on the scene said. It was in the article, how he stumbled upon the scene, new on the job, shaken by the horror of it all—his own jolt into reality, it seemed.

I read it only once. Once was more than enough.

The police said my father didn't even hit the brakes until he was off the road, had probably drifted off, as my grandmother had in the backseat. I thought of that often at night, how we were all sleeping when it happened. How you can hurtle through darkness by momentum alone, without a single conscious thought, with no one to see you go.

Four years later, I'd been brought to the station after the fight with Faith. By then the only person left to call was my grandmother's neighbor, Evelyn.

"Avery?" Detective Collins waited at the entrance to the hall behind me. He nodded as I stood. "Nice to see you again. Come on back." He led me to a small office halfway down the hall and took a seat behind his desk, gesturing for me to take the chair across from him. His office was sparse, with nothing on the surface of the desk, and glass windows to the hall behind me. There was nowhere to look but right at him. "Is this about the dedication ceremony?" he asked, leaning back in his chair until the springs creaked in protest.

I swallowed nothing. "Yes and no." I clenched my hands to keep them from shaking. "I wanted to ask you about Sadie's note."

He stopped rocking in his chair then.

"The note she left behind," I clarified.

"I remember," he said. He didn't say anything more, waiting for me to continue.

"What did it say?" I asked.

After a pause, he sat upright and pulled himself closer to his desk. "I'm afraid that's the family's business, Avery. You might do better asking one of them." As if he knew I'd already tried to find out and failed.

I looked at the walls, at his desk, anywhere but at his face. "I've been thinking about that night again. Is everyone sure the note was hers? I mean completely, totally sure?"

The room was so quiet I could hear his breathing, the faint ticking of his watch. Finally, he drew in a breath. "It's hers, Avery. We matched it."

I waved my hand between us. "To a diary, I heard. But, Detective, she didn't have one."

His eyes were focused on mine—green, though I'd never noticed before. His expression was not unkind, something bordering on sympathy. "Maybe you didn't know her as well as you thought."

"Or," I said, my voice louder than I anticipated, "maybe the note was something else. Luciana Suarez was staying in the house, too. Or it could've been the cleaning company. Someone else could've left it." They could've matched her handwriting in a rush because they wanted to. Making the pieces fit instead of the other way around.

I'd been too caught off guard by the news last year to ask questions. I'd been blindsided by the fact that I had misunderstood things so deeply. That there was something momentous I had failed to see coming once again.

He folded his hands slowly on the top of the desk, finger by finger. His nails were cut down to the quick. "Listen. It's not just that the writing's a match." He shook his head. "It's more like a journal—the inner workings of her mind. And it's very, very dark."

"No," I said. "She didn't mean it." The same thing I had said to Parker. But wasn't that the truth? The way she'd tallied the dangers off to me the day we met, as if she could see them, close to the surface, always ready to consume us. The casualness of death;

something she was courting. *Don't hurt yourself,* she'd said when I stood too close to the edge in the dark. As if, even then, she had imagined it.

He shook his head sadly. "Avery, you're not the only one who missed something, okay? No one saw it coming. Sometimes you can only see the signs in hindsight."

My throat felt tight. He reached across the table, his thick hand hovering near mine before pulling back. "It's been a year. I get that. How things come back. But we've been through all of this. The case is closed, we gave Parker her old personal items today." That must've been what Parker was looking at in his car when I surprised him in the garage—the items returned from the police station. "Everything fits. Write the article, come celebrate her life at the dedication, and move on."

"Everything doesn't fit," I said. "She was supposed to meet us there. Something happened." I reached my hand into my bag, placed her phone before him.

He didn't touch it, just stared at it. A piece he had not anticipated. "What's this?"

"Sadie's phone. I found it today at the rental. The Blue Robin, where we all were the night she died."

His eyes didn't move from the phone. "You *just* found it."

"Yes."

"One year later." Incredulous, eyes narrowed, like I was playing a joke on him. How quickly his demeanor had changed. Or maybe it was me changing before him.

"It was at the bottom of a chest in the master bedroom. I found it when I was taking out the blankets to freshen up. I don't know how long it's been there, but she didn't lose it when she died." I swallowed, willing him to make the leap: that if they were wrong about this, they could be wrong about all of it.

He shook his head, still not touching the phone.

Once, several summers ago, Sadie had tried to get herself arrested. At least it seemed that way to me at the time. I'd taken her down to the docks at night, wanting to show her something. A world she never had access to herself, a way to prove my own worth. I knew how to get inside the dock office from when Connor used to do it—lifting the handle, giving the door a well-angled nudge at the same time—and then taking his father's key from the back office inside, untying the boat and pushing it adrift before turning on the engine.

But someone must've seen us sneaking inside. I'd gotten as far as the front room when the flashlight shone in the window, and I darted in the other direction, toward the rarely used back door. Sadie had frozen, staring at the light in the window. I pulled her by the arm, but by then the officer was inside—I knew him, though not by name. Didn't matter, because he knew mine.

He led us outside, back to his car. He didn't ask me the question I'd grown to expect, about whom to call; he must've known the answer by then.

"What's your name?" he asked Sadie, but she didn't respond. Her eyes were wide, and she pressed her lips together, shaking her head. The man asked for her purse, which she had looped over her shoulder. He pulled out her wallet, shone the flashlight on her driver's license. "Sadie . . ." and then he trailed off. Cleared his throat. Slipped the license back inside, returning her purse. "Listen, girls. This is a warning. This is trespassing, and the next time we catch you, you'll be processed, booked, am I clear?"

"Yes, sir," I said. The relief like that first sip of alcohol, warming my bloodstream.

He returned to his car, and Sadie stood there in the middle of the parking lot, watching him go. "What does a girl have to do to get arrested around here?" she asked.

"Change your name," I said.

108

Her name carried weight. But she didn't throw it around. She didn't have to.

It occurred to me that as long as I was with her, I might be afforded that same protection.

———

HER NAME STILL CARRIED that weight, with her phone on the detective's desk, that he still wouldn't touch. Dead or not, there were things you had to be careful with around here. He picked up his office phone but hesitated first.

"I'm sorry. I wish it didn't have to be this way," Detective Collins finally said before waving me out of the room.

"What? What way?"

He shook his head. "Her note. That's what it said."

CHAPTER 10

'm sorry. I wish it didn't have to be this way.

I slammed on my brakes in the middle of Harbor Drive just as a woman stepped out into the crosswalk without looking. She stood in front of my car, staring back through the windshield. My hands were shaking on the wheel. There were mere inches separating us.

In the rearview mirror, I could still see the police station perched at the top of the hill. The woman in front of me raised her hand like a barrier between her and my car, mouthed *Watch it,* before moving on. As if I hadn't noticed how close I'd come. As if she hadn't yet processed how close *she* had come.

I saw Sadie then, standing at the edge of the cliffs. The blue dress blowing behind her in the wind, a strap sliding down her shoulder, the mascara running under her eyes, her hands shaking. Saw her turn around and look at me this time, her eyes wide—

Stop.

——

I HAD TO CALL someone.

Not the detective, who had just stared at her phone with such disbelief. Not Parker, who hadn't told me he'd just retrieved Sadie's personal items from the police. Not Connor, who had kept things from all of us with his silence—

My phone rang just as I was working it through. Another number not in my contacts. I wondered if it was Detective Collins already, telling me to come back. That they'd discovered something else in her phone, or they needed my help to tell them what something meant. I placed the call on speaker.

"Is this Avery?" It was a girl. A woman. Something in between.

"Yes, who's speaking?"

"Erica Hopkins. From lunch."

"Right, hi."

She cleared her throat. "Justine wanted me to check in. We'll need the piece for Sadie tomorrow—by afternoon at the latest."

Yesterday felt like forever ago. "I can email you the piece tonight, but the photo will probably be a physical copy. I don't have access to a scanner." I would not contact Grant or Bianca to ask for a high-resolution image of their deceased daughter, though it would have to be one of theirs, something that once graced the walls of the Breakers. In truth, I could think of nothing more fitting.

"We've got a meeting at the dedication site with Parker Loman tomorrow around eleven. Right at the entrance of Breaker Beach. Want to meet us there with the photo?"

Somewhere in that house were Sadie Loman's personal items, just returned to Parker from the police station. Parker had said he'd be working from home today, and I could see the lights from the upstairs office from their drive.

111

Tomorrow, around eleven, he would be out. The house would be empty.

"Why don't you stop by after," I said, edging the car to the other side of the garage. "I'll meet you at their guesthouse. Just send me a text to let me know when you're on your way up."

Inside their house was that journal, given back to Parker. The item they used to determine the presumed last words of Sadie Loman. The thing they rested their case on.

And I needed to see it.

Something had worked its way inside, dark and sinuous. Like I had just set something in motion that I now had no power to stop.

———

BACK INSIDE THE BEDROOM of the guesthouse, I opened the closet door, pulling out the single box that had never been unpacked— marked *K* for *Keep,* in Sadie's handwriting. The rest I had steadily unpacked with time, the few things of my own worth bringing. But this was the box that held my parents' things, my grandmother's things.

Though the house itself did not belong to me, I knew no one would dare touch this box. For all the times that Sadie had reached into my closet, she'd never placed her hands on this.

I lifted my parents' wedding album, my grandmother's letters, placing them carefully aside. Until I'd unearthed the small shoebox underneath.

Inside were the photos of Sadie that once were scattered around the Loman house. Replaced each year with a new set. But Bianca had added them without removing the previous photos, stacking them one on top of the next in their frames, so they remained as one. Like layers of paint, slowly growing in thickness, until I'd removed the older images for my own safekeeping.

The surfaces were damaged slightly, adhered to the newer versions, the corners crimped and discolored from the frames.

Where there once were childhood portraits, there were graduation pictures. Where there once were graduation pictures, there were vacation shots—Sadie at the Eiffel Tower, Sadie in red snow gear with mountains behind her, Sadie sitting beside Parker somewhere tropical, with the ocean behind them.

I sorted through these forgotten pictures now, trying to find the right fit for the piece. God, she would hate this. In each photo, she was either too young-looking or too happy. Too disconnected to the purpose of the article. They would want something to appeal to everyone, insider and outsider alike. She had to appear both approachable and untouchable.

In the end, I settled on her college graduation picture. She held the diploma in her hand, but her head was tipped back slightly, like she was starting to laugh. It was perfectly Sadie. And it was perfectly tragic.

This photo captured the beginning of something. It was on the nose, but it would cut hard. The beginning of a laugh, of her life. Something that I now felt had been taken from her.

And then I placed the rest of the photos back inside the box, hidden within the closet, where they would remain alongside all the other people I had lost.

———

SADIE JANETTE LOMAN TO be honored in Littleport memorial

My fingers tapped against the edge of the keyboard, waiting for the words to come. I stared at the photo of her in the graduation gown, the blue sky behind her over the dome of the building.

Sadie Loman may have spent nine months out of the year in Connecticut, but Littleport was her favorite place in the world.

She'd told me that the first time we met. And now she was about to become a part of its history.

For a small town, we had a long past that lived in our collective memory. It was a place filled with ghosts, from old legends and bedtime stories alike. The fishermen lost at sea, the first lighthouse keeper—their cries in the night echoed in the howling wind. Benches in memory of, in honor of; boxes moved from home to home. We carried the lost with us here.

It was a place for risk-takers, a place that favored the bold.

I was trying to find a place for Sadie in this history. Something to be part of.

She was bold, of course she was. But that wasn't what people wanted to hear. They wanted to hear that she loved the ocean, her family, this place.

What I would say if I were telling the truth:

Sadie would hate everything about this. From the bell, to the quote, to the tribute. She'd sit on the rocks, looking down on the beach where we would all be gathered, holding a drink in her hand and laughing. Littleport was unsympathetic and unapologetic, and so was she. As much a product of this place as any of us.

She might demand that she be forgiven. She might compensate for a perceived wrong with an over-the-top counterbalance. She might know it, deep inside, when she had gone too far.

But Sadie Loman would never apologize. Not for who she was and not for what she'd done.

———

I'M SORRY. I WISH it didn't have to be this way.

Two simple sentences. The note they found. Crumpled in the trash.

What was the chance that all of this was a mistake? That the police, and her family, had seen one thing and believed another?

What were the odds that Sadie had chosen those very same words, the ones I had used earlier that summer—the ones I had written myself, folded in half, and left on the surface of her desk for her?

SUMMER

2017

The Plus-One Party

9:30 p.m.

It happened all at once. The light, the sound, the mood.

The power had gone out. The music, the house lights, the blue glow from under the water of the pool. Everything was darkness.

Inside, there were too many bodies all pressed together. My ears still buzzed from the music. Someone stepped on my foot. I heard the sound of glass breaking, and I hoped it wasn't the window. Everything became sound and scent. Low whispers, nervous laughter, sweat and the whiff of someone's hair product as they walked by, and then a spiced cologne.

I felt a hand on my shoulder, a breath on my neck. I froze, disoriented. And then I heard a scream. Everything stopped—the whispers, the laughter, the people brushing up against one another. The light from a phone turned on across the room, and then another, until I pulled my cell out of my back pocket and did the same.

"She's all right!" someone yelled from outside. Everyone shifted toward the back of the house.

117

I pushed my way through the crowd, my eyes adjusting to the darkness. Outside, the clouds covered the stars and the moonlight. There was only the beam of the lighthouse cutting through the sky above, swallowed up in the clouds.

It was Parker, of course, who had her, surrounded by a semicircle of onlookers. At first I could see only a dark shape curled up in Parker's arms. He rubbed her back as she coughed up water. "Okay, you're all right," he was saying to her, and then she turned her face up. Ellie Arnold.

Sadie had known her forever, found her annoying. Said she would do anything for attention, and so my first thought was neither generous nor sympathetic.

But when I crouched down beside her, she was so shaken, so miserable-looking, that I knew she hadn't done it on purpose.

"What happened?" I asked.

She was soaked, clothes clinging to her skin, trembling.

"She couldn't see," Parker answered for her. "She lost her place."

"Someone *pushed* me," Ellie said, arms folded around herself. "When the pool lights went out." She coughed and half sobbed. Her long hair was stuck to her face, her neck.

"All right. You're okay." I repeated Parker's words and smiled to myself, glad for the dark. The pool was four feet deep all the way across—she was never in any real danger, despite her present demeanor. All she had to do was plant her feet.

I was more worried about the sound of her scream carrying in the night.

One of Ellie's friends finally made it through the crowd. "Oh my God," she said, hand to her mouth. She reached down for Ellie's hand.

"Get her inside," Parker said, helping her stand. Ellie wobbled slightly, then leaned on her friend as the crowd parted for them.

"There are plenty of towels in the bathrooms, under the sinks," I said. "Probably a robe somewhere, too."

Parker looked back toward the house. An amber glow flickered in the window—someone's lighter, the flame touched to the wick of a candle.

"I'll go take a look," I said. From here, we couldn't tell whether the power had gone out in the entire town or just on our street. If it was just our street, I'd have to make a call, and this party would be over. Better if it was a town-wide outage. Best if the house had been tripped on its own from the speakers and the lights all running at once—grid overload.

Inside, someone had found the rest of the candles and lined them along the windowsills, placing the pillar from the mantel in the center of the kitchen island. The guy with the lighter finished circling the downstairs, and now everything was subdued in pockets of dim light. The faces were still in shadows, but I could see my way to the breaker panel.

The door to the master bedroom down the hall was ajar—at least the commotion had managed to clear out the people inside.

The breaker panel was inside the hall closet, and I used my phone to light up the grid. I let out a sigh of relief—this was something I could fix. Every circuit was tripped, in the off position. I flipped them back one at a time, watching as the lights came back, as people looked around the room, momentarily disoriented by where they found themselves.

At the last switch, the sound from the speakers blared unexpectedly, and my heart jumped.

"Get someone to turn that down," I said to the guy beside me. The same one who'd accused Greg Randolph of having a fling with Carys Fontaine. "And unplug some of those lights."

"Yes, ma'am," he said with a lopsided salute.

I made my way into the master bathroom, where two of Ellie's friends were hovering around her. Ellie Arnold was clearly both mortified and shaken, and for the first time I doubted Sadie's impression of her.

"Hey," I said, "everything okay in here?" Someone had found the towels, half of which were heaped on the floor beside Ellie's wet clothes. She was wrapped in a plush ivory robe, drying her hair with a matching towel. There were dark smudges under her eyes where her makeup had run. The floor was slick, the water puddling in sections, the mirror fogged. She must've taken a quick shower to warm up.

Ellie shook her head, not making eye contact. "Some asshole's idea of a joke." She leaned toward the open door. "Well, *fuck you!*" she yelled.

"Jesus," I said, half under my breath, though there was no one in the bedroom to hear her yelling.

The taller of her friends grimaced, shared a wide-eyed look with the other. "Calm down, El."

"The power was out," I said. "No one could see. I'm sure it was an accident." Even though I knew attempting to reason with someone fortified by an unknown quantity of alcohol was a lost cause.

But Ellie pressed her lips together. Her shoulders slumped, the sharpness subsiding. "I just want to go home."

I looked from face to face, debating whether anyone in this room was sober enough to give her a lift, before deciding not. "I'll see if anyone out there can take you."

Her face didn't change. She stared at the wall, her eyes unfocused, until I realized that *home* meant somewhere outside Littleport, wherever she'd be heading tomorrow.

"Come on," the shorter friend said, arm on her shoulder. "You'll feel better in dry clothes. Me and Liv have half the luggage in the trunk. Let's see if we can find you something?"

That got a faint smile from her, and the three of them walked out of the bathroom together, despite the fact that Ellie was in nothing more than a bathrobe.

Maybe Sadie was right after all.

I grabbed a few garbage bags from the kitchen, using one to store Ellie's wet clothes, which she'd absently left behind. I stuffed the used towels, splotched with grime, into the other bag, then pulled a few more from under the sink to clean the water and dirty footprints left behind.

"Don't do that, Avie." I turned around to see Parker standing in the entrance of the bathroom, watching me. "Leave it."

His eyes had gone dark, a sheen of sweat over his face, his brown hair falling over his forehead. He smelled like chlorine, and his shirt clung to his chest from the impression of Ellie's wet body.

"Someone has to do it," I said, waiting for him to leave. Instead, I heard the door clicking shut.

He took the garbage bag from my hand, finished stuffing the dirty laundry inside. We were too close. With the humidity of the room, it was hard to take a deep breath, to think clearly.

"Do you think I'm a good person?" he asked, his face so close I could see it only in sections—his eyes, the scar through his eyebrow, the ridge of his cheekbones, the set of his mouth.

Everything about Parker was hypothetical until moments like this, when there was some crack in his facade. Show me a chip in the demeanor and watch me fall. I never met a flaw I didn't love. The hidden insecurity, the brief uncertainty. The waver behind the arrogance.

Here's the thing: I didn't want Parker at first. Not in all the years I knew who he was before we met, and not when I first saw him in that house. Not really until Sadie said I couldn't have him. I knew it was cliché, that I was no different from so many others. But there was something about that—some universal appeal to the thing you could not have. Something that, for a certain type of person, settles in and redoubles desire.

But it was moments like this that focused everything—like I was seeing something that he kept hidden from everyone else. Something shared, just for me.

I pushed the hair back from his face, and he reached for my hand.

"Sorry," I said. But he didn't pull back. We stayed like that, mere inches apart, the room too humid, my vision unfocused at the edges.

Someone knocked on the door, and I jumped. Imagining Luce seeing us in here. "Occupied," I called, standing up.

Someone groaned on the other side, but it was a man. Still, it was enough to shock us both to our senses.

Parker's fingers were looped around my wrist, and he let out a slow sigh. "One day I'll probably marry Luciana Suarez and have beautiful children that are occasional assholes, but they'll be good people."

"Yeah, okay, Parker." I stepped back, my vision clearing. I thought he shouldn't be discussing being a good person while standing too close to me in a bathroom while the woman he was discussing marrying waited somewhere on the other side, but that was just part of his allure.

"Oh," he said, shaking his head. "I came here to tell you. There's some guy out there looking for you." He nodded toward the door. "You go first. I'll take care of the rest."

I cracked open the door, making sure there was no one waiting on the other side, where a rumor could take hold and grow. When I saw the room was empty, I slipped out.

Before I shut the door again, Parker called after me: "Be careful, Avery."

SUMMER

2018

CHAPTER 11

Friday morning, quarter to eleven, and Parker's car was still at the house. At least I assumed it was. I hadn't seen it pull out from the garage, and I'd been watching for it since I woke up.

He could be walking, though, down Landing Lane to the entrance of Breaker Beach. I wouldn't be able to see if he'd left on foot from the guesthouse. I opened the living room windows surrounding my desk and tried to listen, so I'd hear a door closing or his footsteps on the gravel, disappearing down the road.

I'd pushed back a meeting with the general contractor for one of the new homes until Monday. I'd canceled the window replacement for the Blue Robin, telling the vendor we'd have to reschedule. My email sat unanswered; phone calls went unreturned. I did not want to be distracted and miss my chance.

By eleven, I still hadn't heard him, and I started to wonder if he'd been home at all this morning. But at five after the hour, I finally heard the garage door sliding open, the faint turnover of an engine, the wheels slowly easing down the driveway before fading in the distance.

I waited another five minutes just to make sure he was gone.

———

I STILL HAD THE key from the lockbox. I could've sneaked in any of the doors—front or back or side—but thought it would look least suspicious to go straight in the front. I had already come up with an excuse if seen: I was checking the electricity after we'd had a few outages, before calling in a service appointment.

After I entered, I locked the door behind me. The house looked much the same as when Parker arrived. Barely lived in. A single person could leave such little impression here. The house was the definition of sprawling, with large areas of open space. Places to sit and watch the water.

I figured I'd be able to spot a box of Sadie's things pretty easily down here.

At first glance, it seemed that Parker hadn't left her things in any of the common rooms downstairs. His coffee mug was on the counter, an empty carton of eggs beside it.

A pile of neatly stacked mail sat on the corner of the island, most addressed to the Loman Family Charitable Foundation. Parker must've retrieved it earlier in the day—their local mail was always held at the post office until they returned. The envelopes had been slit open, with the receipts and thank-you notes for *your continued support* separated into piles. Each from local causes—the police department building fund, the Littleport downtown rehabilitation project, the nature preservation initiative. All their generosity reduced to a sterile pile of paper.

The only other disturbance to the perfection were the throw pillows on the couch, where Parker had been sitting when we were here together that first night.

I headed upstairs next, taking the wide curving staircase. At the right end of the hall was Parker's bedroom, which I checked first. All the bedrooms upstairs faced the ocean, with sweeping floor-to-ceiling doors that led to private balconies.

Parker's room looked as it always had—bed unmade, empty luggage in the closet, drawers half closed. There was no box in the closet. Just a couple pairs of shoes and the faintly swaying hangers, disturbed by my presence. Same for under the bed and the dresser surfaces. I opened a few of the drawers to check, but it was just the summer clothes he'd brought with him.

The next room was the master, and it appeared untouched, as expected. Still, I did a cursory sweep, looking for anything out of place. But it was immaculate, with a separate sitting area, a bright blue chair beside a stack of books that seemed to be picked more for design than reading desire, all in shades of ivory and blue.

Sadie's room was at the other end of the hall upstairs. Her door was open, which made me think someone had been in here recently. But nothing looked out of place. I knew that the police had been through here, and I wondered what else they had taken. It was hard to know what might be missing if you didn't know what you were looking for.

Her bedspread was smooth and untouched, the corner of the beechwood headboard where she usually hung her purse now empty.

I'd assumed her family had taken her personal items, along with her clothes, back to Connecticut. But the back of my neck prickled. There was just enough of Sadie left behind for me to feel her still. To look over my shoulder and imagine her finding me here. Sneaking up on me, light on her feet, hands over my eyes—*think fast*. My heart in my stomach even as she was already laughing.

I turned around, and the air seemed to move. It was the layout.

The acoustics. A design that showcased the clean lines but also revealed your presence.

The first time I'd slept over here, I'd woken to the sound of a door closing somewhere down the hall. Sadie had been asleep beside me, one arm thrown over her head—completely still. But I thought I saw a flash of light through the glass doors to her balcony. I'd slipped out of bed, felt a floorboard pop beneath my feet.

I stood in front of the windows, so close, my nose almost pressed up against it, peering out. My eyes skimmed the darkness beyond my reflection, straining for something solid. It was then that I saw the pale shadow over my shoulder, in the second before I could feel her.

What are you looking at? Sadie stood behind me, mirroring my position.

I don't know. I thought I saw something.

Not possible, she'd said, shaking her head.

I understood what she meant as I stepped away. The only thing you could see in the windows at night was yourself.

Now, when I peered out those same windows, I felt the shadow of her there, watching.

Her attached bathroom still had an assortment of products, shampoos, conditioners. A hairbrush. A container of toothpaste. An assortment of glass vials, more for decoration than practicality.

Her desk had gotten an overhaul in the last couple years, tucked into an alcove that used to be a sitting area. She had started working full-time remotely last summer, and her desk was sleeker now, wired for a laptop and a printer. It was the place I'd once left that note, along with a box of her favorite fudge, that I'd driven an hour down the coast to get. An apology and a peace offering.

At the start of last summer, Sadie had been my boss, technically. The person I reported to, at least. Before Grant decided I could handle all of the logistics of the Littleport properties on my own, and she had been reassigned.

Right now the surface of her desk was completely bare. Nothing here appeared out of place.

The last room I thought to check was Grant's office—now Parker's. It was the only upstairs room that faced the front of the house, other than the laundry room and a bathroom. There were blinds covering the window here, to fight the glare off the computer screen, which was now on the surface of the desk, red light glowing.

I could see Parker subtly taking over, everything just a little different than I'd remembered. *A junior asshole,* Sadie had called him. The desk was the same, situated on top of a red ornamental rug, but the surface layout was different. A yellow notepad to the side of the laptop, a single pen, a sloppily written list, half the items crossed out. Grant used to keep everything inside the drawers when he was out, a meticulous dedication to clearing the desk, both figuratively and literally, every time he left.

Parker's leather satchel was tucked under the desk. I peered inside but saw only a few paper files he must've been working on. The laptop screen was black, but it was clear that Parker had left in a rush, maybe losing track of time. I carefully slid open the side drawers, but they were mostly empty, except for the items that must've been left from last summer: a stack of fresh notepads and a container of pens.

The bottom-right drawer was locked, but it seemed to be the type that held files—not a place I'd expect a box of Sadie's things to be hidden. Still, I opened the top drawer to check for a key and found one tucked away in a pile of flash drives, all bearing the logo for Loman Properties, which they used to hand out as giveaways in lieu of key chains. Something more likely to be used and appreciated.

But this key was too large for a desk lock. Too small for a house key.

I sat in his chair, surveying the room. The closet was situated beside the window, tucked into the corner. I'd never looked closely before, never had cause to spend time in this room—but that doorknob was the only one in the house that didn't have the same smooth antique look. There was a keyhole in the metal doorplate, just below the knob. The only place in this house afforded privacy, it seemed.

The key fit perfectly, the latch disengaging.

Opening the door now, I expected to see the box of Sadie's things. Secrets worth keeping. Details worth hiding. But the shelves were stacked with bound-up file folders, each labeled in blocky print—a file for each of the rental properties, contracts and blueprints inside; another marked *Charity Receipts,* where the letters downstairs would inevitably be filed; another marked *Medical*. Nothing belonging to Sadie. Just the normal documents for safekeeping, kept out of sight. Nothing secret about them.

Chances were, the box of Sadie's things was still in the trunk of Parker's car. I'd surprised him there, and he'd left it all out of sight, safely locked behind the garage door.

I'd just stacked the files back together when I heard the sound of tires on gravel. I spun abruptly and caught the glare of sun off metal through the slats of blinds. I stepped closer. There was a dark car driving down the lane toward the garage, with a second car right behind, but it stopped before reaching the garage. Someone stepped out of the driver's side. Brown hair falling past her shoulders, beige lightweight sweater. Red glasses. Erica.

Dammit. She raised her hand to her eyes, turning toward the house, and I jumped aside, hoping she didn't see my shadow up here. She was supposed to text me first, so I'd have fair warning.

I locked the closet door and dropped the key into the top desk drawer, moving the flash drives around, hoping it looked natural. A quick scan of the room, making sure I'd left everything as I'd found it. Straightening the chair, making sure his bag under the desk was closed. Then I raced downstairs, holding my breath, listening for them. Parker's voice carried from somewhere out front, one half of a conversation I couldn't decipher.

If I sneaked out the patio door at the back of the house, I risked being caught trying to let myself out the black iron gate. I opted for the side door, located just off the kitchen, through the mudroom.

I eased the door shut as I stepped outside, then slid the key silently into the lock, making sure to secure the house once more. I heard the rise and fall of Erica's voice, Parker's laugh in response. But I was hidden by the garbage can and the lattice fencing. I waited until I heard laughter again, and then I darted the distance to the garage, keeping in the trees, hoping no one noticed.

Ten seconds to slow my breathing, and I stepped out from the other side of the garage, waving my hand over my head. "Hey there. Erica? Thought I heard you guys."

They both turned to look at me, their faces giving nothing away. Erica smiled first. "Sorry, I was just about to text you."

"No worries," I said. "Are you ready? Come on in."

———

ERICA STOOD IN THE middle of the living room, making no effort to hide the fact that she was appraising the place.

My heart was still racing, and I opened the fridge to cool my face. "Can I get you something to drink?" I asked.

"No, thanks." She made a show of checking her watch as I pulled out a drink. "I've got to get back to the office soon."

I took the picture of Sadie from my desk, handing it to her without looking. "Will that work?"

Erica stared at the photo in her hand, eyes unmoving, so close I could see the colors of the picture reflected in her glasses. I hoped it was gutting. "Yes. It's good." She slid it into her bag, then leaned over my desk, peering out the window. "It is pretty up here, I'll give you that," she said. Like she was picking up from a conversation I'd missed.

"It is. You living in Littleport full-time now?"

She nodded, still looking out the window. "Moved up after I got my degree in May. Staying with my aunt until I can get on my feet. She set me up with this job in the meantime."

"You should see the view from the main house," I said.

"I have," she said, then turned to face me, hands on her hips. "You really don't remember, do you."

I shook my head, eyes wide, desperately trying to fit her face into a memory of the Lomans.

"No, I guess you wouldn't. I worked that party with you here. Right after you graduated high school?"

"Oh." My hand to my mouth. I did remember. Not her specifically, but I remembered Evelyn assigning each of us a role. *Erica, patio. Avery, kitchen.* But those moments had gotten overshadowed by the parts that had shone so brightly: the blood, the bathroom, Sadie. "Sorry. It was a long time ago."

"It's okay, my aunt told me what happened back then. She warned me to keep my distance, no offense." Erica cleared her throat, her gaze drifting off to the side. "But looks like you're doing pretty well for yourself here."

I nodded. What did one say when faced with an embarrassing past? I wanted to brush it away, tell her it was a long time ago, that I barely remembered it myself. That it was a matter of her aunt being overprotective, blowing everything out of proportion.

Instead, I leaned in to it, like I'd learned from Sadie, because as she'd taught me, there was no use hiding from myself. Especially not here. "It was a bad time," I said.

She blinked once, then nodded. "Well, we all grew up, I guess."

"Your aunt was good to me when I didn't deserve it. I can't imagine most people would've hired me for something like this around then."

She smiled then, like there was a joke she was remembering. "Don't give her too much credit. She would've done anything the Lomans asked. Probably still would."

I shook my head, not understanding.

Erica jutted her thumb toward the main house. "Sadie Loman, your friend, right? She called before the party, asked for you by name. I thought you knew?"

"No," I said. That was wrong. Erica had it backward. "I met her that day. At the party."

Erica tilted her head as if trying to read something in my words. "No, I remember. I remember because my aunt was not happy about it. Said I'd have to keep an eye on you, make sure you were keeping up." She shrugged. "Like you said, it was a long time ago." As if forgiving me for my lapse in memory.

But no. That moment had sharpened and heightened over the years. Erica was wrong. Sadie did not know me then. It had been an accident. Sadie had caught me in the bathroom, when I'd been hiding, trying to stop the blood.

A chance encounter, and my world changed for the better because of it.

"Well, I'd better be going." Erica patted her bag with the photo. "Thanks for this, Avery."

She walked down the path toward her car, and I stood in the doorway, watching her drive off. She had to be mistaken. Confused. Swapping one memory for another, her visits to Littleport blurring.

I started to close the door, but something caught my eye. Parker, standing at the edge of the garage, watching me.

I jumped. Hand to heart. Uneasy smile. "This is getting to be a habit," I called, going for levity. I had no idea how long he'd been standing there.

But he didn't smile in return. "Were you in the house?"

My heart rate picked up again, and I felt the flush of my cheeks, glad for the distance between us. "What?" I asked, trying to buy some time, come up with the right excuse. Had I left something out of place? Or had they added a security system? Did the camera of his laptop capture me in the office as I searched the desk drawers?

"The back door," he said, coming closer. "To the patio. It was open."

I shook my head. That hadn't been me. I hadn't touched it. "Maybe you forgot to lock it," I said.

He pressed his lips together. "I mean, it wasn't even closed."

A chill ran through me. When I had searched the downstairs, everything had appeared exactly as it should've been. "If you don't lock it, sometimes it's not really latched all the way. The wind can do that," I said. But there was a waver in my voice, and I was sure he heard it, too.

He shook his head as if clearing a thought. "I know that. I thought I locked it. I just—I don't remember the last time I went out there. Does anyone else have a key? I mean, other than you."

I ran my fingers through my hair, trying to unravel his words—subtly accusing but also the truth. "The cleaning company has the code for the lockbox. I have the key right now, though. From the other night. It's the one for emergencies. I'll get it for you." A show of good faith to prove that I hadn't abused my position, and that I would not in the future, either.

He waved me off. "No, it's fine. I just wanted to check. I wouldn't have been angry if it was you."

But from the look on his face when I first saw him standing at the edge of the garage, I didn't think that was true at all.

And now I was thinking that someone else had been up here with us. Had been inside that house just as I had been. A presence I had felt while standing in Sadie's room. Who had almost been caught and had left the door ajar in the rush to leave.

Someone who'd had the same idea I had and was looking for something, too.

CHAPTER 12

Someone was snooping around the Loman property. Someone *had been* snooping around. From the noises at night, to the power outages, to the fact that Parker had arrived home today to an open back door.

Whatever they were searching for, I had to find it first. And now I was pretty sure I knew exactly where to look.

The garage was always kept locked. There was a separate key just for that building—so the Lomans could leave the landscapers access without worrying about their home. I had no way inside on my own. The most logical way to get into the trunk of Parker's car was to get the car out.

"Parker," I called when he was halfway back to the main house. I jogged the distance between us, closing the gap. "Let me take you out tonight." I framed it like an apology. A welcome-home. A Friday night. "You should get out."

He looked me over slowly. "I was planning to, anyway. It's so quiet up here all the time."

He'd never stayed here alone, I realized. Bianca was usually in Littleport all summer. And when she left at the end of the season, Sadie stayed behind with him.

"Eight?" I asked. "I can drive."

"No, I'll drive," he said. Which I'd known would happen. No way he'd be caught in the passenger seat of my old car, which had been left exposed to the elements over the years, snow and ice and saltwater winds. "The Fold?"

I hadn't been to the Fold in nearly a year. It used to be my very favorite place to go with Sadie. It was part of her world, one of those places that operated only in the summer months, like the ice cream shop.

Now the bars I visited were mostly the local ones. My closest acquaintances were the people I worked with in one capacity or another. The property inspector, Jillian. The general contractor, Wes, though I was a representative of the Lomans, so I was never sure where I stood with him. Only that any time I texted him to meet up, he'd arrive. And the one time I'd asked if he wanted to hang out at his place after, he'd said yes. I didn't initiate again, and neither did he.

Then there were my contacts from the various vendors around town, who were always friendly when they saw me out, but always from a remove.

Other friendships had not survived over the years. I'd never reconciled with Connor and Faith. And I'd drifted from the group I met when I started business courses at the community college, made excuses, turned down an offer for a shared apartment lease in a different town. I was set up to work in Littleport. And nowhere else would've had this view. This perspective, looking out over everything I'd ever known. Nowhere else would've had Sadie.

———

IT WAS AFTER SIX P.M. when I got the call from a woman who introduced herself as Katherine Appleton, staying at the Sea Rose—a small cabin down by Breaker Beach, not too far from here. She said it was her dad who'd rented the place, but she was the one staying. I hated when people did this—rented in the name of someone else. As long as nothing went wrong, I let it slide. As long as it wasn't a group of college kids with no respect for others' property, who would leave the venue with more damage than it was worth. The Lomans had an express rule against homes being rented in someone else's name, but I only partially enforced it. I was more interested in keeping the weeks booked: my bottom line, I supposed. The rest was up to me to handle. I was always on call, regardless of the fact it was a Friday night during the last week of August.

"I found your number in the paperwork," she said. Her words were unnaturally stilted.

"Yes, I'm the property manager. What can I do for you, Katherine?" Fingers to my temples, hoping this could wait.

"Someone lit our candles," she replied.

"What?"

"Someone. Lit. Our. Candles," she repeated, each word its own sentence. "And no one here did it. So they say." I heard laughter in the background.

They were drunk. Wasting my time. Calling me up when no one would fess up, on a dare—*Tell me or I'm calling the owners.* But then I remembered the candle left burning at the Blue Robin, the scent of sea salt and lavender.

"Okay, Katherine, hold on. Were there any signs of forced entry?"

"Oh, I don't remember if we locked up. Sorry." More talking

in the background. Someone asking for the phone, Katherine ignoring the request.

"Was anything taken?" I asked.

"No, I don't think so. Everything looks the same. Just spooky, with the candles."

I couldn't figure out what they wanted from me. Why they were calling on a Friday night; why they were still on the line.

"We were just—we were wondering," she continued. Another laugh in the background. "If there were any ghost stories about this place?"

I blinked slowly, trying to catch up. "You're calling for a ghost story?" It wasn't the most ridiculous call I had received on a Friday night, but it was close. What was wrong with people, that they would imagine a ghost first and not something real? Either way, I figured I should be grateful they weren't threatening to leave, demanding a refund or my immediate attention.

The laughter in the background made me think it was probably one of them. That I'd swing by and find too many people in the space, evidence of air mattresses, an overflowing recycling bin.

"I'll be by in the morning," I said. "To check the locks."

———

AFTER HANGING UP, I pulled out the stack of current rental agreements. Tomorrow I'd have to check all the properties, just to see. There were two definite break-ins that I knew of, and now this.

Saturday was when most of the turnovers happened anyway, unless a family was staying for longer than one week. Anyone leaving tomorrow should be out by ten. I lined up the cleaning companies to hit the properties first that had visitors expected the following week. Saturday was chaos: We had six hours to turn a place over, make sure it was ready for the next batch.

I checked the list of homes, making a schedule for myself. There were twenty-two units I oversaw in Littleport, and eighteen were currently occupied. Sixteen would be taken the following week.

I flipped through the list again, wondering if I'd misplaced something. I didn't have a listing for Sunset Retreat. Not for last week or the coming one.

Sunset Retreat, across from the Blue Robin, where I'd seen a curtain fall, seen someone watching after I found the phone.

No one was supposed to be there.

My stomach twisted. Someone had been watching. Not just the Loman house. Not just the rentals. But me.

CHAPTER 13

A *sharp thrill ran through* me as Parker and I walked from the parking lot into the Fold. It was the dark, the promise, the man beside me. It was my place, restored. It was the Friday night, the crowd. The anticipation of what I hoped to uncover and could feel hovering just inches away.

The bar had the feel of a local joint—the distressed wooden beams, the thick wood high-top tables, the laminated plastic menus. But it was all for show. The prices, the bartenders, the view, this was a place geared for the visitors. The owners knew what they were doing. A hidden gem, tucked away up a rickety flight of wooden steps, behind a weatherworn sign. An exposed balcony overlooking the rocky coast, a promise that this was the true Littleport, uncovered just for them.

It had been marketed exactly this way. The owners accrued enough income on four months alone, boarding up the windows and the balcony come October, and moving their operation back to their main headquarters—a burger-and-beer place two miles inland.

The room was loud and boisterous, but the volume dropped as soon as the door shut behind us. It was a reaction to Parker. They hadn't seen him here all summer, and now they came to pay their respects, one by one. Girls in jeans and fitted tops. Guys in khaki shorts and polos. Each of them blending in with the next. Hands on his shoulder, fingers curled around his upper arm. A sympathetic smile. A caress.

I'm all right.

Thanks for thinking of us.

Yeah, I'm here for the memorial.

In the silence that followed, one of the men raised a shot glass and said, "To Sadie."

Parker was pulled into a group at the corner table. He peered over his shoulder at me, raised two fingers, and I made my way to the bar.

The bartender raised his eyes briefly to meet mine, then went back to wiping down the countertop. "What'll it be," he said absently, as if he knew I didn't belong.

A man took the seat beside me as I ordered—a bourbon on the rocks for Parker, a light beer on tap for me—and I could feel him staring at the side of my face. I wasn't in the mood for small talk, but he knocked on the bar top to get my attention. "Knock knock," he said, just in case I hadn't noticed, and then he added, "Hi there," when I finally faced him. Greg Randolph, who had taken such delight in telling me about Sadie and Connor at the party last year. "Remember me?"

I nodded hello, smiling tightly.

He asked it as if he hadn't seen me around for the last seven years. As if he hadn't met me beside the Lomans' pool many summers ago, at a fund-raising party hosted by Bianca when I'd been dressed up in Sadie's clothes, tugging at the bottom of the dress, which suddenly had felt two inches too short, when Greg Randolph had stepped between the two of us, telling Sadie some trivial gossip that she seemed wholly disinterested in. He paused to politely address every adult who walked by.

Don't let the nice-guy act fool you, she'd said when he turned away. *Underneath, he's a mean drunk, like his father.*

She had not lowered her voice, and my eyes widened, thinking someone might've heard. Greg's dad, maybe, who was probably one of the adults in the group behind us—if not Greg himself. But Sadie had smiled at my expression. *No one listens that hard, Avie. Only you.* She'd waved her hand around in that airy way, as if it were all so inconsequential. *All this. This nothingness.*

I never knew what happened between Sadie and Greg.

The bartender placed the drinks on the counter, and I left my card to keep the tab open.

"That for me?" Greg asked, jutting his chin toward Parker's glass.

"Nope," I said, turning away.

He grabbed my arm, liquid spilling over onto my thumb as he did. "Wait, wait. Don't go so soon. I haven't seen you around all summer. Not like we used to."

I could sense the bartender watching, but when I looked over my shoulder, he had moved on, wiping down the far end of the bar.

I stared at Greg's hand on my arm and placed the drinks back on the counter, so as not to make a scene. "I'm sorry, do you even know my name?"

He laughed then, loud and overconfident. "Of course I do. You're Sadie's monster."

Everything prickled. From the way he used her name, to the leer of his whisper. "What did you just say?"

He grinned, didn't answer right away. I could tell he was enjoying this. "She created you. A mini-Sadie. A monster in her likeness. And now she's gone, but here you are. Still out here, living her life."

Parker was standing just a few feet away. I lowered my voice. "Fuck off," I said.

But Greg laughed as I picked up the drinks again. "That drink for Parker?" he said as I turned to leave. "Ah, I see how it is. From one Loman to the next, then."

I kept moving, pretending he'd said nothing at all.

Parker smiled as I set the drinks on the high table where he was standing. "This was a good idea," he said. "Thank you."

I sipped and shivered, trying to shake off the conversation at the bar.

Parker had barely raised his glass to his lips when three women approached us from the side. "Parker, so good to see you here."

Ellie Arnold. Last I'd seen her was the party the year before, shaken from her fall into the pool. Now her long blond hair was both wavy and shiny, her makeup expertly done. Her fingers curled around his lower arm, perfectly manicured nails in a subtle shade of pink. Two of her friends stood between us, offering their condolences while filling him in on all he'd missed.

It was time. I patted my pockets. "Parker," I said, interrupting them all. "Sorry, I think I left my phone in the car. Can I get the keys for a sec?"

He absently handed me his key ring, and I wove my way through the crowd, pushing out the door. The night was silent as I strode for his car in the packed lot, except for the one time the bar door swung open, a burst of sound and light escaping as someone else went inside.

I unlocked the car, the beep cutting through the night, and

opened the passenger door, fishing my phone from the cupholder. I'd left it here just in case he insisted on coming with me.

Then I looked over my shoulder and walked to the back of the car, pressing the button on the key to pop the trunk, unprepared for the light glowing from within.

I looked around quickly, but the lot appeared empty.

I opened the trunk farther, my hands already shaking with anticipation. There was a single crate jammed in the corner. It was covered by a felt blanket, like one that might be stored in the trunk for emergencies. This had to be the box of personal items returned from the police station.

The first things I saw when I removed the blanket were Sadie's sandals. The same ones I saw that night, so close to the edge of the bluffs.

I ran my fingers over them. They had been her favorite, and they looked it. Gold but scuffed at the tops. Stitching showing where the straps had pulled from the base. The hole stretched from the buckle, the left shoe missing one side of the intricate clasp. A low heel, and the sound of her steps echoing in my memory.

The door to the bar opened behind me again, a burst of sound momentarily flooding the lot. I twisted around to see, but there was no one outside that I could tell. I stared into the darkness, watching for any sign of movement.

Eventually, I turned back to the trunk, pushing the shoes aside—and saw it. A journal. Purple, with black and white ink swirls on the front. A corner of the front cover missing, so the tattered pages rippled below.

My stomach dropped, the edges of my vision gone blurry. And suddenly, everything made sense. Why the note matched her diary. Why the diary gave the police pause. I hadn't seen this in years. The familiar, angry pen indentations on the cover, the tattered corners, the blackened edges.

I shoved it quickly into my bag, then shut the trunk again, jogging the rest of the way back inside, feeling as unsteady as I had that night.

The note matched the journal perfectly, yes. Because they were both mine.

CHAPTER 14

Parker was waiting for me when I returned. Ellie and her friends had left him alone. "Find it?" he asked.

I handed him his keys, showed him my phone. "Got it. Thanks."

Greg arrived at our table, balancing three shot glasses between his fingers. "Here we go," he said, like they'd both been waiting for me.

"No, I shouldn't," I said. "I'll drive us back."

But Parker wasn't out to relax or reminisce, and apparently, neither was I. "Just the one," he said, sliding it my way, his eyes on mine.

I raised it in the air, just as they did. "Hear, hear," Parker said, staring right into my eyes as the glasses clinked together.

The shot glass collided with my teeth. As the liquor slid down my throat, goose bumps formed on my arms, even though the room was warm.

I stared back into his eyes, wondering what he knew. "There, there," I answered.

———

THREE HOURS LATER, WE were finally on the road back home. Though I hadn't had any more to drink, I felt parched, dehydrated by the talking, the mindless laughter.

"What was that about back there?" Parker asked, his head resting against the passenger seat as I drove.

"With what?" I asked, holding my breath. My bag was in the backseat, and the journal was inside, and I was scared that he knew everything.

"I don't know, you've been acting weird ever since we got there."

"That guy," I said, scrambling. "Greg."

"What about him?"

"He was an asshole," I said, my teeth clenching.

Parker let out a single laugh. "Greg Randolph *is* an asshole. So what?"

"Sadie couldn't stand him."

"Sadie couldn't stand a lot of people," he mumbled.

Sadie's monster. I twisted in my seat. "He always had a thing for her," I said, and Parker frowned. I could see him thinking it over. All these people who loved her, yes. But these were all people who couldn't have her, too.

———

THE PORCH LIGHT WAS off when I pulled into the drive. The bluffs were nothing but shadows in the darkness. I left the headlights on while Parker slid open the garage door. He may have been intoxicated, but he had the frame of mind to lock up his car inside.

After parking his car in the garage, I waited outside while he locked the sliding door back up, the night nothing but shadows.

"Good night, Parker."

"Are you coming in?" he asked, restless on his feet.

"It's late," I said. "And believe it or not, even though it's the weekend for you, I have work in the morning."

But that wasn't what he was asking, and we both knew it. "Sadie's gone, Avery." He knew then, too, the edict from Sadie, keeping me back. Maybe she said the same to him. When Sadie told me *Don't*, he became all I could think about. Whenever I passed his room, whenever I saw his shadow behind the glass windows.

An active restraint was something to do, a practice, something to focus on. It was a new sort of game, so different from yielding to impulse, as I had grown accustomed. I was forged of resilience, and I let the tension stretch me tight as a wire.

But now Sadie was gone, and Luce was gone, and Parker was here, and what was there left to ruin, really? Without the others here, there was something simmering and unfulfilled, and nothing to stop me. Something, suddenly, within my reach.

He was wavering in the pathway, his eyes darting off to the side, tentative and unsure, and that was what did it for me. That was what always did it. The way an insecurity stripped them back, revealing something that put me in temporary power.

I stepped closer, and he ran his fingers through my hair. I raised my hand to his face, my thumb brushing the scar through his eyebrow.

He grabbed my wrist, fast. The imperfection made you believe he had fought his way through something on his way to this life.

His eyes looked so dark in the shadows. When he kissed me, his hand trailed down my neck, so his thumb rested at the base of my throat. My neck, in his grip.

I couldn't tell whether it was subconscious or not. With him, it was hard to tell. But I couldn't shake the vision of three steps from now—pressed up against the side of the garage, his hands tightening, the memory of Sadie's voice: *It can happen, you know. You can't swallow, you can't breathe. It's not a quick way to die, is what I'm saying.*

I gasped for air, pulling back. My hand to my throat, and Parker looking at me curiously. I wondered what else I had missed in this house—if Parker was capable of harming me. If Parker was capable of harming *her.*

I had grown up an only child, didn't understand what a normal sibling dynamic should be. Thought the bursts of animosity, the casual cruelty, were the expected result of a pair of siblings fighting their way out of each other's shadow.

But maybe Sadie knew something I didn't. Maybe when she said *Don't,* she was saving me instead.

More and more, I was convinced someone had harmed her. That note wasn't hers. That journal wasn't hers. Without those, the police would still be interviewing all of us, over and over, until something broke. Someone's story. A lie. A way in.

Parker's breath was hot and sharp, and there was no one up here but us. "What's wrong?"

I cleared my throat, took another deep breath of cool night air. "You're drunk," I said.

"I am."

"I'm sober," I said.

He tipped his head to the side, the corner of his mouth quirking up. "So you are."

I never knew how to say no to him, to any of them. How to navigate the nuances of their words and mannerisms.

But there was too much at stake here now. Too much I hadn't seen clearly the first time.

"Let's go back thirty seconds," I said, stepping back, feigning levity. "Good night, Parker. See you in the morning."

Even in the dark, I could see his wide smile. I felt him watching me as I walked away.

———

I LOCKED THE DOOR to the guesthouse behind me. When I flipped the light switch, nothing happened. I tried again, but there was only darkness.

Shit. I wasn't about to go back out there to reset the breaker. Not with Parker standing nearby, watching. Not with whatever was happening at the rental properties.

I pictured the shape of the shadow inside Sunset Retreat and shivered. Using only my phone for light, I circled the apartment, pulling all the curtains closed. Then I collected the tea lights from the bathroom, the ones at the corners of the tub, and lit them around the bedroom. I locked that door, too. Pulled the journal from my bag. Felt the familiar grooves in the cover and opened the notebook.

The cliffs, it began.

The road.

The bottle in the medicine cabinet.

The blade.

The writing was so angry, the pen leaving deep indentations in the page; I could've felt the emotion in the words, running my fingers over the lines in the dark. I turned the page, my hand shaking. There were more lists, page after page of them, just like this. The times death was right there, within reach. The times death had come so close.

Walked to the edge, balanced there.

Top of the lighthouse, leaning forward.

Woke up on the beach gasping for air, dreamed the tide had risen.
Slip of the blade. The blood in my veins.

I tried to see this as the police would, reading these pages. Pictured Sadie doing these things, writing these things. Staring at her veins, like Parker had told me. Listing the ways she could die.

I hadn't seen this journal in years. Not since that winter. When the spark of spring never caught, and summer rolled in just the same as winter, empty and endless. It was the story of grief, of disappointment, of a soul obliterated.

It was the story of who I had been until the moment I met Sadie Loman, and I chose her. My life in her hands, restructured, recast. No longer adrift or alone.

This was my journal from a time in my life I would have rather forgotten—but which had colored everything that followed. When I had sunk beneath the surface and all I wanted was to slide deeper into it, like there was something I was chasing, waiting at the bottom. You could tell where I had been by the destruction in my wake.

Within these pages, I could see exactly where I'd lost Connor, where I'd lost Faith, and where I'd lost myself.

When had Sadie found this? I couldn't remember where I had kept it. It had maybe been in my closet, at my grandmother's place. It had been forgotten after I'd met Sadie and a new world had opened up to me. The world, through her eyes.

I wondered if Sadie had found it when she and Grant were helping me move. Even so, I didn't understand why she'd kept it.

But the police had found it in her room and decided a person like this, she would do it. *It was very, very dark.* That's what the detective had told me. A person like this, they believed, didn't want to live. She existed in the darkness and would step off the edge.

This journal, sad and angry, was just a moment in time.

Looking back at these pages, I knew that I had been trying to find my way through it.

Only now that I was past it did I see how close I truly came. The darkness that I was ready to dive headfirst into.

I kept looking at all the places death might be lurking. In so many lists, I ended with the blade. I remembered, then, the feeling of my blood pulsing underneath my skin. The image of a car crash, bodies versus metal and wood. The pressure of the blood in my grandmother's skull. Staring at my veins, at the frailty of them, so close to the surface.

The blade, the blade, I kept coming back to the blade.

The sharp glint of silver. The empty kitchen. The impulse and chaos of a single moment.

I hadn't anticipated the amount of blood. The sound of footsteps. I couldn't get it to stop.

I hid in the bathroom, pressing the toilet paper to the base of my hand.

Thinking, *No. No.* Until Sadie slipped inside.

You're lucky, she'd said. *You just missed the vein.*

———

I BARELY SLEPT. FEELING so close to the person I'd been at eighteen. Like my nerves were on fire.

At the first sign of light, I took my car down through town, at the hour when it was just the fishermen at the docks and the delivery trucks in the alleys. I drove up the hill, past the police station, up past the Point Bed-and-Breakfast, to where I could see the flash of the lighthouse beckoning, even in daylight. And then I turned down the fork in the road, heading for the homes on the overlook.

Most of the Loman rental properties were located along the coast. A view drove up the cost of rent nearly twofold—even more if you could walk to downtown. To compensate, the homes on the overlook were more spacious, typically renting out to larger families. And with school starting up soon, these were usually the first homes to go vacant.

I had all the keys with me, each labeled with a designated number that corresponded to a specific property. By this point, I knew them all by heart.

Someone had broken in to the home called Trail's End last week at the edge of downtown, smashing a television. Someone had sneaked inside the Blue Robin up here, looking for something. And someone had lit the candles at the Sea Rose, down by Breaker Beach.

I was starting to see the pattern not as a threat to the Lomans but as a message.

Someone knew what had happened that night. Someone had been at that party and knew what had happened to Sadie Loman.

As I drove up the lane of the overlook, I saw a dark car parked in front of the Blue Robin, lingering at the curb.

A shadow sitting inside. Eyes peering in the rearview mirror.

I parked behind it, waiting, my own car idling in a dare. Until Detective Ben Collins emerged from the car. He walked in my direction, frowning.

"Funny seeing you here," he said as I exited the car.

"I have to check the properties each weekend. Before the new families arrive," I said.

"Someone staying here next week?" he asked, thumb jutting at the Blue Robin.

"Yes."

"No." He shook his head. "Move them. We're gonna need to see inside."

My heart plummeted, but I clung to his words. "Are you reopening the case?" I asked. Maybe he believed me after all.

Detective Collins stood back, assessing the house—quaint and unassuming, like a birdhouse hidden amid the trees. "I was trying to see how someone might leave without notice. There's a path behind the house, right?" Not answering my question but not denying it, either. He believed it was possible, then, that something else had happened that night.

"Right. To the bed-and-breakfast." You could walk it in five to ten minutes. You could run it much faster.

"Show me inside?"

I led him in the front door, watched as he peered around the vacant space. He hadn't been one of the officers who'd come to get Parker that night. But he'd taken the call from the Donaldsons about the break-in earlier this week.

"Show me where you found the phone," he said.

I opened the door to the master bedroom, pointed to the now closed chest at the foot of the bed. The pile of blankets sat beside it, untouched. "In there," I said. "I found it in the corner. Seemed like it had been there a long time."

"That so," he said. The lid creaked open as he peered inside. He stared into empty darkness, then closed it again. "Here's the thing, Avery," he said, pivoting on his heel. "We got a good look at her phone, and it's really nothing we didn't know."

"Other than how it ended up here?"

He paused, then nodded. "Exactly." He paced the room, peering into the bathroom where I'd once cleaned the floor alongside Parker. "There was one thing I noticed, though. In all those pictures on her phone, you weren't there."

I froze. Sadie and Luce; Sadie and Parker; Connor; the scenic shots. Everything but me.

"I thought you were her best friend," he said. "That's what you told me, right?"

"Yes."

"But you're not in her pictures. She didn't respond to your text that night. And we got a lot of conflicting information during the interviews."

I felt something surging in my veins, my fists tightening of their own accord. "She didn't respond because *something happened to her*. And I'm not in the pictures because I was busy that summer. Working." But I could feel my pulse down to the tips of my fingers as I wondered if there had been rumors—about the rift, about me, about her. I thought no one had known—I thought Grant had kept it quiet.

"About that. Your work," he continued, and my stomach dropped. "Luciana Suarez provided us with some interesting details. This was her first summer in town, wasn't it?"

"Yes. She'd started dating Parker the fall before."

"Is it true that you took over Sadie's job?" And there it was. Luce. I should have known.

"Luce said that?" I asked, but he didn't respond. Just held eye contact, waiting for the answer. I brushed the comment away with a wave of my hand in the air, like Sadie might do. "They didn't need two people to do it. She was reassigned." Not fired.

"But, to be clear, you have her role."

I pressed my lips together. "Technically."

"You know what else Luciana said?" He paused, then continued like he didn't expect me to answer. "She said she'd never heard of you before." A twitch of his mouth. "Said that she didn't know anything about you until she arrived. No one had seen fit to mention your existence. Not even Sadie."

"Because Luce was Parker's girlfriend," I snapped. "There was no reason I would've come up." I was being blindsided yet again. This was an interrogation, and I'd walked right into it.

"She told us she'd been a friend of the family first."

"So what? That doesn't mean she and Sadie were close."

He looked at me closely, steadily. "Rumor has it you and Sadie were on the outs."

"Rumors are shit here, and you know it."

He smiled then, as if to say, *There you are.* That girl they all remembered. "I just think it's odd, is all, that Sadie never would've mentioned you."

Luce. She had complicated everything. Always with a quizzical look in my direction—something dangerous that kept me second-guessing myself. Luce became the unwitting wedge that summer, leaving everything off balance. If anyone understood what had happened in that house, it was her. Always there when I thought we were alone. I had no idea what she'd told the police during her interview. It hadn't mattered then, because of the note.

Detective Collins paced the room again, the floorboards creaking under his feet. "If I had to make a professional assessment, I'd say the friendship was a little one-sided. If I'm being honest with you, it seems a little like you were obsessed with her."

"No." I said it louder than I meant to, and I lowered my voice before continuing. "We were growing up. We had other responsibilities."

"You lived on their property, worked for their family, ran around with her crowd." He held up his hand, even though I hadn't said anything. "You considered them family, I know. But," he continued, lowering his voice, "did they consider you the same?"

"Yes," I said, because I had to. I trusted them because they chose me. Taking me in, welcoming me into their home, into their lives. What other choice was there? I had been adrift, and then I was grounded—

"I know who you used to be, Avery. What you've been through." His voice dropping, his posture changing. "Shitty hand to draw, I get it. But are you saying you never thought, just once, that you wanted to be her instead?"

I shook my head but didn't respond. Because I did, it was true. Back then, when I met her, I wanted to crawl inside someone else's head. Stretch their limbs. Flex their fingers. Feel the blood pulsing through their veins. See if they could hear it, too, the rhythm of their own heartbeat. Or if something else surged in their bones.

I wanted to feel something besides grief and regret, and I did. I had.

"This phone does raise some questions, in more ways than one. Of course, your prints would have to be on it, since you were the one who found it. Right?"

I jerked back. Did he think I was lying?

I wanted to tell him: *The note wasn't hers, the journal wasn't hers.*

But I knew what they would have to ask next: *"I'm sorry. I wish it didn't have to be this way." What were you apologizing for, exactly, Avery?*

I knew better than to give any more of myself away.

"Well," he said, "this has been enlightening. We'll be in touch." He tapped the bedroom door on the way out.

CHAPTER 15

was shaking as I watched the detective drive away, looping his car too fast around the cul-de-sac, passing Sunset Retreat on the way down the street.

They would be back. That's what he was implying. They would be back, and they were looking at how someone might've left the party that night.

I had been at the party the entire time—I'd proved it. But the phone meant something. It meant that being at the party did not absolve us. Chances were, if her phone had been left there the night of her death, she'd been murdered by someone *at* the party.

That list Detective Collins had handed me, the details I had given him in return—

Me—6:40 p.m.

Luce—8 p.m.

Connor—8:10 p.m.
Parker—8:30 p.m.

What had once been our alibis now became a cast of suspects.

———

IT DIDN'T LOOK GOOD that I was there for so long alone. It didn't look good that I was the one who found the phone. Detective Collins was fixating on my role in the Lomans' lives as if the rumors had reached him as well.

There had been no public fight. Nothing people could've witnessed and known for sure. Just a lingering chill. A feeling, if you knew what you were looking for. A brief shrug-off in public at her planned birthday lunch, when I'd tried to catch her after—*I can't talk to you right now*—where she looked at my hand on her arm instead of me. And a humiliating moment the next night, though I'd thought we were alone.

I'd been heading toward the Fold—she hadn't been answering my calls, my texts—when I saw her slip out the entrance with Luce. They were standing close together, Sadie a head shorter than Luce, who was relaying a story in a voice too low and fast to hear clearly, her hands moving to accentuate her points. But they parted at the corner, Luce heading for the overflow of cars, Sadie walking toward downtown.

I waited until Luce was out of sight to call her name, then again: "Sadie," the word echoing down the empty street. She stopped walking just under a dim corner streetlight. Her skin looked waxy pale, her hair more yellow than blond in the halo of light. She ran her fingers through the ends of her hair as she turned around, eyes skimming the road and then skimming right over me—pretending she didn't see me standing there, looking back. The casual cruelty she'd perfected with Parker. Like I was invisible. Inconsequential. Something she could both create and unmake at her whim.

She turned away again without a second thought.

I wondered now if Greg Randolph had whispered those words before—*Sadie's monster*. If others had, too.

If it was blinding the detective to everything else.

I had to nail down my time line, and everyone else's, before everything got twisted.

But first I needed to clear this house. I'd thought about moving the family who was supposed to stay at the Blue Robin into Sunset Retreat across the way—there was even more space, and I didn't think they'd complain. But I needed to check it out first, especially since I was sure I'd seen a shadow watching me the day I found the phone.

The key for the property was in my car. As soon as I stepped across the threshold, I knew something was wrong. The air had a thickness to it, some unfocused quality I couldn't quite put my finger on, until I drew in a slow breath.

My hand went to my mouth even as I was backing away on pure instinct. The scent of gas, so thick I could practically taste it.

The room was full of it. I shut the door behind me, running down the front path.

I dialed 911 from the front room of the Blue Robin across the street, safe behind a layer of wood and concrete.

———

I WAS WATCHING OUT the window when the fire truck arrived—expecting to see an explosion, everything reduced to rubble. But a stream of people in uniform entered the home, one by one. Eventually, another van arrived, delivering a crew of maintenance workers.

After they came back out, removing their gear, conferring with one another, I walked out front, meeting them in the street between the properties. "Everything okay in there?"

"You the person who called this in?" the closest firefighter asked. He still wore the bottom half of his uniform but had removed the rest and was wearing a T-shirt and ball cap. He looked a good decade older than the rest, and I assumed he was in charge.

"Yes, I'm Avery Greer. I manage the property."

He nodded. "A connection at the back of the stove, come loose. Probably a slow leak. But must've been going on for a while, with nobody there to notice."

"Oh," I said. I felt nauseated, sick. The shadow inside the house—had they been waiting for me to walk inside next?

He shook his head. "Lucky nothing made a spark." Then he motioned for the maintenance crew that it was safe to enter. "Still, I'd give it some time to air out," he said. Then, as if he could see something simmering within me, some fear made clear, he put a hand on my shoulder. "Hey, it's all right. You did the right thing, and we caught it in time. Everything's okay."

———

I'D BEEN DEBATING CALLING Grant on the drive home. I hated to do so unless it was urgent, didn't want him to think I couldn't handle things on my own.

As I was passing Breaker Beach, I decided to do it.

He would know whom to contact, and his name would carry more weight than mine. We were taught to always consult with the company lawyer before engaging. I'd already failed when I let Detective Collins inside. If the gas leak was a crime, I needed Grant's input on how to proceed before involving the police further.

His cell rang until it went to voicemail. I turned the car up the incline of Landing Lane, leaving him a message on speakerphone. "Grant, hi, it's Avery. Sorry to bother you, but there's a problem. With the rentals. I think I need to talk to the police. Please call me back." When I turned down the stone-edged drive, I tapped my brakes. There was another car in the driveway—dark, expensive-looking, familiar.

I swung around the corner of the garage, parked in my spot, hidden out of sight. I could hear voices coming from the back-yard—Parker's and someone else's, deep and firm.

I moved as quietly as I could, hoping no one noticed my arrival. So I wasn't paying attention as I approached the door of the guesthouse.

The front door was unlatched. A sliver of light escaping from inside. I held my breath, pushed the door slowly open.

The living room was in disarray. My box of things in the middle of the room. My clothes pulled out of the closet, heaped on the couch. And waiting in the center of the room stood Bianca.

"Hello," she said. Her blond hair was pulled back so severely it seemed to blend in with her scalp. She was imposing, even at Sadie's height, both of them at least four inches shorter than I was.

"Hi, Bianca," I said. I'd been waiting for Bianca and Grant to return since the start of the season.

No one had mentioned anything about my job in all the time since Sadie's death. The money kept coming. I thought maybe it was just a moment when we'd said things that each of us would rather take back, and we could chalk it up to grief, on both sides.

The state of my living room suggested otherwise.

Bianca's face remained expressionless, and I knew I'd had it all wrong. "I thought I told you to leave," she said.

SUMMER

2017

The Plus-One Party

10 p.m.

The police were coming. That was what everyone was whispering when I stepped outside the master bedroom, joining the rest of the party at the other end of the darkened hall.

The blackout. Ellie's scream as she fell into the pool. Someone had heard it, called it in. Three people told me in the course of two minutes. I didn't know any of them by name, but I assumed one of them was the person Parker had told me about who'd been looking for me. It was a small thrill to realize that they knew who I was, that I was the one to turn to. That I was the person in charge here.

Depending on the source, there was either a police car outside, or an officer out front, or one of the guests had received a call in warning. But the message was clear: Someone was coming.

Okay, okay. I closed my eyes, trying to focus, trying to think. Parker's family owned the house; Ellie Arnold was fine. I scanned the sea of faces until I saw her—there—across the room, half in the kitchen, half in the living room. Hair wet and now braided over her shoulder, face clean of makeup, in a loose-fitting blouse and ripped jeans that hung a little low on her hips. Enough to give away that they weren't hers. But she was here, and she was fine. Laughing, at that moment, at something Greg Randolph was saying.

I let myself out the front door, the hinges squeaking behind me as I pulled it shut, in hopes of interceding if the police had already arrived. I'd explain what had happened, retrieve a safe and unharmed Ellie Arnold, a witness or two, and keep everything outside.

But the night was empty. It had dropped at least five degrees in the last hour, maybe more, and the leaves rustled overhead in the wind. There was no police car that I could see—not with the lights on, anyway—and there was no officer on the doorstep. Just the crickets in the night, the soft glow of the porch light, and nothing but darkness as I stared into the trees.

I walked down the front porch steps, waiting for my eyes to adjust to the night so I could see farther down the road. The stars shone bright through the shifting clouds above. It was part of the town bylaws to keep the lights dim, to opt for fewer streetlamps rather than more, leaving the town untouched, poetic, one with the surroundings, both above and below. It was why we had the dark winding roads in the mountains. The beach lit only by bonfire. The lighthouse, the sole beacon in the night.

From the edge of the front lawn, I saw a quick flash of red at the end of the road. Brake lights receding and then disappearing. I kept my focus on the distance, just to make sure the car wasn't coming back. That it hadn't been turning around and parking. I stared for minutes, moments, but no one reappeared.

My hope: Maybe the police did come. Maybe they got the call and drove up the street and realized this was just a party, just a house. The Plus-One party, they must've realized. And when they saw the street and realized the house belonged to the Lomans, they left it well enough alone.

Worst case, I had the key for Sunset Retreat. I could move everyone if needed.

Back inside, I saw exactly what needed to be done, could see everything playing out, three steps forward. The liquor coursing through my veins only heightened my sense of control. I *had* this. Everything was okay.

"Hey, can I talk to you?" Connor shifted a step so he was blocking my path. His breath was so close I shivered. His hands hovered just beside my upper arms, like he had meant to touch me before thinking better of it.

Connor standing before me could go one of two ways. There could be the slide to nostalgia, where he turned his head to the side and I caught a glimpse of the old him, the old us; or there could be the slide to irritation—this feeling that he had secrets I could no longer understand, an exterior I could not decipher. An entire second life he was living in the gap.

He held my gaze like he could read my thoughts.

Look again, and now I couldn't see Connor without picturing Sadie. The arch of her spine, the smile she'd give, the scent of her conditioner as her hair fell over his face. And him—the way he'd look at her. The crooked grin when he was trying to hide what he was thinking, giving way as she leaned closer.

I started to turn but felt his hand drop onto my shoulder. I shrugged it off, more violently than necessary. "Don't," I said. This was the first time we'd touched in over six years, but there was something about it that felt so familiar—the emotion snapping between us.

He stood there, eyes wide and hands held up in surrender.

———

SIX YEARS EARLIER, CONNOR had found me on Breaker Beach kissing another guy. I'd stumbled after him, clothes and skin covered in wet sand, soles of my feet numb from the night. I reached a hand for his shoulder, to get him to stop, to wait. But when he spun, I didn't recognize his expression. His voice dropped lower, and a chill ran down my spine. "If you wanted me to see this," he said, "mission accomplished. But you could've just said, *Hey, Connor, I don't think this is going to work out.*"

I'd licked my lips, the salt water and the shame mixing together, and, my head still swimming, said, "Hey, Connor, I don't think this is going to work out." Trying to get him to laugh, to crack a smile and see how ridiculous the whole thing was.

But all he heard was the cruelty, and he nodded once, leaving me there.

The first time I saw him after that night was at Faith's, when she broke her arm. The second time, at the bonfire at Breaker Beach, where Sadie found me and our friendship began. After that, for a small town, it had been surprisingly easy to avoid each other. I kept away from the docks and the inland edge of town, where he lived. He kept away from my grandmother's place at Stone Hollow and from the world the Lomans occupied—the orbit in which I soon found myself.

After a while, it was less an active process than a passive one. We didn't call, didn't seek each other out, so that eventually, we didn't even nod in passing on the street. Like a wound that had thickened as it healed. Nothing but rough skin where nerve endings once existed.

But on this night, at the Plus-One party, when I'd just learned he'd been seen with Sadie earlier in the week, it was harder to feel nothing when his hand dropped on my shoulder. Suddenly, his interest in Sadie felt like a personal slight meant to hurt me.

And maybe it was. But it worked both ways; Sadie knew exactly who Connor was. We'd crossed paths a few times over the years. I'd glanced in his direction, then looked away, and she'd done the same; when I'd fallen silent, so had she, in a show of understanding. Though maybe I had understated his importance. She should've read it on my face, seen me then as I had seen her. I felt my teeth grinding, because she must have. She *must* have known. And she'd done it anyway. Taking everything, even this—owning it all.

Connor looked around the party and shook his head to himself. "I should go. I don't belong here," he said, but I had to lean in to hear him. Could feel the blade press against my ribs the closer I got.

Then leave, I wanted to say. *Before Sadie gets here. Before I have to see it, too.*

"I'm sorry," I said. What I should've said the first time but never did.

Connor frowned but didn't respond.

I heard voices from the second floor, the sound of something dropping. "I have to . . ." I gestured toward the staircase, turning away. "Just—" But the word was lost in the chaos, and when I turned around to try again, he was already gone.

Upstairs, there were three doors set back from the open loft. The door to the bedroom on the left was open but the light was off. Inside, a heap of jackets and bags were piled on top of the bed. The second bedroom door was closed, though a strip of light escaped from the gap between the door and the floorboard. In between the two rooms, the door to the bathroom was slightly ajar, and I heard a whispered "Shit."

I pushed the door open farther, and a young woman inside jumped back from the mirror. "Oh," she said.

"Sorry. You okay?"

She had her hand over her eye, and she leaned over the sink again, undisturbed by my presence. It took me a second to realize she was trying to remove a contact lens. "It's stuck, I can feel it."

171

She talked to me like I was someone she knew. Maybe she was expecting someone.

"Okay, okay," I said, taking her wrists in my own. "Let me see." I had done this once before, for Faith. When she got contacts our freshman year of high school. Back when we trusted each other with the most fragile parts of ourselves. *You poked my eye. No, you moved. Try again.* And again, and again.

This girl held perfectly still until it was over, then blinked rapidly, giving me the type of sudden hug that simultaneously revealed her blood alcohol content.

"Thanks, Avery," she said, but I still had no idea who she was. I blinked, and she was Faith again, falling away from me. But then she came into focus—dark brown hair, wide brown eyes, somewhere in her twenties, probably, though I wouldn't bet money on it. I didn't know whether she was a resident or a visitor. In which context she had heard my name. I couldn't orient myself here. Not tonight, not when we were all playing at people who didn't exist.

Maybe it was seeing Connor. My past and present blurring. The old me and the new me, both fighting for the surface.

"Are you—" I began, just as something banged against the wall, hard enough to rattle the mirror.

Her head darted to the side. "That's the second time that happened," she said. We held perfectly still, listening. Low voices, growing louder.

I realized that was what I'd heard from downstairs—not the sound of an object hitting the floor but something else. A door slamming shut; a fist making contact with the wall.

I stepped out into the loft, listening, and the girl continued on, down the stairs. Light on her feet, like a ghost. Not interested in the secrets hidden behind closed doors.

Something scratched against the loft window, and I jumped,

peering out into the darkness. But it was just a branch brushing against the siding.

I headed to the closed bedroom door, trying to work up my nerve to knock. I didn't know what I'd be walking into.

As I approached, the door swung open, and a woman barreled straight out of the room.

It took me a moment to realize it was Luce, wild and unlike herself. Up close, her eyes looked dark and imperfect, the makeup running; her lipstick smeared, and the strap of her top slipped halfway down her shoulder.

She slammed the door shut behind her as she readjusted her top, backpedaling when she saw me there. Then her face split, and she laughed as she leaned in close. "What is it about this place?" she said, and I was so sure I'd smell something foreign on her, something strange and unfamiliar that had taken her over. Something that had stripped the facade and made her one of us. Her eyes locked on mine.

Right then I thought she could see everything: me and Parker in the bathroom; me and Connor by the stairs; every thought I'd had, all summer long. I didn't know whether she meant the party or all of Littleport, but at that moment, it felt like there wasn't any difference between the two.

"Are you okay?" I asked, and she laughed, deep and sharp. She took a step back, and it was like the last minute hadn't happened at all. She was Luciana Suarez, unshakeable.

"You would know better than me, Avery."

I closed my eyes, could feel Parker standing over me in the bathroom, watching. "Let me explain—"

Her eyes sharpened, as if something new had just shaken loose and become visible. "You, too?" she asked. "My God." She leaned in closer, her lips pulling back into a grin or a grimace. "I have never seen so many liars in one place."

SUMMER

2018

CHAPTER 16

In the end, I backed out of the driveway of One Landing Lane with nothing more than I'd arrived with seven years earlier: a laptop on the seat beside me; the box of the lost and my luggage tossed into the backseat; the remaining items from the kitchen, bathroom, and desk hastily thrown into a few plastic garbage bags that fit on the floorboard. I didn't even have to open my trunk.

———

SADIE'S SERVICE THE YEAR earlier had been in Connecticut, an unseasonably warm day with a traitorous bright blue sky.

I'd picked my outfit because it had been hers first, because I could feel her beside me as I slipped my arms into the short bell sleeves of the dress, could imagine the dark gray fabric brushing against her legs. I thought it would help me blend in. But I felt too large in her clothes, the zipper cinching at my waist, the hemline more festive on me than serious, as it had been on her. I felt the sideways glance from the couple beside me, and the fabric prickled my skin.

I heard once that you can't dream a face until you've seen it in real life. That the figures in dreams are either real people or, blurry and unformed, things you can't recall when you wake.

But that day it felt like I must've dreamed up the whole town. Row after row of flat, stiff expressions. Everywhere I looked, a sense of déjà vu. Names on the tip of my tongue. Faces I must've conjured from Sadie's stories of home.

When everyone reconvened at the Lomans' stately brick-front home after the service, there was an odd familiarity to it, like something I almost knew. Maybe it was the way Bianca had decorated, a similar footprint to the homes. Or a familiar scent. The background of photos throughout the years that had pieced together subconsciously in my mind. So that I could open a door and know what would be there in the second before it was revealed. On my right, the coat closet. The third door on the left down the hall would be the bathroom, and it would be a shade of almost blue.

I believe that a person can become possessed by someone else—at least in part. That one life can slip inside another, giving it shape. In this way, I could judge Sadie's reaction before it occurred, picture an expression in the second before she shared it. It was how I could anticipate what she would do before she did it, because I believed I understood how she thought, and the push and pull that would lead her to any given moment—except her final ones.

As I moved through the house, the only person I suspected could see that possession in me was Luce, standing beside Parker on the other side of the living room, glass in hand, watching me closely. Ever since Parker had introduced us when they pulled up in the drive that summer, she'd been watching me. At first, I thought, because she didn't understand my history with the Lomans and therefore Parker. But lately, I felt it was something else: that she could sense things from a remove. As if there was something I had believed invisible that only she could see clearly.

Parker leaned down to whisper something in her ear, and she flinched, distracted. Her face was stoic as she turned to face him, and I used the moment to slip away, taking the steps to the second-story landing. The hallway was bright and airy, even with the darker wood floors and closed doors. I knew as soon as I put my hand on the knob, second one down the hall, that this room was hers.

But the inside was so different than I'd imagined. There were relics from childhood lingering, like the horse figurines on a high shelf. Photos tucked into the edge of her dresser mirror—a group of girls I might've seen downstairs. Sadie had spent her high school years at a boarding school and summers in Littleport. Her room was as temporary a place as any, filled with the things left behind, never fully growing with the person who returned to it each time.

Her quilt was designed in bursts of color—purple, blue, green—the opposite of her bed in Littleport, which was all in shades of ivory. She hadn't been here since before the start of the summer season, but I kept searching for some sign of her, something left behind that could fill the void she once occupied.

I ran my hand over the ridges of wood grain on the surface of her dresser. Then over the jewelry box, monogrammed with her initials, painted peach on white. Beside it, a pewter tree was positioned in front of the mirror, its branches bare and craggy, meant to display jewelry in a child's room. A single necklace hung from the farthest point. The pendant was rose gold, a swirling, delicate *S,* and set with a fine trail of diamonds. I closed my fist around it and felt the edges poking into the flesh of my palm.

"I always knew you were a thief."

I saw her in the mirror first, pale and unmoving, like a ghost. I spun around, releasing the necklace, coming face-to-face with

Bianca. She stood in the doorway; her black sheath dress hit just below her knees, but she was barefoot. Her toes flexed while I watched.

"I was just looking," I said, panicked. Trying desperately to hold on to something that I could feel slipping away.

She swayed slightly in the doorway, her face fracturing, like she was overcome—picturing Sadie here, seeing me instead, in her daughter's room, in her daughter's dress. But then I wasn't sure—whether she was the one moving or whether it was me. She looked so pale, I thought if I blinked, she might fade away into the bone-colored walls.

"Where does your money go? I wonder," she said, shifting on her feet, the hardwood popping beneath her soles. I could feel the mood shifting, the room changing—a new way to channel her grief. "You make a living wage directly from us. You have no bills, no expenses, and I know exactly what we paid for your grand-mother's place." She took a step into the room, then another, and I felt the edge of the dresser pressing into my back. "You may have had my husband fooled, but not me. I saw exactly what you were from the start."

"Bianca, I'm sorry, but—"

She put a hand out, cutting me off. "No. You don't get to talk anymore. You don't get to roam my house—*my* house—as if it's your own." Her eyes caught on a photo of Sadie, wedged into the corner of the mirror. Her finger hovered just over her daughter's smile. "She saved you, you know. Told Grant that stealing the money was her idea, that she was the only one responsible. But I know better." Her hand moved to the necklace, the delicate *S,* enclosing it in her palm.

I set my jaw. Bianca was wrong. She believed I had stolen from their company, taken Sadie's job, let her take the fall for it, but it wasn't true.

In mid-July, over a month before Sadie's death, I'd been reconciling the rental property finances when I realized the numbers didn't line up. That money had gone missing, systematically and quietly, and had never been flagged.

For a brief moment, I considered asking Sadie about it first. But I worried I was being set up—all summer I'd felt she'd been holding me at a distance. It was the reminder that everything in my life was so fleeting, so fragile. That nothing so good could last.

I summarized the details, passed them along to Grant, didn't say what I knew to be true: If it wasn't me, it was Sadie—who was technically the person in charge. I was many things, but I wasn't a thief. I would not lose everything I'd worked for because of her misplaced rebellion.

The fallout was handled behind closed doors, and I never asked Sadie about it. She shut me out when I tried to mention it. Back then I thought it was just her recklessness. Like her fixation on death—something to grab attention. She was always striving for an edge, seeing what she could get away with, never stopping to consider the collateral damage.

For a month afterward, she'd avoided me, not responding to my texts or my calls. Latched herself firmly on to a friendship with Luce. With Parker, they became an impenetrable group of three. One month and I'd been cast out of everything I'd known, as I had been once before. But I was older this time. I could see things three steps forward and back, and I knew exactly what Sadie would do when presented with each move.

I left her a note, an apology, beside a box of her favorite fudge. Positioned in the center of her desk, so I was sure she'd see them.

I'm sorry. I wish it didn't have to be this way.

So she would know I wasn't upset and didn't think any worse of her. I understood her, of course I did. Any apology would need to come from me. I wasn't even sure she knew how to apologize, how to feel it. But that was the thing about loving someone—it only counted when you knew their flaws and did it anyway.

The very next night, she sent me a text—*Avie, we're going out, come!*—never mentioning what had happened, and I was back; everything was fine.

She'd knocked on my living room window—her face pressed up to the glass, her cheek and one hazel eye, crinkled from laughter. She reminded me of Sadie at eighteen, and maybe that was the point. I could hear Luce and Parker in the driveway.

She had a bottle of vodka in her hand when I opened the door, and she pulled down a few glasses from my cabinet herself, poured at least two shots' worth into each. "I thought we were going out," Parker said, standing in the open doorway.

"We *are*. In a minute. Don't just stand there," she said, rolling her eyes so only I could see. Luce crossed the room, following orders, glass raised to her lips.

"Wait!" Sadie said, hand out, and Luce froze. "Wait for everyone." We each picked up a glass. "Hear, hear," Sadie said. She clinked her glass against mine. Her eyes were large and unblinking, and I believed I could see everything reflected inside, everything she never said.

"To us," Luce said, and Parker repeated in echo. I could feel my heartbeat in my toes, my fingers, my head. Sadie stared back at me, waiting. The silence stretched, the moment intoxicating.

"There, there," I said, and her smile cracked open.

———

THE NIGHT SHE DIED, she traipsed into my room without a thought, or so it seemed at the time. We'd been back to normal for two weeks, and I didn't want to shake the foundation. If something was off, I'd been too focused on my work to notice.

But to Bianca, I had set everything in motion. I'd gotten Sadie fired. I had ruined her. Taken her job. Revealed her to her parents. Pushed her to this inevitable outcome.

Standing across from Bianca, I thought I finally knew the real reason Sadie had taken that money—not as a reckless act of rebellion at all. It was something she had said after I'd been welcomed back into her life, when we were all out at the Fold. From a corner of the bar, Parker had Skyped in to a board meeting he'd forgotten about, with a drink in his hand, laughing sheepishly.

Parker can get away with literally anything. I can't even get away, Sadie had said. The closest she had come to mentioning the fallout of her missteps.

In retrospect, that was what I had missed. She wanted out. Out of the Lomans' grip, out of her life, by any means possible. Out—into the directionless, limitless wild. So she stockpiled the money. And that wasn't my fault at all. No, the blame could be traced back a few more steps.

"*You* did this," I said, stepping toward Bianca, my voice rising. "I can't imagine what it must've been like for her, growing up in this house." The same way grief had taken hold of me years earlier. Except I wasn't sinking but sharpening. Wasn't chasing something at the bottom but letting something free instead.

I had been armed for attack with all the things Sadie had ever told me. Her whisper in my ear, one of the first things she'd said about her mother: *All must worship at the shrine of Bianca Loman.* "Why do you think she did it there?" I asked. "At the place you were so desperate to live? It wasn't safe, isn't that what Grant thought? Living so close to the bluffs? But you insisted." Push and push until something shatters.

"And now look," I went on. I was shaking, my expression ferocious in the mirror. Did Sadie's parents ever see her for the person she was and not the one they expected her to be?

Bianca's face did not change. A mask of fury. "Out," she said. "I want you out."

"Yeah, I'm going." I edged by her, but she reached out to grab me, her cold fingers firm on my wrist, her nails grazing the surface, as if to let me know that she was only choosing not to draw blood.

"No," she said, "I mean out of this family. Out of our house. You are no longer welcome at One Landing Lane."

———

HER WORDS HAD HELD. But when I returned to Littleport that night, no one was there to tell me to go. The distance made everything hazy and ungrounded.

No one called, no one checked. And the time, like the distance, only softened things.

I continued overseeing the properties, and the money continued coming into my account.

It was a mistake. A fight, then, like in any family. Words not holding, emotion that would settle.

———

FOR NEARLY A YEAR, I'd been wondering if Bianca had really meant it. And now I knew.

I eased my car down the hill, passing Breaker Beach, heading into downtown. Like my mother, driving through town, looking for a reason to stop. Every earthly possession in the car beside me.

As I tapped my brakes at the crosswalk, I heard the rattle of metal under the passenger seat. I reached down, felt the edges of the metal box—the keys that I hadn't brought back inside on my return earlier.

Like a sign. Like Sadie calling my name. All the ghosts reminding me that this was my home. Reminding me of all the reasons I still had to stay.

THE SEA ROSE WAS set three blocks back from the water, in a row of closely built one-story homes with pebbles in place of grass yards. At one point, the cluster of homes made up an artists' colony, but now they were mostly quirky yet exclusive second homes, occupied only in the summers or on long weekends in the spring and fall—and they rarely went on the market.

It was a place I could've imagined my mother choosing in another life. Where she could carry her supplies down to Breaker Beach and work uninterrupted back at her house—the life she must've envisioned for herself when she set out in her car. Instead of the discordant one she had lived—working in the gallery, raising me, and painting only at night, in the hallowed silence. Torn between two worlds—the one in front of her and the one in her head that she was continually trying to uncover.

Still, she never could've afforded a place like this here.

The Lomans' company outbid the nearest offer for the property by almost a third to compensate for the fact that it would be a seasonal rental, but so far, it had paid off. Being so close to the downtown, on a historic street, in a place where others once crafted famous poems and art, offset the smaller size and the lack of a view.

There were no driveways here, just homes set back from the sidewalk in a semicircle, with first-come, first-served street parking. We called them bungalows, but that was only because no one wanted to pay so much for a cabin.

Unlike the Donaldsons, Katherine Appleton and friends had not followed protocol. There was no key in the mailbox, and the front door was unlocked. No surprise that someone had gotten inside the night before. I was starting to think whoever was messing around at the properties was just picking the easy targets: The broken window latch at the Blue Robin. The electrical box outside at the Breakers. And Katherine Appleton failing to lock up. The only house I couldn't figure out how they'd gotten inside was Sunset Retreat.

The cleaners weren't scheduled to arrive until later in the day—there were no guests scheduled for the following week—but it was even worse than I had expected inside.

Even though it was midday, a dimness fell over the house— the curtains pulled closed, the trash bags in the corners. And the scene left behind in the living room, like a seance. "Jesus," I said, running my finger along the counter, then recoiling, wiping the residue against the side of my jeans. The key was in the middle of the counter, beside the laminated binder, where they must've found my number the night before. A mystery how they'd seen that yet failed to notice the checkout procedure.

I caught sight of the candles mentioned in the call, one still burning on the kitchen windowsill. I leaned close and blew it out. The rest of the candles had been gathered in the living room, clumped together on the end tables and fireplace mantel, as in some sort of occult ritual. There was no way they'd be getting back the cleaning deposit.

I was scrolling through the contact information on my phone to send an email to the man who rented the place—with a note about the state his daughter had left it in—when I saw a stack of twenty-dollar bills on the coffee table. I pictured the guests opening their wallets, pulling out the contents, absolving themselves in the process. As if money could undo any slight.

Fanning through the bills, I realized the sum was more than I would've asked for on my own. I deleted the email and called the cleaning company instead. "Canceling the appointment for the Sea Rose today," I said.

Then I went to the closet by the laundry room, pulling out the supplies. I stripped the beds, threw the sheets in the washing machine, and began scrubbing the counters as the wash ran.

It didn't take too long, all things considered.

There was no garage, but cars lined the grid of streets in the blocks from here to downtown. No one would notice an extra car. I nodded to myself, dragging in the last of my things.

This would do.

———

SETTING MY LAPTOP UP at the kitchen table, I logged on to the Wi-Fi and sent Grant an email, referencing the voicemail I'd left him earlier. I kept things businesslike and to the point, nothing but facts and figures as I listed the issues with the houses. I told him about the window that wouldn't latch at Blue Robin, the gas leak at Sunset Retreat, the property damage at Trail's End the week earlier, and the report of someone in the home from the Donaldsons. I asked if he wanted me to make the replacements—asked if he wanted me to file a report.

I told him, even, about the power outages up at his property. Said he might want someone to look into that, let him decide what to make of it all.

Then I pulled the shades and opened the folder on my screen where I'd copied Sadie's pictures. I started piecing through them one by one. Looking for something that I hadn't seen the first time around. Believing, without a doubt, that something terrible had been done to her. I clicked the photos one after another, trying to retrace the steps she'd taken in the weeks leading up to her death.

The police had access to these, too, now, but Detective Collins seemed focused only on the thing that wasn't there. When Sadie was showing us something *right here*—the world, through her eyes.

There she was with Luce, laughing. There was Parker, by the pool. The view of the bluffs, where she'd stood at least once before. The shaded mountain road, with the light filtering through the leaves above. Breaker Beach at dawn, the sky a cool pink.

Next, a photo of Grant and Bianca standing side by side in the kitchen, in the midst of a toast. Bianca looking up at Grant, her face open and happy. The smile lines around Grant's eyes as he stared out at the hidden guests.

And then Connor. Connor on the boat, shirtless and tan. The piece that didn't fit. I kept coming back to this shot. The shadow of her, falling across his chest. A strand of blond hair blowing across the lens as she leaned over him.

I zoomed in on Connor's sunglasses until I could see Sadie herself in the reflection. Her bare shoulders, the black strap of her bathing suit, her hair falling forward, and her phone held in front of her as she caught him, unaware.

CHAPTER 17

I knew I'd find Connor at the docks, even though most of the day's work would be over—the crates weighed and shipped, the boats tied up to the moorings. Connor was the type who would lend a hand to whomever happened to be working down there.

He was cleaning his boat, currently tied to the farthest post. Even turned away, he was hard to miss. I could see the sinew of his back as he worked, the late-afternoon sun hitting the curve of his shoulders, darker than all the rest of him.

My footsteps echoed on the dock, and Connor turned as I approached, pushing the hair off his forehead.

"You busy?" I asked.

"A bit," he said, rag in hand.

"I need to talk to you about Sadie," I said, my words carrying in the open air.

He frowned, focusing somewhere beyond my shoulder. He dropped his rag, then started untying the rope holding his boat to the docks. "Get on the boat, Avery," he said, voice low and unsettling. Like when he'd get angry. I shivered.

I planted my feet on the last board of the dock. "No, I need you to answer my questions. It won't take long."

He started the engine then, not even pausing to look at me. "Ask me on the boat, or would you rather have this conversation with Detective Collins?"

My shoulders tightened, and I started to turn.

"Don't look," he said. "He's heading this way."

I felt him coming then, in the shudder of the wooden planks under my feet. Last year, when I was questioned, I had told Detective Collins that Connor and I didn't talk anymore, and that was true. But here I was, face-to-face with him, seeking him out even—and the detective had probably seen us. I wasn't sure whether he was coming for me or for Connor, but after our last conversation, I didn't want to wait to find out. He was looking into the case, yes, but he seemed more interested in how I'd found the phone—as if, once more, I'd been keeping something from him.

That list of names, it meant something, though. And Connor was on it. He'd told me when he arrived at the party, but all I had to go on was his word—and he'd already lied to me once.

I swallowed, stepping down onto the boat. Connor offered a hand without looking, but I steadied myself on the rail, taking the seat next to his behind the wheel, just as he pulled in the rope. He angled the boat away from the dock, no rush, like we had all the time in the world. But his jaw was set, and he kept his gaze on the mouth of the harbor.

I didn't look back until we were in line with the rocks of the Point to our right. And when I did, Detective Collins was standing there, just a dark shadow on the edge of the pier, hands on his hips, watching us go.

—

IT HAD BEEN A long time since I was out on a boat made for function instead of comfort. The thing Connor promised with his charters and tours was authenticity. Nothing had been changed for the comfort of his guests, but that was the excitement. This wasn't the same boat we'd taken out when we were younger—that had been his father's—but this one was newer, and slightly larger, and cared for meticulously.

He cut the engine when we were still in the protection of the harbor, with the steady rise and fall of the sea below, and all you could hear was the hull dipping in and out of the water, the water gently lapping against the sides. "It's nice," I said, meaning the boat.

"It's going to turn soon," he said, looking up at the sky, then back at the water. Both were in shades of dark blue, but the wind blew in from offshore with an unexpected chill. Fall storms approached like that, with a colder current from both the sky and the sea. "What is it you wanted to ask me, Avery?" He sat across from me, bare feet and khaki shorts, arm slung on the back of the seat, every word and mannerism chosen with care. Like he was pretending to be the person I thought I knew.

I knew the dangers of the water, had known them half my life, growing up here. But I had not considered the dangers inside other people. That kept me from trusting myself. Wondering what else I'd gotten wrong.

"Your picture was on her phone," I said, circling cautiously rather than asking outright.

His eyes narrowed, but he didn't move. "What phone?"

"Sadie's phone. They found it. I found it. At the Blue Robin." I watched him carefully as I spoke, looking for a tell in his expression.

His face remained impassive, but the rise and fall of his chest paused—he was holding his breath. "When?"

"When I went to check the property, after the break-in."

His eyebrows rose sharply. "You mean when I was there with you?" His voice dropped lower, and I knew I'd struck a nerve. I didn't answer, and he closed his eyes, shaking his head. "I don't know what you expect me to say."

"I expect you to . . . I want you to tell me the truth," I said, my own voice rising. To anyone nearby, it would've sounded like a one-sided conversation: me, growing louder; Connor, falling softer. Both of us on edge. "You told me at the house that you weren't seeing her. But your picture is on her phone. *And* you were on this boat together. Someone saw you last year, which I guess you could've tried to explain away, but Sadie had your picture. Why else would she take your photo if she didn't . . ." I took a deep breath, said what I'd come here to say. "You *lied,* Connor. You lied to the police, and you lied to me."

"Don't get all sanctimonious on me, Avery. Not you." His lip curled, and he stood abruptly, pacing the small open deck. We were alone on a boat in the middle of the harbor. I looked around for other vessels, but Connor had picked a secluded area. To anyone else, we were just a blur in the distance, as they were to us. "I told the police this," he said. "She paid me to take her out once, for a tour. That's all."

"Your number is in her phone. With an asterisk. Try again."

He stopped pacing, fixed his eyes on mine. "Once," he said. "Just once," he repeated, like he was begging me to understand something more. But I wasn't catching on. He ran a hand through his hair, squinted at the glare of sun off the water. "She found me on the docks. Called me by name, like she knew who I was already."

"She did know," I said quietly.

He nodded. "She asked how much it would be to take her on a private tour." He frowned. "I don't like to do private tours so much, honestly. Not just one person, and not someone like her."

"Like what?"

He widened his eyes, like I knew better, and I did. "But," he continued, "she told me a friend had given her my name. I assumed it was you." His gaze met mine, waiting, and I shook my head just slightly. "You didn't give her my number?" he asked.

"I didn't." He looked out at the sea again, like he was thinking something through. "You gave her the tour?" I asked, dragging his attention back.

"Yeah. I did it right then. She had the cash on her, more than I usually would've charged, but I wasn't gonna complain. She asked me to tell her about the islands, all the stories from the charter tours, you know?" He shrugged. "Guess that's why she came to me."

These were the islands the locals escaped to when we wanted to get away. Anchoring the boat offshore and swimming the final few meters with the current. One of them had an old cabin, deteriorated and rotted, only the walls left standing, last I saw. But at one point someone had carried in the stone and the wood and made themselves a secret home. Connor and Faith and I spent one evening there, waiting out a storm.

"Where did you take her?" I asked.

"I took her to three. The two in Ship Bottom Cove first, because the tourists usually like to see those. But she wanted one that she could explore herself off the boat, said she'd heard there were plenty of hidden places. So we went to the Horseshoe." I felt my jaw tensing as he spoke. "I stayed on the boat," he said, as if he needed to defend himself from the implication.

The Horseshoe was what the locals called the horseshoe-shaped band of rock and trees that at one point had been connected to land by a bar, at low tide—so went the stories. The waves broke over the rise of land you couldn't see, creating a sheltered cove, which made it a favorite of kayakers and locals alike. Any connecting land had long since disappeared, but we used to tell stories of travelers trapped there when the tide came back in.

"She swam there, though?" I asked, confused. Sadie did not like cold water. Or sharp sun. Or uncertain currents. She did not like being alone.

"Yeah, well, she waded out to it, just had a small backpack with her, figured it held her phone, maybe a towel. It was low tide, and I anchored there, it was easy enough. But she was gone so long, I took a nap. I probably would've been worried if I hadn't fallen asleep. I woke up to the sound of a camera. She was standing over me, in her bathing suit, shivering from the cold." He ran his hand through the air, like he knew the outline of her. Like he'd committed it to memory.

But none of this made sense. Why would Sadie need to come out here, with Connor? I could've told her anything she wanted to know about these spots. I would've come out here with her myself. Told her the stories, not only about the history of town but my own. Listened to her laugh at my stories of getting stranded; watched her eyes widen at the time we tried and failed to sneak a boat back to the docks at dawn. The parts of Littleport only I could show her, proving my own worth. *Did you get in trouble?* I could imagine her asking. Feel my smile as I told her we didn't. We were kids of Littleport, and you protected your own.

Sadie may have forgiven me for turning her in to her father, but she still hadn't trusted me—not with this. She'd come here alone. Without telling any of us—something she'd kept secret. Something that would've remained that way, if Greg Randolph hadn't seen her and Connor together.

"That's it?"

"That's it," he said, jaw set. But I didn't expect he'd tell me the truth, not after all this time. "I don't know why she took my picture." He pressed his lips together. "I know better than to get involved with a family like that." He gave me a look, as if I should've understood this, too. "This is why I told the police nothing. Because just one thing—one private tour—and suddenly, I'm dragged into this whole mess."

"This whole mess? She's *dead,* Connor." My voice broke mid-sentence.

He flinched. "I'm sorry, Avery."

"She had your *number.*"

"She called me after. I didn't pick up. I didn't like . . . It was weird, okay? Why she was there, what she wanted with me. Why she took my picture. I couldn't figure it out. At first I thought you had sent her, but . . ."

He had an answer for everything. Quick with an explanation—and yet. Sadie was out here in the week before her death. If Connor was telling the truth, what could she possibly have been looking for?

"Can you take me there?"

He narrowed his eyes, not understanding.

"To the island. Please. Will you take me there, too."

———

OUTSIDE THE PROTECTION OF the harbor, the waves dipped, and the spray of the water coated my arms, the back of my neck, as he cut a path to the arc of land in the distance.

There was no way to avoid the past as we got nearer. Time snapping closer as the land mass grew larger. It was the place we'd come seven years earlier, just before the start of the summer season.

Connor had shown up at my grandmother's house. "Come on," he'd said. I hadn't left the house in two days. I hadn't slept, my hands were shaking, the house was a mess.

When we stepped off the dock onto his father's boat, I asked, "Is Faith coming?"

"Nah," he said, "just us." And the way he smiled, keeping his eyes cast down, told me everything.

Before my grandmother died, it was where things were sliding. Connor and me. An inevitability that everyone could see coming but us. The knowing looks that we'd railed against our entire lives. As we grew older, a playful nudge with a shoulder or a hip, a wry joke and a fake laugh and a roll of the eyes. And then one day he blinked twice, and refocused, and it was like he was seeing something new. I saw something reflected in his eyes—of what else might be possible.

The touch of his hand became more deliberate. A play kiss in front of everyone late that last fall, when we were drinking down on Breaker Beach, while he bent me back, and his eyes sparkled in the bonfire as he laughed. And I'd said, *That's it? That's everything? That's what I've been waiting for all these years?* And took off down the beach before he could catch me, my heart pounding.

When he said, hours later, *You've been waiting?*

So we'd come here with a cooler of beer and takeout from the deli and a blanket, wading out to the island together, gear held over our heads to keep dry. We never got to the food or the drinks because I knew exactly what this was, and there was too much in the lead-up. But I wasn't capable of feeling anything then, just my own bitterness. A disappointment that, even then, he wanted something from me. How he couldn't see that I was so far beneath the surface, he might as well have been anyone.

I was a tight ball of resentment when he came over two days later with a lopsided smile, thinking somehow that this fixed everything: not only me but us. Even worse was the new fear I'd only just uncovered, that maybe he liked me this way—watching me slide to the edge and unravel, so he could make me back into the person he desired. It was the beginning and also the end.

Connor anchored the boat offshore now, turning off the

engine. Both of us looking at the mix of tree and rock and pebbled shore before us instead of at each other.

I pictured Sadie standing here, in her wide-brimmed hat, deciding to strip herself down and wade out to the island. The goosebump prickle over her skin. The red-pink tone where the cold touched her flesh. The softness of her feet on the crude shore. The determination that had brought her to this moment.

I pulled my shirt over my head, and Connor narrowed his eyes.

"I'll be right back," I said.

"The tide is up. You'll have to swim," he said.

But I continued undressing, and he looked away, opening the bench seat and pulling out one of the orange flotation devices. We'd stripped down to our underwear in front of each other a hundred times since we were kids, whenever we were out on the water. I'd never felt self-conscious about it until he looked away. Never used to think of myself in comparison to Sadie until I saw us both through Connor's eyes.

I grabbed the orange flotation device hastily and jumped straight in, the shock of cold seizing everything up to my rib cage as my toes brushed the rocky shore.

"Okay?" Connor called from above. I must've let out a gasp.

I had to slow my breath, just to relax the muscles around my lungs. "Fine," I said, using the flotation device as a kickboard, letting the current push me the rest of the way to shore.

———

IT HAD BEEN SEVEN years since I'd stepped foot on the island, though I could always see it in the distance on a clear day: a copse of dark trees. The terrain was rough in person. A rocky beach giving way to the hard-packed dirt and the green of the trees. The horseshoe shape created a small protected cove, so kayaks would often stop here to rest. But there were no other boats here now.

There was evidence of people who had been here, though—glass bottles half buried in the rocks that lined the dirt and roots. A log that had been dragged over and fashioned into a bench at the edge of the brush. There was an overgrown trail from back when the island had a dock.

I shivered as I walked the path that I imagined Sadie taking. My steps in her steps. The thorny roots, the sharp edges of rocks, the branches reaching for her legs.

I felt a prick on my shin, saw a bead of blood rolling toward my ankle, nicked from a loose vine. Connor said Sadie had been in her bathing suit. Would she have kept going, barefoot and bare-legged? Her unmarred skin, the fact that she couldn't even stand walking barefoot on hot pavement—I couldn't imagine it. Couldn't imagine what would have driven her here in the first place.

She had a backpack, a camera—did she think there was something here worth finding? A secret worth holding? Did she see something she shouldn't have while she was here?

The terrain was too unyielding. She wouldn't have kept going, not if she didn't have to—but Connor said she'd been gone a while. In her bathing suit, with a backpack.

I stopped walking. Or was it something she was bringing? *Lots of hidden places,* she'd told Connor. That's what she was looking for.

A safe place to hide something of her own.

I traced my steps back to the clearing, spun around, my eyes catching on the makeshift bench once more.

The log had been partially hollowed out, and I dropped to my hands and knees beside it, peering inside. There was moss growing on the underside, insects and things I didn't want to think too hard about. But I reached my hand into the dark and felt the slickness and rustle of plastic. I shuddered, imagining what might be inside.

It scraped against the base as I pulled it out. There was a layer of sludge and grime covering the surface, but it was a plastic freezer bag, airtight and watertight. Maybe someone's trash but maybe not.

I wiped off the mud with my bare hands, opened the top, and saw a brown wooden box inside, like something that would hold a necklace. It remained dry. I dragged my hands against the edge of the log, trying to clean them. Then I opened the top of the box. Set in the midst of the maroon lining was a silver flash drive, cold to the touch.

The trees rustled in the wind, and I looked over my shoulder, feeling the chill rise up my neck.

Sadie had been here. I could feel her, in this same spot, opening her backpack, pulling out this bag. I could see her reaching an arm into the hollowed log, nose scrunched, eyes pinched shut, holding her breath.

Why, Sadie?

Why here? Why across the expanse of a sea, inside a log? What sort of fear could've driven her here—to this level of secrecy? Where the walls of her home were not enough? A place, I had once thought, with no locks, no secrets.

I wished I had something to hide this inside now. Pockets, clothes, a way to keep it for myself. But there was no way to swim back to the boat, no way to keep it hidden without Connor seeing. He'd told me the truth, at least—maybe not all of it, but enough to get me here. To her.

He wouldn't have brought me here if he truly had something to hide, right?

———

CONNOR WAS WATCHING AS I waded out toward him, holding the freezer bag on top of the flotation device.

"What's that?" he asked, reaching a hand down for me.

"Not sure." I dripped water onto the boat, shivering, and looked for a towel, but Connor already had one out on the bench for me.

"Is that hers?"

"Not sure," I repeated, leaning over him for the towel. "There's a flash drive inside, though, and I can't figure out why else it would be out here."

His hand touched my stomach, and I flinched. But his fingers didn't move. His gaze was fixed on the spot just above my underwear, on the inside of my left hip. I stepped back, shaking him off, and he frowned. "Why do you have that?"

I looked down to where his gaze was focused. "It's a tattoo, Connor."

"It's the same as Sadie's."

My stomach twisted, and again I wondered if he was playing me. How he would have noticed that so clearly if he'd seen her only the one time.

Once, just once, he'd said. As she stood over him in her bathing suit. "I know. We got them together."

Sadie was all pale pink skin that freckled in the summer. She was wide-brimmed hats and oversize sunglasses and SPF 50 in every lotion she used; a collection of freckles on her forearms that almost looked like a tan from a distance. I was a color that bordered on olive, even in the winter, like my mother. I never had to worry about the summer sun this far north. The only similarity between me and Sadie was the color of our eyes, a shade of hazel. And this ink, binding us together.

But Connor was shaking his head. "But why *that*."

Sadie had picked it. Drove us out to the shop the day she returned, our second summer. "Incomplete infinity," I told him. Because there was nothing that lasted forever. The ends of the symbol stretched toward each other but never met. The curved line, looping with promise, truncating at a point—so I couldn't look at it without feeling a yearning, too.

Connor's head drifted to the side as he leaned even closer. "All I see is the letter *S*."

CHAPTER 18

Dusk began to settle on the ride back. All I could think about, with the thin towel wrapped around me, was the shape of the tattoo. The shape of the *S* of Sadie's necklace, left behind in her room in Connecticut. The gold edges lined with diamonds, digging in to my palm.

Do you trust me? she'd asked when she found me waiting for her on the bluffs. And I did. What other choice was there? I had been adrift and alone, and then I chose something else. I chose her. That day, she drove us straight up the coast to the tattoo parlor. She'd had the design ready, something she had thought about all winter, I had believed. Something that would be permanently etched onto both our bodies, bonding us together—for infinity, or as long as our bodies should last.

How many times had I felt another person tracing the lines, told them with confidence: *Nothing lasts forever.* Meaning: Not you, not me, not this.

I believed it had bonded me not only to Sadie but to my place in the world. Given me a purpose, a reminder.

But the necklace. The one I'd found when Bianca caught me in Sadie's room—I strained to see it clearly in my memory—the looping *S,* the edges curling toward each other—

Connor cut the boat sharply to the right, so I had to grip the railing. All that remained were Connor's warning words—and this creeping realization that maybe I had branded myself not with a promise of who I would be but who *she* was from the start.

I gripped the jewelry box tight in my hand as we veered away from the mouth of the harbor, where the water funneled and calmed all at once. We were heading north, toward open sea.

"What are you doing?" I called to his back, but my words were swallowed up by the wind.

Connor kept the boat heading diagonally, and as the sun dipped below the bluffs in the distance, I knew exactly what he was doing. He cut the engine abruptly, and I leaned forward from the change in momentum. Not Connor, though. He never broke stride as he walked across the boat, dropping into the seat beside me.

My ears buzzed from the change of equilibrium—the sudden stillness, without the raging wind. We were at the whim of the current, the creaking of the hull below us as we moved untethered in the waves. In the distance, on the bluffs, one house grew brighter as the sky turned a dusty blue, plummeting to night.

"I remember sitting here at night with you," Connor said, feet up and crossed at the ankles. "So I think if anyone should be asking questions here, it's me."

I gestured my free hand toward him, trying to keep it from shaking. "It was a long time ago, Connor."

"So," he said, "was it everything you imagined?"

I shook my head. "It's not like that."

"No? It's not everything you hoped it would be?"

"No, I mean, *it's not what you're thinking.*"

Those summers when we were fifteen, sixteen, seventeen, sometimes at night, we'd take his dad's boat from the harbor, just beyond the bluffs. Anchored here, far enough offshore, you could watch them in the dark, and no one could see you doing it.

They weren't close enough to see clearly, but it was enough: The girl in the upper-right window, staring out. Shadows behind the screens. Bodies moving in time to some rhythm we couldn't understand, on opposite sides of a door. On opposite ends of the house. Every light on, every shade pulled open—they were a beacon in the night, calling us closer.

She sees us, I'd said, so sure from the way she was standing there, looking out.

Not possible, Connor had promised. The light from the boat was out. We were invisible, as we were taught to be.

If I lived there, I wouldn't spend all day staring out.

If I lived there, I'd hang some curtains already, he said, laughing.

We watched their lives from a distance. Imagining what they were doing, what they were thinking. We were captivated by them.

So when Connor asked if it was everything I hoped it would be, I knew what he was thinking—that I had wormed my way into their lives, become the thing I once only imagined.

I could almost forgive him the implication. The tattoo on my body, the way I was living up there. The way I seemed to slide into her life. I was following the ghost of her footsteps even now. "It was a coincidence that we met," I said. "She walked in on me in the bathroom when I was working. Evelyn hired me." It was what I'd always believed until Erica told me someone from the Loman house had requested me to work that party. But that didn't make sense.

"And yet," he said.

And yet here we were again, in a place we hadn't been together in years. "Did you ever see me in there?" I wondered then if he had continued on without me.

He cut his eyes to me briefly, but he didn't move his head. "I don't watch people, Avery. I've got better things to do."

"Then what the hell are we doing here now?"

"Because I was a suspect until a note was found, and I've been living under a cloud for almost a year. I'm sick of it. I don't know what's the truth anymore."

I blinked slowly, taking a steady breath. "I don't know anything more than you do. I'm the one who told you about the phone."

He shifted to face me, one leg tucked up on the bench seat. "You know, just because you don't talk to us anymore doesn't mean people don't talk about you."

"I know. I've heard it all."

He tilted his head back and forth, as if even that was up for debate. "Most people seemed to think you're fucking the brother. Or the father." He said it sharp and cruel, like he intended to hurt me with it. "I say you're smarter than that, but what do I know."

"I wasn't. I'm not."

He raised his hands. "Faith always thought it was the sister," he continued. "But I told her you only wanted her life. Not her." He dropped his hands abruptly. "Anyway, mostly she was just pissed at you, so no one really listened."

My stomach squeezed, hearing his words. Even though I'd imagined them, heard the whispers, gotten the implication from the snide comments—like Greg Randolph's. It was different hearing them from someone who knew me, from the people who once were my closest friends. "It's not true. Any of it."

He narrowed his eyes. "I covered for you once before, you know. Told the police it was an accident when you pushed Faith."

I flinched, though he hadn't moved. "It *was* an accident. I didn't mean to hurt her."

"I was there, Avery. I saw." In the dusk, I couldn't read his expression. Everything was falling deeper into shadows.

I closed my eyes, seeing her fall in my memory. Feeling the surge in my bones, as I had back then. The rage fighting its way to the surface. "It was just . . . I didn't know she would trip."

His eyes grew larger. "Jesus Christ. She needed *surgery*. Two pins in her elbow, and God, I covered for you, even after everything."

"I'm sorry," I said, my throat catching on the word. It needed to be said, now and then. "Back then, you should know, I used to think about dying. All the time." I thought of the journal, the things I had written; the nightmare of my life. "I dreamed about it. Imagined it. There was no room for anything else."

"You wanted to die?" he said, like it had never occurred to him.

"No. I don't know." But, the blade. The list of things I had done—leaning forward from the lighthouse, falling asleep at the edge of the water—the time he had found me on Breaker Beach, drinking so I wouldn't have to make a decision either way.

Salt water in my lungs, in my blood. A beautiful death, I had believed.

But it had been Sadie's death instead, and the reality of it was horrible. All I could give him was the truth. "It was a bad time."

He sighed, ran his hand through his hair. "I know. I knew it was bad timing." He saw it the other way—that it was his fault. *Timing,* not time. "You weren't yourself." Except I was. In one way or another, I was never more myself than right then. Desperately, terrifyingly, unapologetically myself. And I'd just discovered the power of it, how it wreaked destruction, not only on myself but on others.

"When I saw you on the beach," he continued, "I wanted to die, too." A smirk to soften the truth.

"I didn't go there to hurt you. Some nights I'd sleep out there."

"I know. That's why I went there. You weren't home, and I was worried."

They had just shown up. Two guys, a bonfire. I knew them, a year older, but I knew them through Connor. "Everything just went to hell."

I thought of that journal, how fast I was sinking, at the whim of some current I couldn't see.

He sighed, then spoke quietly, as if someone else might be listening in. That detective, somewhere on the dark beach in the distance, watching us. "I need to know, Avery. What role you're playing here. It's not just *your* life, you get that? It's mine, too."

I didn't understand what he was implying. "I'm not—"

"Stop." His entire body changed, no longer feigning nonchalance. Everything on high alert. "The police kept asking why I was there that night, at the party. And I didn't know what to say."

"Why *were* you there?"

"Are you kidding me?" His eyes went wide. "You sent me the address. Why did *you* want me there?"

"I didn't." I pulled out my phone, confused, even though this was a year ago.

"You did. You sent me the address. Listen," he said. He leaned forward, close enough to touch. "It's just me and you here. No one can prove what you say to me right now. But I have to know."

I shook my head, trying to understand. "It must've been Sadie," I said.

The same way I'd just accessed her phone. I checked the password settings on my own phone now. She'd programmed her thumbprint, just as I'd done on hers—we'd done it together, years earlier. Because we shared everything, for years. And when that changed, we'd forgotten to redefine the boundaries.

Now I was picturing Sadie getting Connor's number from my phone. And then sending him a text about the Plus-One from me.

She wanted him at the party that night. Which meant she was planning to be there, too.

"It was from your number," he said, his hand braced on the bench between us.

"I didn't send you that text, Connor. I swear it." And yet he had shown up, thinking it was me. It was a startling confession. But Connor always saw the best possibilities in people.

"It's not over, Avery."

"I know that."

"Do you? Collins questioned me, sure. But I'm not the only one they want to know about. Not back then, and not now." Even in the dark, I could feel his eyes on the side of my face. I pictured that list. The one I'd been filling in to make sense of things. But also: the one Detective Collins had slid in front of me the very first day. He'd written out each name. *Avery. Luciana. Parker. Connor.* A list of suspects.

Mine was first on that list. He'd practically told me from the start: *You.*

And I'd gone straight to him with the phone, hoping he'd reopen the case.

"Did you tell the police about the text from me?" I asked.

"No. I didn't mention it." His eyes slid to the side. "I didn't mention you at all. So don't worry."

"Why not?"

"Maybe I'm a better person than you." He shook his head. "I loved you once." Changing his tune but proving the first comment true in the process.

"You hated me, too," I said.

He grinned tightly. "I don't even know who I'm talking to anymore. What you're like."

An echo of Greg's thoughts, claiming I was Sadie's monster instead of someone fully formed. There were pieces of others who gave everyone shape, of course there were. For me: my mother, my father, my grandmother, Connor and Faith, even. And yes, Sadie. Sadie and Grant and Bianca and Parker. How bizarre to expect a person to exist in a vacuum. But more than any of them, I was a product of here. Of Littleport. Same as Connor beside me.

"I don't live up there anymore," I said. He turned his head quickly, in surprise. "Long story."

He leaned back. "I've got nowhere else I need to be."

I tried to think of something to give him. Something true that would mean something to him. I pictured Sadie standing behind me in the window of her bedroom—and how we'd seen her standing there before, looking out. "At night, from the inside," I told him, "the only thing you can see is your own reflection."

As we were watching the house, the lights shut off unexpectedly, all at once. Not like someone was flipping the switches one by one. Like a power outage. Everywhere I looked, darkness.

"And I still get seasick at night." As if there was one thing that could bridge the time. A place to start.

"Keep your eyes fixed on something," he said.

"I remember." He had said the same thing to me when I'd gotten sick over the side. But there was only the lighthouse in the distance, and the beam of light kept circling, appearing and vanishing as it moved.

I scanned the distance for a steady object as Connor started the engine again.

There. On the bluffs. A flash of light in the dark. Near the edge, moving away from the Loman house, down the cliff path.

Another person, watching. Moving. Someone was there.

"Connor. Someone's up there. Watching. You see that, right?"

"I see it," he said.

CHAPTER 19

The twinkling glow of lights along Harbor Drive came into view as we neared shore. The lights of Littleport, steadying me—guiding me back. The docks were empty at this hour, no more workers milling about. Just a handful of visitors out for a stroll after dinner.

How many times had Sadie and I been out there together, imagining ourselves alone? Walking back toward Landing Lane, the sound of the waves as we passed Breaker Beach. Not noticing the people around who might be watching. Laughter in the night, stumbling in the middle of the street—oblivious to the fact that someone could've been lurking around their house. Blinded to the true dangers that surrounded us.

Not tetanus, sepsis, or a misstep near the edge. Not a warning to be careful—*Don't hurt yourself*—and a hand at my elbow, guiding me back.

But *this*. Someone out there. Watching, and waiting, until she was left all alone.

———

I HOPPED OUT OF the boat as Connor tied us up to the dock, checking to make sure the detective wasn't anywhere in sight. "Avery," Connor called, "you tell me what's on that." He nodded at the box tucked under my arm.

I was trembling with cold, the dried salt water coarse against my skin, my hair stiff at the edges. The ground shifted beneath my feet, as if we were still out on the water. In the distance, the lighthouse flashed over the dark sea. I just wanted to get home, get warm. "I will," I said—but honestly, that depended on what I found.

———

WHEN I GOT BACK to my car, I had a missed call and voicemail. The sound of a throat clearing and then a man's voice, professional and serious. "Avery, it's Ben Collins. I was hoping to run into you today, wanted to check in on some things. Give me a call when you get a chance."

I hit delete, stored his number in my phone, and drove toward the residential section behind Breaker Beach. I decided to park a few blocks from the Sea Rose and walk, just in case the detective was still prowling the streets, looking for me.

As I walked the two blocks toward the circle, the outside lights of the homes illuminated my path, making me feel safe, crickets chirping as I passed. I'd just turned onto the front path of the Sea Rose when I heard the sound of footsteps on rocks—coming from the dark alley between homes. I froze, unsure whether to run or move closer.

A shadow suddenly emerged—a woman with her hand on the side of the house for balance. She was in platform shoes, a skirt that hit just above her knees, a top that draped low in front. Unfamiliar but for the red glasses. "Erica?" I asked.

She stopped, narrowed her eyes, then took one more step. "Avery? Is that you?"

She had something in her other hand, and she twisted it out of sight, looking over her shoulder into the dark alley, then back at me. Her face nervous and unsure—like she had something to hide.

"What are you doing here?" I asked, walking closer. I had to see what was in her hand. What she was hiding.

"Just walking. For my car." She stepped back as I approached, as if I were something to fear.

And then a voice from deeper in the alley. "What's going on?"

I saw it then—a phone held out in her other hand. Like I might do when walking in an unfamiliar place, the light guiding the way. A man jogged the rest of the way through the alley, calling, "Erica? You okay?"

He slid an arm around her. She looked shaken, confused by my presence here. Like she was remembering the stories her aunt must have told her. The things I had done and therefore was still capable of doing. "You guys scared me," I said. "Someone's been messing with the properties around here."

She blinked twice, slowly, as if unsure about what had just happened. Whether to trust her own instincts. She gave me a small smile, her eyes drifting to the side. "I was just cutting through. From Nick's."

"Nick's?" The guy she was with, maybe. But he didn't react.

"The bar behind Breaker Beach," she said. "Straight shot from here." She extended her arm like an arrow down the dark alley.

"We were just . . . going to get my car." She cleared her throat. She was drunk, I realized.

"Oh. *Oh*."

The break-in the other night could've been a crime of opportunity, then. A house on the way back from the bars. Unlocked.

The man beside her watched me carefully. He had sandy blond hair, the shadow of a beard that matched; taller than Erica but not by much—I didn't recognize him. I was thinking of the image of the person on the bluffs with the flashlight. The fact that I'd seen the power go out, and now Erica was here with a strange man, slipping beside this house where someone had been the night before, lighting candles.

"What are *you* doing here?" she asked.

"I was visiting a friend. Heading home now."

She nodded once and shifted her weight, leaning in to the man beside her. She kept looking down, and I realized it wasn't nerves—she was embarrassed that I had seen this other side of her.

I wanted to tell them not to drive. But Erica was maybe a year younger than I was, and there were a lot of dangers in Littleport. You learned them by living them.

Still. "I can give you a ride," I said.

"No, no . . ." she said, waving me off.

"She's fine," the guy answered. "Well," he corrected, "I'm fine. And I've got it."

———

I WAITED UNTIL THEY were out of sight, the sound of their laughter drifting farther away, before letting myself in to the Sea Rose. The place was just as I'd left it—dark but warm. I wasted no time in emptying my purse, opening the Ziploc bag, pulling out the box, and removing the flash drive.

When I held it to the light, I saw a small circle engraved on the front with the logo for Loman Properties. I'd seen a collection of these at the Lomans' house in the desk drawer of the office upstairs.

My God, this was hers. This was definitely hers.

My hands shook as I inserted it into the USB port of my laptop, waiting for the folder to pop up. There was only one file inside, a JPEG, and I leaned closer as I opened it.

It was a screenshot, a long horizontal bar with two rows in a spreadsheet, slightly out of focus, all blown up on my screen.

Sadie had majored in finance, interned with her father in the process. Before she died, she'd been working with the cash flow of his company.

There were three columns, each containing a string of numbers, but only one made sense: the one with a dollar amount—$100,000.

The other two I recognized as bank account and routing numbers. I pulled out my checkbook from my purse to confirm. And yes, it all made sense.

Account numbers. Payments. Something she'd felt the need to hide away, outside the reach of all of Littleport. But there wasn't enough information. No names, no dates. It all meant nothing in a vacuum.

Maybe this was where the stolen cash was going? Maybe what I'd uncovered last summer was just a small part of it all—

My phone rang, jarring me. A name I'd never thought I'd see again lighting up the display.

"Hey," I answered.

"Hi. Sorry I was a little impatient." In all the years that had passed, I'd never deleted Connor's name from my phone. And Sadie had found him here. In the things I had lost but held on to.

"It's hers, Connor. It's bank stuff. Two payments. I don't know what any of it means or why she hid it." The words coming without a second thought, a habit of trust. He'd covered for me once before, he claimed. Like a promise that he was on my side. But I wanted to take the words back as soon as I said them, no longer sure of his intentions—of anyone's. Things were moving too fast, and I kept making mistakes.

The sound of laughter from the window over the sink made me bolt upright and freeze. But the footsteps continued past. Another group cutting through from the bar after being out near Breaker Beach.

"Avery? You there?"

I kept my eyes on the dark window. "I'm here. Maybe I can track it, see why this was important?"

A pause. "I think you should stop," he said.

"What?" She had hidden this on an island, paid Connor to bring her there, and now she was dead. And Connor thought *this* was the place to stop?

"Payments? Avery, come on. Every family has secrets. And that's one family I don't want to touch. She's dead, and we can't change that."

But it wasn't just that she was dead. If she had fallen, yes. If she had jumped, even, yes. But there was a third option, and it was the only one I could believe anymore. "Someone *killed* her, Connor. And I think the police suspect one of *us*. Are you just going to sit there and hope for the best?" Silence, but he didn't object. "That person is still here. That person was at the party with us." My breath caught—couldn't he see? We were living with evil. Someone who was still out there.

Even tonight, just outside our reach. The flashlight on the bluffs. Shutting down the electricity at night. He was a shadow behind the window. Watching me to see what I'd do. Or maybe: to see what I knew.

I double-checked the locks around the house, the phone pressed to my ear, glad I'd parked a few blocks away.

"Where are you?" he asked, voice flat.

I paused. It didn't seem like he wanted to help. It seemed like he wanted to talk me out of something. "I'll call you when I know more."

I saved the file to my laptop, then rifled through my purse for the closest piece of paper—the list with all of our names and the times we arrived at the party. And then I flipped it over and copied the account details down. I spent the next several hours staring at those numbers. Willing them to mean something. I knew only that the information must've come from somewhere in the Loman house, and Sadie did not feel safe leaving it there.

I fell asleep on the couch, the sound of footsteps periodically passing through the night. A side of Littleport I'd never known. A side of Sadie, too.

Something new I'd just uncovered, even after all this time.

CHAPTER 20

woke to the sound of gravel footsteps outside again, and it took a moment to remember where I was. To place the furniture with the room, the window with the light slanting in through the curtains.

The footsteps receded—someone walking to the beach, maybe. Heading in the opposite direction from last night.

I had fallen asleep on the couch, the open laptop, already low on charge, draining while I slept. I fumbled my way through the dim room, finding my bag with the cable to recharge it. While it was charging on the kitchen table, I cracked open the window so I could smell the ocean on a gust of wind. The phone buzzed from somewhere in the couch cushions, and I took my time finding it, expecting Connor again.

But it was Grant's name on the display. Like he could sense me opening that file last night.

"Grant, hi," I said as a greeting.

"Good morning, Avery," he said, his voice the same monotone as always, businesslike and unreadable. So that I was constantly trying to please him, to see my worth reflected in his expression. "Not too early for a call, then?"

"No, not at all," I said, my eyes focusing on the nearest clock. There, over the kitchen sink—frozen in time at noon.

"Tell me what's been happening."

"Well," I began, "like my email said, there've been some petty break-ins, not anything major. A television that needs to be replaced at Trail's End, and a new window at Blue Robin. But there was a gas leak at Sunset Retreat, and I'm worried it's all related."

He didn't respond, and I cleared my throat, waiting.

"Have you called the police?" he asked.

"Well, I had to. I called 911 when I smelled the gas, and the fire crew came straight up." A pause. "It wasn't safe."

"I see. And what did they say?"

"A loose connection behind the oven. We should replace that, obviously."

"Obviously," he repeated.

He waited to see if I'd say more, but I knew this was a tactic—silence and waiting for someone else to fill it, to reveal the things they'd wanted to keep hidden. I'd learned a lot from Grant over the years, nearly everything I knew about the business and how to conduct myself within its boundaries—the rules both spoken and unspoken.

He once told me I had something his own children lacked. The secret to success that eluded even Parker, he said, was that you had to take great risks for great rewards. That to change your life, to truly change it, you had to be willing to lose.

Parker will be good at the job, he explained. *He'll keep the company strong. He's good at working with what we have. He understands the game, the ins and outs of it all. But what he gambles, he hasn't built on his own.*

Your risk must come at some counterbalance. Neither of my children is truly willing to take the risks.

Because, I thought then, they already had everything.

"You mentioned the main house," he said now. "Something about the electricity?"

And suddenly, I understood what had made him call me back. It wasn't the email I'd sent or his concern about the properties. It was the lights going off at night; the flashlight I'd seen on the bluffs. The fact that he also suspected something was happening up there.

"Yes," I said, "it's happened a few times. The grid going out. I've had to reset the fuse box. You should probably have that looked at."

"All right, well, thank you. Is there anything else?"

What have you risked, Avery? He'd asked me that, too, when he called me into his office. When he gave me Sadie's job. Because I knew he understood. I had risked my place in their world. I had gambled my friendship with Sadie. Where I was for where I might be.

There were no gains without some great risk to yourself. And now I was desperate to hold on to what I was losing.

"I wanted to explain about Bianca. About—"

"That's really not necessary, Avery." His voice remained even and controlled, and I felt my pulse slowing, my fingers relaxing. "Listen," he continued, "we appreciate your help through this very difficult year. The truth is, I don't think we would've been able to keep things going without you. Not like you've done for us. But we'll be moving the responsibilities to one of the management companies for the next season."

I waited for a beat, two, seeing if he would continue, if his words were leading anywhere else—a new position, a new opportunity. But the silence stretched so long, he had to call my name again, just to make sure I was still there.

"I see," I said. I was being fired. A quick one-two. My home and my job, both gone.

And then his voice did change. Something lower, more personal, more powerful. "I took a chance on you. Thought you had something different, worth the time and energy. But it seems I overestimated you—my fault, really. A weakness of my own, I suppose."

The sting was sharp and deep—I could imagine him saying those same words to Sadie as she stood on the other side of his desk in the office upstairs, when he took her job and gave it to me. I didn't respond, because there was a line between drive and desperation, and he respected only the former.

It was all I could do to keep my breath steady, bite my tongue—as I had learned. And then he was back, even-toned and professional, expecting me to keep on going. "I've had a look at the schedules, and this is just about the last week of the season, isn't that right?"

"It is," I said. Next week was Labor Day weekend, and the town would clear out soon after.

"Right. Let's go ahead and close out the year, then. At the end of the season, we'll repay you for your time." And then he hung up. I listened to the empty air, even though the call had disconnected.

How had I not seen this coming? Three steps ago, when Parker arrived. Two, when Bianca kicked me out. One, the flash drive file on my computer. Sadie, trying to show me something. Waiting for me to notice her. In the entrance to my room, in her blue dress and brown sweater, and those gold strappy sandals, worn out and left behind.

I felt something surging in my bones. The same thing I felt when I pushed Faith, when Connor had found me with someone else—some prelude to destruction. I'd felt it again when Greg had called me Sadie's monster. But wasn't I? Who could understand, better than me, the push and pull that guided her life? That set the path for her death?

The laptop light turned green, the screen flickering as it booted back up. I shivered, heard the echo of Connor's warning, telling me to *stop*. Because he understood the danger immediately. A hidden file and Sadie dead. Something potentially worth killing over.

———

I SAT AT THE kitchen table, trying to make sense of things.

It was possible this wasn't even about something in Littleport. First step, I could find out if the routing number was for one of our local banks. Even if it wasn't, that didn't necessarily mean anything—there were plenty of national chains and online banks. But it was a place to start. There were two local banks in town, and I was a client at one. I had already checked last night—the number didn't match the routing number in my checkbook.

I drummed my fingers on the surface. Thought about calling Connor, *Hey, which bank do you use? Can you tell me your routing number?* I wondered if I could call the bank, but it was Sunday, and they were closed.

I pushed back from my seat at the kitchen table. My grandmother had used the other bank. She'd added my name directly to her account so that, when she died, I didn't have to wait for any will to be sorted out—I had direct access to the money, not that there was much. But I knew I had this information somewhere. In that box, I'd kept all the paperwork transferring our assets. Everything that had been hers, and my parents' before, becoming mine.

The paperwork still existed. I dug through that box until I found the old file.

Inside, I found a canceled check—the one I used to transfer the money from my grandmother's account to mine.

I brought the check to the computer, reading the numbers off, double-checking.

The paper was shaking in my hand. Yes, yes, they matched. This was the bank. A Littleport branch.

But I couldn't stop looking. Back and forth. The screen. The checkbook. Back to the screen.

I leaned closer, holding my breath. Reading them twice.

It wasn't only the routing number that matched. It was the account. One of the account numbers, one of the recipients of this money—it was my grandmother's.

The room spun.

"Wait." I said it out loud, though I didn't know whom I was talking to. Just. *Wait.*

Every family has secrets, Avery. Connor had said those very words last night, but I had never considered my own.

Erica's words in my living room—that Sadie had requested me by name. I had never considered that this could be true. Never stopped to think what could've drawn her to me in the first place.

But here it was.

I pushed back from the table, reimagining the scene. The bathroom. Sadie turning around, finding me there. The red creeping up her neck.

Had she known, all along, I was in there?

The slip of the blade. The toilet paper pressed to the blood.

Don't hurt yourself. She had said that so clearly, so earnestly, when I'd stood too close to the edge.

As if, all along, she had known.

She had seen me in the kitchen of her house. Followed me. Known what I had done.

Later, she'd found that journal, and she knew the hidden things I dreamed and feared. Keeping it all a secret for herself.

What did she *want* with me? Did she know I'd once sneaked into her house? Shimmied inside with Faith and Connor?

Or that I had watched from Connor's boat, staring in those big portrait windows—her life, her body, that I wanted to inhabit?

She had sought me out on the beach after, inviting me back. Into her home, into her life. Welcoming me—

Or. *Or.*

Something that belonged to her. Oh. Oh, no. No, Sadie.

Bringing me to dinner, watching her parents' faces, the stiff expressions. Her guileless smile. *Do you see me now?*

A sad story to share: Look what has become of this girl. No family, nowhere to live. Won't you help? Grant's voice when they offered me the guesthouse: *It's the right thing to do.*

The ink on my body, same as hers, the shape of an *S*—I have found you, and you belong, here, with me.

Don't, she said when her brother walked by.

She believed I was the secret. And, like the locals would gossip, she planted me right out in the open. *Look what I have found. Look what I have done.*

She believed I was a Loman.

SUMMER

2017

The Plus-One Party

10:30 p.m.

The threat of the police was now a distant, alcohol-infused memory. As much a nonconcern as the power outage, or stepping into the pool, or your secrets exposed for all to hear over a game at the kitchen island. The second round had begun.

I had been waiting to see what Parker would do after the scene upstairs—Luce spilling out of the room, tinged with the remnants of anger. Of violence.

Parker never played the game, I realized. Never had his secrets exposed for all to hear. Not in all the years I'd known him. Always too busy hopping from person to person.

Or maybe the rest of us were scared of him. What he would do. There were enough rumors about his past, his reckless teenage years. How he had gotten into fights—that's what Sadie said. He had the scar, and the gleam in his eye, to prove that he used to have a wild streak. Which, unlike mine, only added to his appeal now that it was gone. But there was an understanding that it had existed, and therefore still existed, somewhere at his core.

Parker finally rounded the corner from the front foyer, alone. He saw me watching and paused. Then he redirected his path, coming to stand beside me at the entrance of the kitchen, his hands restless without a drink to hold. He cracked his knuckles one by one. I imagined them in the shape of a fist.

"What happened up there?" I asked, nodding toward the front foyer, where the staircase was tucked just out of sight.

He scanned the room instead, ignoring the question. "Where is she?" This was not the type of place where you could call a cab or an Uber and get home. Luce was stuck here.

Parker stepped away from me, into the crowd.

"Parker," I said, loud enough to get his attention—on the cusp of making a scene. "What the hell happened? I heard something. I heard you guys."

He looked at me curiously, his eyes shimmering, the scar through his eyebrow reflecting the light overhead. "She's drunk. She'll cool off."

Like there was a hot, simmering rage in all of us. I laughed. "You want me to believe that Luce—*Luce*—is the one to blame?"

I tried to picture it. Luce, in her heels, throwing something against the wall. Or barreling into him, knocking him backward. Luce, uncontained.

He inhaled slowly. "Believe what you want. I don't care." Like my thoughts were inconsequential. Because his was the story that would matter, that would count.

I spotted her through the patio doors, sitting in a chair beside the pool, the glow from the underwater lights turning her skin a sickly pale. Her shoes were kicked off and her legs tucked up underneath her. Parker seemed to spot her at the same time. He started walking, but I reached for his elbow. "Did she see?" I asked. Meaning us. In the bathroom.

Parker flinched. "Did she see *what*?" he asked, like I was not permitted to mention things that had happened in the past. That it was up to him to decide whether something existed or not; that the narrative of his life was no one's business but his own, and he could erase it at will.

"Nothing." Because it *was* nothing. With Luce in town, with Sadie here, that moment with Parker could never happen.

Maybe that was my mistake. Maybe all I needed to say to Sadie about Connor was *Don't*. But who could say that to her?

To be Sadie Loman was to do exactly what you wanted. If it had been Sadie who had pushed Faith, watched as she fell to the ground, her arm held out awkwardly to break the impact—all would be forgiven. If I had been the one to steal money from the Loman company, I would've been kicked out of their world immediately. But not her. She was just given a different job. A better one. And what had happened to the money? Who knew. She'd probably spent it.

She took what she wanted and did what she wanted—they all did. Parker, Grant, Bianca, Sadie. Living up at the Breakers, looking out over everything. Deciding what would be theirs for the taking.

The crowd moved on around me, a blur of faces, sweat and heat, the prickle on the back of my neck—this feeling that I had to get out of here. But I had no idea where to go.

How long had I been standing perfectly still, watching the lives of others play out around me? Leaning against a wall, drinking what was left of the Lomans' whiskey?

The Lomans' house, the Lomans' rules, the Lomans' world.

Like sitting in Connor's boat, watching from the outside in. No matter how close I got, I was always the one watching.

There was Parker, whispering into Luce's ear, crouched beside her while she sat in a low chair near the edge of the pool. Her gaze fixed somewhere in the distance.

There were Ellie Arnold and her friends sitting on the floor together in the corner of the den, cross-legged, like a memory of a time long past—girls at a sleepover like Faith and I used to have, the rest of the world fallen away.

It took me a moment to realize one of the girls in the group was passed out, her head tipped back against the wall, and that her friends had remained with her, here. A large salad bowl rested beside her, and I realized it was in case she vomited. Ellie placed a wet washcloth on the girl's forehead, and I looked away.

There was Greg Randolph sitting on the couch, his arm behind a girl who appeared to be on the cusp of eighteen, her gaze turned up to his, like he was everything worth knowing.

And there was Connor crossing the room, heading for the door, his phone out in his hand.

"Connor," I called before I could think better of it. When he turned, I saw him as Sadie might, without the layers and years that had come between us. I saw him as a girl looking out over the balcony of Harbor Club, watching a man step off his boat, self-assured and perfectly himself. A man who would act exactly the same whether someone was watching or not. The rarest thing.

He didn't care who Sadie was, who any of them were. He was someone, she knew, who once was mine. The only thing left here that still belonged to me, and me alone. And I knew she had to have him.

I pushed off from the wall, met him in the foyer. "Don't go yet," I said.

His head tipped to the side, but he didn't say no. For all our history, I knew his weakness as well as he knew mine. Connor believed in a linear life. He'd known what he would do from the time he was a kid: He would finish school, he would work summers for his dad and for any fisherman looking for a second deckhand. He would fall in love with a girl he'd known his entire life, and she with him, just as his parents had done before.

He was unprepared when his life veered off track.

I smiled as I had once before, when he tipped me backward at the bonfire, kissed me in front of our friends—his mouth, a grin.

I knew, same as he did then: Things like this required a bold move. Me, in a crowd of people—in front of Parker Loman and everyone in their world—whispering in his ear, asking him to follow me down the hall.

My hand trailed down his arm until my fingers linked with his, and he did not resist. I walked slowly, in case anyone wanted to see. In case Greg Randolph would turn from the couch, raise an eyebrow, say, *That's the guy I saw Sadie with*. But no one did, and I didn't even care. I was high on the knowledge that he wanted me still, even after all this time.

It was dark in the downstairs bedroom, and I turned the lock. Didn't say anything, for fear it might break the trance.

I pulled his face down to mine, but the feel of his kiss was still a surprise. I could taste the liquor on him. Feel the looseness of his limbs as I pushed his shirt over his head. The malleable quality of him, where I could slide myself into his life. The power I held— that I could alter the course of everything to follow.

But he was the one who guided me toward the bed. Who whispered in my ear—*hi*—like he'd been waiting all this time just to say it.

In the dark, I wasn't sure whether he was imagining me or Sadie, but it didn't matter. His fingers just below my hips, brushing over a tattoo he couldn't see.

Nothing lasts forever. Everything is temporary. You and me and this.

Connor was no longer the Connor I knew—and neither was I. Six years had passed, and we had become something new. Six years of new experiences, life lived and learned. Six years to sharpen into the person you would become. But there were shadows of the person I knew: In the arm around my waist, holding me to him. And his fingers faintly drumming against my skin after, before his hand went still.

Neither of us spoke then. We lay there, side my side, until a noise from out in the hall jarred us both. A hand at the locked doorknob. I bolted upright.

"Avery—" he said, but I got up first, scooping up my clothes, so I wouldn't have to hear the excuse. I walked straight for the attached bathroom, so I wouldn't have to see the regret on his face. Stood in the bathroom that was still damp from when I'd cleaned the mess of towels and water earlier in the night with Parker.

I waited until Connor had enough time to get changed, to leave. He knocked once on the bathroom door, but I didn't respond. I turned on the shower, pretending I hadn't heard. Kept staring into the mirror, trying to see beneath the fog to the person I had become.

When I finally stepped outside, he was gone. I didn't know where he went after that. Couldn't find him in the sea of faces all blurring together in the living room.

I imagined him driving back to see Sadie, telling her. I imagined her finding out what I had done. What I would say: *You never told me you were with him. Sorry,* a shrug, *didn't know.* Or: *I was drunk—* absolving myself. *He didn't complain—*to hurt her. Or the truth: *Connor Harlow is not for you.* What I should've said long ago: *Don't.*

Don't forget that I once burned my own life to the ground piece by piece. Don't think I won't do it again.

Everything's easier the second time around.

It was then, as I was running this conversation through my

mind—all the things I would say to her, my resolve tightening, strengthening—that Parker caught my gaze over the crowd, tipping his head toward the front door. Warning me.

Two men in the open doorway, hats in their hands.

The police were here after all.

SUMMER

2018

CHAPTER 21

I *paced a circle in* the living room of the Sea Rose, phone held to my ear. All the information fighting for space. My grandmother's account. The way Sadie and I had met, even. Everything was shifting.

Connor's line kept ringing, and I hung up just as the call went to voicemail. He'd be working now, even though it was Sunday. *People need to eat.* What he'd always say when we were younger, when I was annoyed by his hours and his commitment to them.

The ocean was an addiction for him—a shudder rolling through him, like that first sip of alcohol coursing through the bloodstream.

I locked the front door to the Sea Rose when I left, but I brought the flash drive with me, scared to have it out of my possession. It was the closest I'd felt to Sadie since her death. My footsteps tracing her path, my hands where hers had been. My mind struggling to keep up.

All the secrets she'd never shared with me—but she had been wrong about this one. If she'd asked, I would've told her: I was not a Loman.

I would've explained that I looked like my mother, yes, with the dark hair and the olive skin, but my eyes were my father's. That my mother stopped here and put down roots not for that thing she was chasing, as she claimed, but because she met a guy, a teacher, and he was so *earnest* in his beliefs, so sure this was the place he belonged and that he was doing the thing he was meant to be doing. And his earnestness made her drop her guard, see the world through his eyes: that nothing would happen that hadn't been planned—and then she ended up pregnant with me.

It was not a perfect marriage, not a perfect life. It was always there, in the unspoken places of every argument—the reason she had stayed. The life she was living and the one she seemed to be searching for still.

She had given the last fourteen years of her life to my father, and Littleport, and me. They did not have money, I knew, because it was in their arguments, voiced aloud. The line between art and commerce. The side hustle. My mom worked in the gallery where her paintings hung, made more behind the cash register than behind the easel.

I remembered my dad dropping me off once at the gallery in the summer when I was young, on his way to go tutor. My mom stood behind the counter, and she seemed surprised to see us there. *You were supposed to be home by now,* he'd said. Her face was pinched, confused. *We could use the overtime,* she'd said. Then, looking down at me, her face slipping, *Sorry, I forgot.*

There was no hush money coming in. There was no strain of a man in the shadows.

There was only me, running free in the woods behind our

home, learning to swim against a cold current, with the buoy of salt water. Sledding headfirst down Harbor Drive before the plows came through, believing this world was mine, mine, mine.

My way of seeing the world, to my mother's disappointment, was always more like my father's—pragmatic and unbending. It was why I was so sure she would've loved Sadie. Here was someone who could look at me and see something else, something new.

Only now I understood what Sadie believed she was seeing that very first time.

Six years, she must've thought she knew who I was. Parading me around her house, taunting her parents with it, claiming me as her own. A dig at her mother; a power move with her father. Six years, and she'd finally discovered the truth.

At the start of her last summer, she'd bought two of those commercial DNA test kits that report your genealogy while also screening for a bunch of preexisting diseases. *Just to be sure,* she'd said. *We'll feel so much better after. Who knows, maybe we have some long-lost relatives in common.*

I was hesitant. As much as I liked to track things forward and backward step by step, I didn't know if I wanted to see something like that coming. Something untreatable, an inevitability that I had no power to stop. But how did one say no to Sadie, sitting across from you on the bed of your house that was really her house, really her bed? Spitting into a test tube until my mouth was dry, my throat parched. Handing over the very core of my being.

It took over a month to get the results back, and by then I'd almost forgotten about it. Until she barged in and told me to check my email. *Good news, I'm not dying. At least not of any of these eighteen conditions,* she'd said. *And surprise, I am very, very Irish. In case my sunburn led you to believe otherwise.*

She watched over my shoulder as I checked, then showed me

how she entered her info into a genealogy database. *Maybe we're distant cousins,* she said. Waiting, holding her breath, while I did the same.

We weren't.

I saw the reflection of her face in the screen of my laptop, the brow knitting together, the corners of her mouth turning down. But I was too preoccupied with the fact that my family tree branched outward suddenly. I was the only one left of the relatives I knew. My mother had cut off contact with her family before I was born, and they hadn't even come to the funeral. But here, I saw something new stretched before me—the tie of blood, connecting me to a world of people out there whom I'd never known existed.

I didn't realize then that Sadie had been expecting something different. That she wanted me to know the truth, and this was the way to do it. There would be no turning back then. No more secrets. Everything and everyone exposed.

But she'd been wrong.

I couldn't reconcile the payment to my grandmother with anything that made sense. And there was a second payment to someone else who used the same bank.

The summer after her first year of college, Sadie had interned for her father—that was when I met her. She had been working in his office, in his accounts. Had she stumbled upon this and found me because of it?

What did she understand when she realized she was wrong after all?

———

HARBOR DRIVE WAS BUZZING with midmorning activity. It was the last Sunday before Labor Day weekend—and by the time I found a place to park, I probably could've walked from the Sea Rose.

Though the streets were crowded, everything felt vaguely unfamiliar. A sea of ever-changing faces, week by week, somehow shifting the backdrop with their presence. I wove through the crowd on the sidewalks, headed toward the docks, but saw a familiar figure standing still in the bustle of activity across the way. Dark pants and a button-down, sunglasses pulled over his eyes, feet shoulder width apart, head moving slowly back and forth—Detective Ben Collins was here.

I sucked in a breath, dipped into the first store on my right. The bell chimed overhead, and I found myself in the long, snaking line of Harbor Bean—the favorite coffee shop of locals and visitors alike. In the fall, the hours would shift and the prices would change. It was mostly a place for the visitors right now. None of us wanted to pay more than something was worth.

I peered over my shoulder as the line shifted forward, but I had lost sight of the detective through the front glass windows. There were too many people passing back and forth, too many voices, too much commotion. "Next?"

"Coffee," I answered, and the teenager behind the counter raised an eyebrow. He tipped his head to the chalkboard menu behind him, but the script all blurred together. "I don't care," I said. "Just pick something with caffeine."

"Name?" he asked, pen poised over a Styrofoam cup.

"Avery."

His hand hovered for a second before he resumed writing, and I wondered if he'd heard something. Knew something.

"Well, hey there." A woman's voice from a table against the brick wall. It was Ellie Arnold, smiling like we were friends. She was sitting across from Greg Randolph, who grinned like he was in on some joke. There was a third man hunched over the table with his back to me.

The teenager handed me my credit card, and the third man

stood as I approached. And then I understood: It was Parker Loman, empty cup in hand.

"Avery," he said, and then continued past. As if I were an old plot point. As if I were just someone caught living on his property when I shouldn't have been there; as if I weren't his sister's best friend, hadn't worked with him for years; as if he hadn't kissed me two nights earlier.

It was a skill of the entire family, creating the story and owning it. Sadie herself, welcoming me to the Breakers. And now Parker, probably spreading this new story about me. I wondered if everyone at the table, behind the counter, out on the docks, knew that I had just, an hour ago, been fired.

Still, I almost felt bad for him, thinking about what his own father said of him. Parker had been robbed of the chance to want something badly.

Ambition wasn't just in the work. Ambition, I believed, was tinged with a sort of desperation, something closer to panic. Like a dormant switch deep inside that could be forced only by necessity. Something to push up against until, finally, you caught.

"Here, have a seat." Greg Randolph pushed Parker's now empty chair with his foot, the metal scraping against concrete. I perched on the edge, waiting for my order. "How've you been?" he asked, grin firmly in place. "I mean, since Friday."

The teenager behind the counter called my name, and I excused myself for my drink. It was something mixed with caramel, steaming hot, a spice I couldn't place. When I sat down again, I ignored his last question.

Greg gestured toward Ellie. "We were just talking about the party next week. Will you be joining us at Hawks Ridge?" He tilted his head to the side, and I took a sip. The Plus-One party must be at his place this year. Hawks Ridge. A group of exclusive estates set on a rise of land closer to the mountains, with a distant view of the sea.

"Probably not," I said.

"Oh, come on," he said, fake-sighing. I knew why I was wanted. For the drama, for the scene, so someone could say: *Look, Avery Greer, can you believe she showed her face?* So someone could corner me with a shot of liquor and say: *I know a secret about you.*

"It won't be the same," Greg went on, stuffing the last bite of a messy muffin into his mouth. "First Ellie, now you," he added, even as he was chewing.

"You're not going?" I turned to Ellie, surprised.

She shook her head, looking down at the table, then pressed her pointer finger to a crumb on the table, dropping it onto her plate. "Not after last year."

Sadie, I thought. Finally, someone with the sense to know this was in bad taste. Another year, another party, as if nothing at all had changed.

No one else seemed to know the truth: that one of them had done something to Sadie.

"It was an accident, love," Greg said to Ellie, voice low. "And I have a backup generator. The power's not going to go out up there."

"Wait. You don't want to go this year because you fell in the pool?" I asked her.

She cut her eyes to me, sharp and mean. "I didn't *fall.* Someone *pushed me.*" Angry that it seemed I had forgotten her claim, and I had. Last year, I'd thought she was being overdramatic, wanting attention, like Sadie had warned. But nothing about that night was as it seemed.

"Sorry," I said.

But even Greg Randolph wasn't having it. He smirked as he

raised the cup to his lips. "Probably bumped into you in the dark, by accident." And then to me, in a fake whisper, "She had quite a bit to drink, I seem to recall."

"Fuck you, Greg," she said. "I remember just fine."

Everything was shifting then. My memory of that night: The lights going out, the power grid tripped. A commotion. A scream.

Did someone leave in the chaos? Was someone coming back?

I pushed away from the table abruptly. "I have to go." I had to talk to someone else who had been there, who had seen everything. Connor, maybe. Except he didn't understand all the intricacies. The ins and outs of the Lomans' world.

But there was someone else. Someone who was there. Who saw everything. Who was dangerous, I thought, in the things they had noticed.

And who, after all of that, did not come back.

CHAPTER 22

Sadie once said she never knew whom to trust. Whether someone wanted to be her friend because of what she stood for. Whether they were drawn to the girl or the name. That life I'd watched from outside Littleport. The promise of something.

She had loved a boy once, at boarding school. She told me about him that first summer, like she was whispering a fairy tale. But he lived overseas, and after graduation they had broken up; he did not come back for her. I heard other names over the years, during college. But never with that same fervent whisper, the gleam in her eye, the belief that she loved and was loved.

I'm lucky I found you, she'd said at the end of that first summer.

I believed it was I who was the lucky one. A coin tossed into the air, one of hundreds, of thousands, and I had fallen closest to their home. I was the one she had picked up when she needed one.

How lucky I had been to find this girl who looked at me like

I was someone different than I'd always been. Who sent a gift on my birthday or just because. Who called when I could hear other people in the room, or late at night, when I heard just the silence and her voice. Who confided in me and who sought my opinion— *What do we think of this?*

She had become my family. A reminder, always, that I was no longer alone, and neither was she. I knew better than to trust that anything so good could be permanent, but with her, it had been so easy to forget.

Every summer, year by year, I was all she needed. And then Luciana Suarez was there.

———

WHEN I JOINED THE family out back at the pool that first night as they toasted to summer, every time I looked across the way, I'd find Luce watching me back.

She told me she'd known Sadie and Parker for years, that their families had been friendly since they were teenagers, though none of them had gone to school together. As if to let me know that her relationship with the Lomans superseded my own, based purely on the factor of time.

Luce had just finished up her master's degree when she arrived with the Lomans at the start of the summer. She'd put off the starting date of her new job until mid-September. She was moving anyway, she'd said. Out of graduate housing, closer to the hospital where she'd be working as an occupational therapist.

She'd told me everything I needed now. I only had to spend ten minutes looking through the staff directories of several local hospitals in Connecticut before I landed on her name—Luciana Suarez, office hours Monday to Friday, 8:30 to 4:30.

I mapped the hospital, found a nearby hotel, booked myself

the cheapest room I could get in a hotel chain I was familiar with—all from the front seat of my car, which felt as permanent a place as any.

I didn't even stop at the Sea Rose before heading out of town. All I had with me were the items in my purse—the paper with the list of names and account numbers, and Sadie's flash drive. I left behind the boxes, the bags, my laptop, the keys. Maybe leaving was for the best, anyway.

I could imagine someone finding those items next season if I never returned. Wondering what had happened to me. The rumors about that girl who was obsessed with the Lomans. Who must've had something to hide.

The same way we had crafted a story about Sadie—a person who wanted to die.

It was a thought that had me calling Connor again—just so someone would know—but his phone kept ringing. I debated not leaving a message, knowing how it would look, but there was already evidence of the calls. Detective Collins had seen us together.

There was nothing incriminating about tracking down the truth.

"Hi. Didn't see you on the docks this morning but wanted to let you know I'm heading out of town." I didn't know how much more to say—about the payment and the bank accounts on the flash drive in my purse. I didn't know whether to trust my instincts or him. But Connor knew my grandmother. He knew my family. And he was always, always better at this part—at looking again and seeing something new. "I was trying to find out which bank the accounts were from." I took a breath. "I discovered that one of the accounts," I said, "belonged to my grandmother."

And then I drove out of Littleport—through the crowded streets of the downtown, rising up and away from the harbor; winding through the mountain roads, the pavement cut like switchbacks in sections; through the greenery and the barren roadsides, nothing but trap shops and ice cream shops and gas stations with a single pump—until the highway.

I headed south, like everyone else leaving town, sat in the traffic heading back to the cities, until we connected with 95 and the roads opened up in Portland, highways splitting off in various directions, like a spiderweb.

It was dinnertime when I pulled in to the hotel parking lot in a town that looked like every other town I'd passed through on the way. Connor had left me a voicemail, which I listened to while sitting in the car, as if there were someone who might be eavesdropping.

"Just back at the docks and got your message. Call me when you get this. No matter what time."

———

THE HOTEL ROOM WAS standard, simple, a box room like a thousand other box rooms all across the country. I had forgotten how everything about Littleport carried a reminder of where you were, even the motels up and down the coast, with the seashells and the candle votives floating in sand. Lobster traps refurbished to create benches and artwork. Nets and buoys decorating the lobbies of restaurants farther inland, even. Here, there was nothing but ivory walls and a generic flower painting.

Maybe this was how to do it. How to live a life of even-tempered safety. Where nothing harms you, but nothing thrills you. Where you have risked nothing.

It took this—stepping outside Littleport and looking back in—to see my home through the eyes of a stranger. To finally get a sense of my mother when she was my age. Not what made her stay but what made her stop in the first place.

In Littleport, we had become addicted to the extremes. No matter where you found yourself, you adapted to the highs or you adapted to the lows. Everything was temporary, and so was your place within it. We understood that. It was always there, in the force of the sea and the rise of the mountains. In the crowded chaos of summer and the barren loneliness of winter. The sweet sea roses dying, the quick foot of snow melting. Everything marked a passage of time and another chance for you within it.

I called Connor back once I was settled in my room. When he picked up, I heard noises in the background, like he was out somewhere. "Is this a bad time?"

The noises drifted away. "Just a sec," he said. I heard the sound of a door squeaking closed.

"Are you out?" How could he disregard everything happening for a night out with friends right now? He'd told me to stop looking, and apparently, he'd gone right on with his life.

"No, I'm not out. I just got home. There was a party at the apartment next door. People out in the hall."

"Oh." I didn't even know where he lived anymore.

"God, listen." His voice dropped lower. "That detective was around the docks when I left, and then when I came back. He's been there all day. And he asked if I'd seen you."

"What did you say?"

"What do you think? I said no. But he saw us together yesterday and wanted to know what that was about. I told him, you know, old friends catching up. None of his business."

I leaned back against the headboard, bent my knees, staring at my reflection in the mirror over the dresser across the way. "He thinks it's someone at the party, Connor. That it's one of us. And then I find my grandmother's account listed on that flash drive, and I don't know what to think."

"Where are you?" he asked.

"Connecticut. Talking to someone else who knows the Lo-mans."

"You should've waited. I would've come."

"Connor," I said, because we had to be honest with each other here. Everything was temporary, and so was this. An alliance of necessity, because we had found ourselves tied to either end of it. But something that would drift apart again as soon as we were free of it. "I'm here to talk to Luciana Suarez. Better if it's just me. You said she saw what happened that night at the party, right? With the window?"

Silence. I heard the sound of something popping, could picture his jaw shifting back and forth, and suddenly, I held my breath. Wondering whether I had put my trust in the wrong person, if my instincts were wrong. "Let me know what she says," he finally answered. His voice low and chilled.

"Of course," I said. Though if he could read the tone of my voice as well as I could read his, he would know that this was a lie.

CHAPTER 23

The last time I'd seen Luce was at the service in Connecticut. When she'd been watching me closely. I wasn't sure when she and Parker had broken up—or why. There was the fight at the party, but they appeared to be back together by the service. I didn't know whether it was truly *a break,* as Parker said, or if something else had caused the split.

I was up by five-thirty, with nothing but my thoughts for company. Inside my purse was that folded-up sheet of paper with the details of the party.

Me—6:40 p.m.

Luce—8 p.m.

Connor—8:10 p.m.

Parker—8:30 p.m.

I kept working through the events of that night, trying to see something new. Wondering whether each person was truly accounted for the entire time.

After we had all arrived, there was the game with Greg Randolph; Luce showing me the broken window; the power outage and Ellie Arnold falling—or pushed—into the pool; Parker helping me clean the bathroom after; then his fight with Luce upstairs; and Connor, heading for the exit, until I pulled him back.

And now, at seven-thirty in the morning, I was already at the side door to the hospital medical center, waiting for it to unlock. The gentle automated click, and I was in.

I found her office down the white maze of halls. Her name, on a sign on the door, along with three others. Though the hours were posted from eight-thirty on, I knew she'd have to show up sooner than that.

I saw the shadow first—no footsteps—rounding the corner. Then a woman: rubber-soled flat shoes, dress slacks, a blue fitted blouse. Hair pulled back and clipped low, coffee in one hand, phone in the other. It was Luce. She stopped as soon as she came around the corner, still looking down at her phone, as if she could sense something off. Something out of place.

She looked up and blinked twice, her face giving away nothing.

"Hi," I said.

She kept looking, like she wasn't sure who I was.

And then something seemed to register—putting me in context, dragging out the memory. "Avery?" she said. She looked over her shoulder, as if I could've been waiting for someone else.

"I was hoping to find you before office hours." I tapped the sign on her door, a reminder that I was just following public information. "I was hoping to talk to you."

"Is everything okay?" She stepped closer, and I wondered if she was talking about Parker. Whether they were still close and now she was worried about her boyfriend—the fact that they were just on *a break,* or maybe not a break at all. Maybe she had just stayed behind for work, and Parker had lied. It wouldn't be the first time.

"Yes. No, I'm not sure. Sadie's dedication ceremony is this week, you know? Parker's there. And the investigation, it's not as simple as it seemed after all."

She tucked her phone into her purse, took out her keys, opened the door. "I didn't think it was simple from the start." She held the door open for me with her back foot, beckoning me inside as she flipped on the overhead lights and dropped her bag behind the front desk. It was a small office, a scattering of chairs along the wall across from the reception desk, and a hallway with several open doors visible from where we stood.

She checked her watch. "We probably have ten minutes before the secretary arrives. She's always early."

I kept staring at her, which made her frown. But it was just the surprise of her. She appeared so different from the person I'd met the previous summer, in white capris and gold jewelry and perfect hair curled beneath her collarbone. I figured I must seem different to her as well, outside Littleport. The town itself made people something more. That was why the visitors went there. Surrounded by the mountains and the ocean, you became more than you were elsewhere. Someone who could cut a kayak through the breakers; someone who'd hiked to the top of a mountain, looked out over the forest of trees, straight to the ocean, believing you earned every aspect of it. Who could be home in time to drink champagne over lobster that evening. Someone worthy of everything the place had to offer.

Luce glanced once toward the closed door, clearing her throat. I was losing her now that she had time to think things through. To realize I must've found her name, driven half a day, just to be standing here in front of her.

"When did you last speak to Parker?" I asked.

That seemed to focus her attention, because her eyes widened slightly, her breathing picked up. Almost as if she were afraid. "We haven't spoken much since we broke up."

"When was that?"

She tipped her head. "Last September. Well, technically, that night. The night of the party."

"What?" I saw her again, leaving the upstairs bedroom. That wild look in her eyes. Had he dumped her right then? Or had it been her?

"We got in a fight that night, but that was just the last straw. The thing that makes you say it, you know?"

I'd heard them from the bathroom. The bang against the wall. I dropped my voice. "Did he hurt you?"

"Parker? No. It was nothing like that . . . He opened the door to leave, and I slammed it shut." She shook her head. "I just wanted the truth for once. I was so sick of the lies."

"But I saw you. At the service." Standing beside him, watching me. He'd leaned down to whisper in her ear, and she'd flinched, turning away—

"Yeah, he asked that— Well, he said it *wouldn't look good* if we'd broken up the same night his sister died." She rolled her eyes. "Can you believe it? Even then they were thinking of how things would look. We agreed to keep up appearances until after the service, after everything wound down and I started my job." She gestured around the room. "Mostly, we just sort of . . . drifted after. There was nothing left to say. I've gone out of my way not to cross paths with the Lomans since. So far, I've succeeded."

"I thought you . . . Well, they seemed to really like you. You seemed to like them."

She laughed then, unexpectedly. "Sure. They seem like a lot of things." She chewed the inside of her cheek, considering me. A nervous habit I'd never noticed before. "Have you ever played chess?"

My father had, but his set had disappeared after that first move, and I didn't know how to play, really. "You think they're playing a game?" I asked.

She ran her hand back over her hair, down the ponytail. "I think they *are* the game, Avery. Bishops and knights. Kings and queens. Pawns."

I lost the thread, lost the metaphor. "You think you were a pawn?" Or maybe it was me she was talking about.

She pressed her lips together, not answering. "They will sacrifice anything for the king."

I remembered what Grant had taught me—that you had to be willing to risk in order to win. That you had to be willing to part with something. You had to be ready to lose.

"The family is so screwed up," she continued, her voice barely above a whisper. "They hate each other."

"No . . ." I said unconvincingly. Thinking: *They close ranks. When things go wrong, they cover.* Setting Parker up to take over the company. Moving Sadie's career. Guiding their lives. But I'd also witnessed the animosity between Sadie and Parker. There was no way Luce hadn't noticed. I thought it had stemmed from jealousy, from the expectations of their parents—a typical sibling rivalry— but maybe I was wrong.

"It's all fake," she said. "Imagine the lengths they must go to, all of them, to make you believe. Everything's fake. Nothing's real."

But Luce had pointed the finger at me. Detective Collins told me so.

"You told the police I was obsessed with Sadie."

She took a deep breath. "That detective . . . he was looking for something. And I didn't want him to see it in me. He kept asking for every move I made. Where I was, every second. It's so hard to remember every moment. What you did, what you saw . . ." She closed her eyes, but I could see them moving underneath the lids. "What was I supposed to think, though? When I arrived last summer, you were really not pleased to see me there. It wasn't a lie, what I told him."

"I just didn't know you would be there," I said. "No one told me, either."

She twisted the coffee cup in her hands, took a long sip, then dropped the rest in the trash can beside the desk. "I thought you were after Parker at first. But then I saw—the way you and Sadie were. I don't know what happened between the two of you over the summer, but yes, I told the police. It was a humiliating night for me, and I was sick of replaying it. And then *Sadie,* God. I just wanted to get out of there." A shudder rolled through her as she finished speaking.

"You mean there was a reason they might focus on you?"

Her mouth was a thin line. "No, not me."

Parker, then. She meant Parker. Parker's involvement would drag her down into the mess. The way you could pull someone up into a different world but also pull someone down. It was a lesson we'd both learned from the Lomans.

Luce shrugged on her white coat. Clipped on a name tag. I thought about the ways we dressed to present ourselves. How we slipped into another disguise, another skin. How we shifted our appearance in ways to say something to one another. Luce now: *I am a person who will help you.* Or: *I belong here.*

She looked at the clock once more. "Is this what you came for? Is that enough?"

"Someone killed Sadie. That note wasn't hers."

She stared at me for a long time, her hands frozen on her name tag. Finally, she smoothed her hands down the side of her lab coat. Lowered her voice. "Are you asking if I think one of them could've done it?"

Wasn't I? Wasn't that what I was here for? "You knew better than me how they were." I cleared my throat. "You saw how all of them were." I was too close to see clearly. And, as she'd told me the day we met, she'd known them longer.

"I did."

"I think Sadie wanted to get out of there. I think she found something out about her family." I glanced to the side, leaving my part out of it—that whatever she had found wasn't tied only to her family but to mine. The theft, the payments—how it was all connected, and I was a part of it.

"I don't know that she wanted to leave, exactly," Luce said. "I think she just wanted to be seen, like Parker was. He needs it, you know, from everyone around him. The idolization of Parker Loman." She rolled her eyes. "But Sadie was never having it." *A little star protégé. A junior asshole.* "Her teasing, it got under his skin. I'd never seen Parker's look turn so dark as when Sadie pushed him. It was always something. She kept teasing him about his scar. I didn't think it was that big a deal. We were all young once." She touched her eyebrow, shrugged. "But she wouldn't let up. Said, *Oh, tell Luce about your wild youth. Parker gets away with everything. What was it again, a fight with two guys? A fight over some girl?* He would stay silent, but she'd keep pushing. Say something like, *Parker, your next line is: 'You should see the other guy.' Or do I have it wrong? Come on, tell us.* Or, *The sins of his youth. Locked away forever.*"

I could see Sadie doing it, the expression on her face. Digging and digging until something snapped. *Parker can get away with anything.* She hated him. Of course she did. The life she could never have, even growing up in the same house, with the same parents, the same opportunities.

"Why did you break up, then? Were you afraid of him?"

"No, I wasn't afraid. I was *pissed.*" She looked to the side and sniffed. "It's embarrassing. That night. The window. Remember?"

I held my breath. Held perfectly still.

"I was inside looking for Parker. But I finally saw him through the window. I smiled. I remember, I *smiled.*" She shook her head to herself. "Until I saw that his hands were out. He was talking to another girl, trying to get her to calm down. And the look on her face . . . I know that look. Anger, yes, but also heartbreak. And then she picked up one of those standing pillars around the patio and swung it at his head." Luce swung her arms as if holding a bat—demonstrating or remembering. My mouth dropped open.

Her mouth quirked into a smile. "That was my look, too. He ducked out of the way, but it hit the glass, and, well, you saw. She meant to do it. She was going to hurt him. She was so, so angry . . . Later, when I confronted him, he claimed it was over long ago. That she couldn't let it go. But come on." She flexed her fingers. "I wanted the truth. No more lies. You don't wait until the very last day of summer and attack someone about something that happened a *year* ago. She was so angry, angry enough to hurt him right then." Her throat moved. "That whole place . . . it's like you walk into it, and it's a world unto itself. Nothing else exists. Time stops. You think you can do *anything* . . ." Then she refocused on me. "You didn't know? I really thought everyone was in on the joke but me."

"No," I said. "I didn't know." I had no idea what Parker did when he was off alone.

"Parker begged me to leave her out of it. And I only did because I didn't believe then that he could've hurt Sadie. We were together most of the night, and then there was that note . . . I didn't believe he'd really hurt her. But I don't know anymore. The more time that passes, looking back?" She shook her head.

But I was barely listening. I was picturing the girl out back with a pillar held like a bat. Running through a list of faces I'd seen at the party. Rumors I'd heard or imagined about Parker. "The other girl, did you know her name?"

"No. But I knew who she was. I'd seen her before. Curly hair, sort of brownish red. Worked at that bed-and-breakfast, the one we went to for brunch sometimes." She choked on her own laugh. "He brought me right there during the summer, paraded me around, the sick fuck. I figured, after, that's why he wanted to park there. That's what took him so long to show up at the party. So he could see her first."

I stepped back just as the door swung open. An older woman in a floral dress stood there, half in the entrance, door balanced on her hip. She looked between us. "Is everything okay?" She must've sensed it in the air, the tension, the danger of this moment. A name tag was clipped to the front of her dress. The secretary, then.

"I have to go," I said.

"Avery?" Luce's voice faded away as the door swung shut behind me. I moved fast, practically running down the hall. I pushed through the closest exit, into the crisp morning end-of-summer air, sucking in a deep breath.

Goddamn Connor. He knew. The girl he was arguing with in the shadows—the one who'd swung a pillar at Parker. I saw them through the cracks in the window, near the edge of the yard—her face just out of frame. He saw it happen, and he lied. Choosing his allegiance, then and now.

I could see her perfectly, that girl in the shadows. Knuckles white. I pictured the look in her eyes as she stumbled backward. Could see it clearly, in a way I never could before. Fear, yes, but anger, too.

Faith. It had been Faith.

CHAPTER 24

sat in the car outside the hospital, my hands shaking. Pulling out that sheet of paper with our names, unfolding it again. Adding one more name to the end of the list:

Faith—9 p.m.

She'd been there. Sometime after Parker arrived but before the window was broken.

I could barely focus on the drive home, feeling nothing but a white-hot rage surging through my bones.

If the case was reopened, like I believed, the police were looking at a person who had been at the party. They were looking at that list of names again.

But there was one more name. A name the police didn't even know about. Someone who wasn't even supposed to be there.

———

CONNOR KEPT CALLING WITH a frequency that I found alarming. I had watched each call come through, listened to each ring until it went to voicemail. But then it would start up again a few moments later, and I began to worry that something had happened. Sadie's dedication was the next day. I wondered if the investigation had changed anything. The next time the phone started up, I answered on speaker. "Hello?"

"Where are you," he said by way of greeting.

"On my way back. Is everything okay?" The coastal highway was much emptier heading north on a Monday, so much different from the Sunday commute out of town.

"I was worried. You said you would call, and you didn't."

"Sorry. I started driving straight after talking to Luce."

A pause. "What did she tell you? What did you find out?"

No longer curiosity but a test, and I couldn't tell where his allegiance remained. "Oh, I'm sure you already know."

A stretch of silence, everything unraveling between us in the gap. "No."

"You didn't know Faith was the girl who broke the window?" I came up fast on the car ahead of me, veered around it without pausing. I had to slow down, calm down, but my fingers tightened on the wheel. "You didn't know she was fighting with Parker Loman and took a swing at him?"

"No. No. I mean, I saw her there. I knew she was upset. I knew she was there to confront Parker, but I told her to leave. I sent her home. Jesus, she was furious with me, probably still is. Accused me of being a traitor. She didn't know why I was there."

"Well, you missed it. The fight. She was pissed and took a stone pillar to his head. She missed Parker and hit the window instead."

"Listen, Faith wouldn't hurt someone . . ."

His words trailed off, and in the gap of silence, I laughed. "But I would, isn't that what you mean?"

He didn't answer.

"She swung it at his *head*."

"The window wasn't even broken, right? She probably didn't swing it that hard. Maybe she just wanted to scare him. Let him know she was upset."

"Give me a break, Connor." As if that were the narrative he wanted to believe about both Faith and himself. That he had not latched himself on to two girls from his youth, each of whom had the power to harm, to rage. Because what did it mean for him that he saw something in the both of us that he liked—that he loved?

"You don't know her anymore, she's . . ."

"She's what?"

"Smaller, somehow. Like she surrendered and gave up."

"That doesn't sound like Faith." Not the girl I used to know, sneaking in houses with me, speaking her mind, fearing nothing—the perpetual bounce in her step. But I remembered how she looked when I saw her at the B&B the week before, quiet and reserved. The clipped words, the fake amicability.

But she could harm. Oh, she could harm.

Bend until you find that point. When you're low and sinking faster, and so you do something, anything, in a drastic move, just to get it to stop. The *fuck you* rising to the surface. The scar from Parker's fight. The violent shrug of Connor's arm. My hands connecting with Faith's shoulders. The surge as I felt our shift in balance—the fulcrum on which so many lives were balanced.

"Listen, I'm out making a few deliveries, but let me talk to her first. Let's get together. Let's—"

"No, Connor. No." I would not wait for Connor. Detective Collins clearly had the two of us in his crosshairs. Connor had told me as much—that the detective was asking questions, not only about Connor but about me. And I'd just discovered that Connor's allegiance did not lie with me. If I wanted the truth, I'd have to get there myself, before it was too late. "I'll know the truth when I ask her. I'll know." Same as how Connor and I could still read each other even after all these years. The things we wanted to keep hidden but couldn't. Faith couldn't lie to me. If I asked her, if she'd hurt Sadie—I'd know.

"And then what?" Connor asked.

I didn't know. Couldn't answer honestly. Faith or Sadie. My past or my present. "Promise me you'll let me talk to her first."

"We're too old for promises, Avery." He hung up, and I pressed my foot on the gas, picking up speed as I veered off the highway.

———

I WASN'T PAYING ATTENTION as I eased my foot off the gas, coasting back down the mountain roads toward the sea. Didn't see the approaching hairpin turn and braked too late—the momentum swinging the back of my car off the edge of the pavement, the entire car teetering slightly left. My stomach dropped, and I jerked up the emergency brake. My hands shook, my pulse raced, and it took until the surprise of another car—a honk as it swerved past—before I could focus again.

How easy that would've been, I realized. Death never something I had to look for but something that sneaked up when I wasn't watching. How easy it must've been for my father, drifting asleep on the mountain road, my mother beside him, my grandmother in the back. The dark road, the dark night. Honestly, I was surprised it didn't happen more often.

It was a miracle, it seemed, that so many of us made it this far and kept going.

I took a few deep breaths, then drove back toward the downtown of Littleport. In the distance, the sun hit the surface of the water, and my stomach dropped. I passed the turn for Hawks Ridge on my left, with its stone pillars and iron gates. Then a road to the right—forking off toward the place I grew up, with the one-level homes that backed to the woods, and a view of the mountains. In front of me, the road sloped toward the sea and the center of downtown.

The streets weren't as congested as they were on the weekend, and I could pick out a few familiar faces as I passed. I knew Detective Collins was somewhere out here, looking for me. Waiting for me. Because he believed that I had wanted to be part of Sadie Loman's world, and that when she was set to cast me out of it, I wanted her dead.

They knew what I was capable of when I was angry.

The sea in the distance looked calm. I steered the car back up the incline, past the police station on top of the hill, toward the Point in the distance, and the lighthouse.

The lot was half full, and my wheels slowed on the gravel drive. As I exited the car, I could hear the crash of the waves against the cliffs beyond the wooden fence. The shocking power of the ocean. A reminder that one place could become both a nightmare and a dream.

Watching a family empty their luggage from the car beside me, I almost missed it: a woman walking from behind the B&B into the woods. Down the path I'd raced the year before.

It was the speed at which she moved that made me follow her. That hair, wild and untamable, piled in a ponytail high on the top of her head. The quick glance over her shoulder, like she didn't want to be seen.

I kept my distance, following the path, but I couldn't keep her in view without being noticed. And by the time I reached the backyard of the Blue Robin—the high row of hedges surrounding the pool, the flash of the blue siding from the house, peeking out from over the top—I had lost her.

I stood still and listened for signs of her; for anything.

A flutter in the trees. Leaves blowing across the ground in a quick gust of wind. A crash of waves in the distance.

And then: the sound of a door opening.

I stepped around the corner of the Blue Robin just in time to see the door closing in the house across the street. I stood there, staring. She was inside Sunset Retreat.

It wasn't because of a broken window, a missing latch. That wasn't how she'd been getting inside.

She already had the key.

CHAPTER 25

I *waited across the street,* pressed against the side of the Blue Robin, watching. Trying to understand. Faith had been at the party last year, had gotten into a fight with Parker. Now she was inside one of the Loman properties. I tried to match this information to the ghost of the girl I used to know.

I remembered Connor and Faith and me inside the empty Loman house together. The way she'd opened all the cabinets, peering inside—all of us taking stock of the life that wasn't ours. Detective Collins was right—there was someone who had grown obsessed over the years. Who had watched and found a crack—a way into that life. Only it wasn't me.

I hadn't set foot inside Sunset Retreat since I'd discovered the gas leak. This soon after, I wasn't sure if it was safe yet.

I crept across the street, keeping to the trees when I could, and stood on my toes, peering in the front window. Behind the gauzy curtains, Faith was running her hands along the surfaces, opening the cabinets, just like she had all those years ago. She was both different and familiar. Smaller, yes, like Connor had said—quieter in her actions. And yet still the same Faith who was bold enough to sneak into a house that was not hers, run wild through town, like she was part of the product of this place. Invisible, now, as we were taught to be.

I kept watching as she pulled something down from a cabinet. My forehead pressed to the glass before I could understand what she was doing—the matchbook in her hand.

No. *No.* Her name on my lips, stuck in my throat. The push and pull. Stay or run. "Faith!" I called, my eyes wide and tearing, but she didn't look up.

I pounded on the glass just as she struck the match, but the spark didn't take. She saw me then, but her face didn't change. She took out a second match, and I hit the window again. "Stop! Wait!" All I could think of was the smell of gas.

She looked right at me as she struck the match, and I flinched. The flame caught, and she held it between her fingers, staring my way. I was holding my breath, shoulders braced. But nothing happened as she brought the match slowly down to a candle.

"Faith," I called again, but I knew I was muffled behind the glass, my expression softened and obscured. I pounded on the glass again with both hands. "Get out."

She didn't listen, but she didn't stop me when I raced up the front porch, letting myself in behind her. I stood in the doorway, fists clenched, leaning back—as if the extra distance could protect me. "Blow it out," I said, but she just stood there, watching me. "There's gas. There was. A gas leak—"

"Heard that was fixed," she said, blowing out the match. The candle flickered on the counter.

I lunged past her, practically running across the room, and blew out the candle myself. My hands were trembling. "There could've been an explosion. A fire. Faith, you could've . . ." I shook my head, once more hearing Sadie's voice. Tallying all the ways I might die.

Faith blinked slowly, taking me in. "The gas was turned off. It's perfectly safe."

And then we were standing face-to-face, the rising smoke between us. Her face was more angular—sharp nose, high cheekbones, a chin that narrowed to a point. The years had chiseled her out, turning her serious and determined.

"Did you call the police?" she asked calmly, evenly. She didn't try to run. Now that she'd been caught, she didn't even make any excuses. It was as if she'd been waiting for me to walk in the front door.

But I was shaken, too much adrenaline coursing through my veins and nowhere for it to go. "Jesus, Faith, what are you doing in here?"

She shrugged, then took a slow, resigned breath. "I don't know. I like to come here sometimes. It's peaceful. A quiet street."

"You have a key?"

She rolled her eyes. "You tell the visitors to leave the key in the mailbox. Nobody comes for *hours*. Not the best business practice, Avery. Can you blame me? I wouldn't be surprised if there were others. You know how people get in the winter." She stared directly into my eyes, daring me to deny it. Reminding me that I once was one of them, and she knew exactly what we'd done together.

I was thinking about the other properties, the signs of someone else. Not just the gas leak here but the shattered screen of the television at Trail's End; the evidence of someone inside the Blue Robin; the candles lit all around the Sea Rose. How many more were there? "You made a copy of other keys, too, didn't you?"

She shrugged again. "Sure, why not?"

I pushed open the kitchen windows, just in case. To me, this place would always be dangerous. "Is this because of Parker?" I asked.

Her eyes narrowed, the skin pulling tight around the edges. Her teeth snagged at the corner of her lip, but she shook her head. "Fuck him."

Still angry, then. And now in the position to do something about it. "I know you were there last year. At the party. I know you got in a fight with him." I stepped closer, around the kitchen island. "I know you broke the window."

Faith took a step back, her hand going to her elbow on instinct. There was a scar there from the surgery. I stopped moving, and she eyed me carefully.

"I was angry," she said, staring back unflinching. As if that feeling bonded us together. As if we were the same. "He's an asshole, but you probably already know that." She looked to the side. "We're all supposed to know that, right? We're supposed to know better." Then she fixed her eyes on mine, and I understood. How you could get pulled into the orbit of one world, thinking you had a place in it, even if you weren't fully part of it.

"What happened between the two of you?" I asked.

"Parker Loman happened. You should know, right? Waltzed into the bed-and-breakfast like he owned the place. I knew who he was, had seen him every year, but suddenly, he saw me." She smiled at the memory. "That first summer, it was fun, keeping the secret. But then he showed up with *her* the next year."

"Luce."

She waved her hand, as if the name were inconsequential. Put a hand on her hip and leaned in to it. "He didn't stop, you know. Kept telling me it was a mistake, bringing her to town. That he didn't want her there anymore but couldn't just send her home . . . He came to see me *even then,* that night. Dropped his supposed girlfriend at the party and came to see me."

I could believe it. The way he'd stood over me in the bathroom with Luce somewhere outside. Sadie's words—that he could and did get away with everything. How he needed it, the idolization of Parker Loman.

"So you were tired of being a secret?" I asked.

"I thought it would be fun to play the secret out in public. More at stake, you know? He got so mad when I said I'd see him at the party later. Like there were some rules that I didn't know about. He thought he was calling all the shots. But he's not. It's not just his decision. We argued about it at my place, but then he said he had to go. Another car pulled into the lot of the B&B, and it spooked him. He said he didn't want to be *seen*." She shook her head. "Seriously, even the thought of being seen with me was too much . . . Well, it didn't seem so fun anymore."

Parker Loman, living so many lives. His lies, then and now, so effortless. Did he know, all along, it had been her? Did he suspect her of sneaking around, causing damage to the properties, and was keeping quiet to save face? So he wouldn't have to admit he had been seeing a local who had lost her mind?

"But you followed him," I said. "To the party. Luce saw you there, you know."

She crossed her arms over her chest. "Well. I didn't go over right away. Spent some time stewing in my anger. But then, yes. I followed him. I knew where he was going. Where you all were. Though I didn't expect Connor." Her eyes widened. "This town convinces you all you're better than you really are."

"Faith," I said, and she jarred back to reality. "You've been destroying his properties to get back at him?"

"I'm not that petty. A woman scorned. *Really,* Avery?" She

strode through the foyer, threw open the front door, and gestured down the empty road. I stepped out front, looking into the trees, but I didn't see anything. "Do you know what's happening here while you act like Grant Loman's little puppet? Do you know what's happening to the rest of us as you watch him buy up more and more and more?"

I shook my head, because I didn't. I knew Grant's accounts deeply. Knew his hopes and aspirations for this place and my role within it. I knew people had been pissed when I sold my grandmother's house to him, but I did not know what Faith was talking about.

"I finished my degree this May, and I come back home to work, and I discovered the B&B is totally in the red. Not just a little. Like unsalvageable. My parents took out a second mortgage for the expansion a couple years back, thinking they could recoup it with the new units. But we can't. Not with all the other options out there." She looked out the window. "We were supposed to expand here, did you know? We put a bid on these properties, were going to have this be an annex of the main building. But we didn't get them. The properties are all under contract, some LLC." Her upper lip pulled up past her teeth.

"I'm not working for them anymore. Believe me, I—"

"And you." She stepped closer, fixing her anger on me. Walking down the front porch step, forcing me back in the process. "You, this complete fuckup . . ." She cringed, then shook her head to herself. "I'm sorry, but you were. This complete *nobody*. Now you're running the show? When people like me, who do everything right, get the degree, serve their time—we come back here to nothing? Excuse me for doing something about it. I'm just trying to reclaim what's mine."

"By what?" And then I understood. She was trying to spook the visitors. Hit the Lomans' bottom line where it hurt. *Our* bottom line, as far as she was concerned. I didn't know whom she was angrier with—them or me. Or maybe everything was all tied up together, feeding off one another. Me, the person who had hurt her physically; Parker, the one who had broken her heart; the Lomans, destroying her future. Everything broke here.

"Have you been up there? At the Lomans'?"

She threw her hands in the air, as if it were all so obvious. "I'm just trying to find something. Anything. I just want something I can use. I want them out of here." She was trembling then. "I wanted *you* out of there. It isn't fair." Her voice broke on the last word.

The nights when the electricity had gone out and I'd believed myself alone. Footsteps in the sand, the back door left open, and the feel of someone in the house with me. The flashlight on the bluffs. "You could go to jail," I whispered. "They could ruin you." The truth, then. They could ruin anyone.

She sat down on the first step, looking down the undeveloped street, legs stretched out in front of her and crossed at the ankles. "Are you going to tell the police?"

I had come here to ask Faith about Sadie, thinking that if I looked her in the eye, I'd know. Instead, she was confessing to something else. Something perhaps unconnected. Meanwhile, I'd given the police the phone, told them everything I knew, and all it had done was turn their focus on me. I didn't know what else I owed them. Or her.

"I don't know," I said. That, at least, was the truth.

"What about them, then?" she asked. "Are you going to tell the Lomans?"

"I'm not speaking to them right now. They're not speaking to me. I don't work for them anymore. I was fired." I didn't owe the Lomans anything. Maybe I never did.

Her eye twitched with some emotion I couldn't understand. "I want him to know it was me," she said.

She had no idea, the depths of my own anger. Or maybe she did. She tipped her head to the side, watching me closely.

"No one's stopping you," I said. "Do what you want. But the Lomans, they think they control everything. People, properties, this entire town. They think they've earned that right. They think they deserve to know everything. Maybe they don't."

If it were me, I'd let them wonder. Let them wake up to footsteps and not be sure. Let that fracture split their night, their lives.

"You need to leave," I said. "You need to get out of here. Please, just stop. You almost . . . This place, it was full of gas. Someone could've gotten hurt."

"No, no one was supposed to get hurt. Just—no one was even noticing. You didn't, even, until the candles. No one was doing *anything*."

A chill ran through me. All these invisible lives, hidden just out of sight. Even that night at the party, when she was *right there,* she remained out of frame, hidden behind shadows and broken glass.

"Did you see what happened that night?" I asked.

She looked at me out of the corner of her eye. Then pressed her lips together. What did she think had happened? Did she, like the police, believe I could've been involved in Sadie's death?

"No. Connor told me to leave. I wasn't about to hang around after that."

Had those been the footsteps I'd heard that night in the woods? When I called Sadie's name? Forgetting how so many of us could move like a ghost, undetected and invisible—as we were taught to do.

Still, it was her word. Her word that she'd left the party, gone back home. I stared at her face, trying to see—

The sound of a car engine in the distance pulled my focus. I peered down the road but couldn't see past the trees.

"Faith, let's go back." I pulled her by the sleeve, trying to get her to stand, but she was staring at my hand, clenched in the fabric of her shirt. "The police have been keeping an eye on the house across the street." I nodded toward the Blue Robin. I wondered if it was the detective even now. If he would find us here and know.

She stood then, her gaze following mine down the road. "I don't see anyone," she said.

"Still. We need to go back."

We walked quietly, side by side, around the side of the Blue Robin, back through the path of trees, like two friends. To anyone else, it probably looked like a friendly hike. I waited until we were out of view of the Blue Robin, until I was sure we were alone again, to ask. I kept my voice low. "None of this—the candles, the damage—it's not about Sadie?"

She stopped walking for a second before continuing. "Sadie? No. *No*. You thought I could hurt her?"

Could she? I closed my eyes and shook my head, but that was a lie, and she knew it. Anyone could do it. That wasn't the question here. "If I was going to hurt someone," she said, not breaking stride, "she would be the last Loman on my list."

I had missed Faith. She was fierce and honest—how had I not seen her there in the shadows? What was happening at the properties this year had all been about Parker and what the Lomans stood for—not Sadie.

As we emerged into the clearing of the parking lot, she headed toward the back of the house, overlooking the sea.

"Faith. Please. Hate them all they want, but they lost their daughter last year. Is that not enough?"

She looked off to the edge of the cliffs, but I knew how it could be—how you could become so lost in your own anger and grief and bitterness that you can barely see anything else. When she turned back, her eyes were watering, but I didn't know if that was from the sting of the saltwater wind. "I know you were close to her, and I'm sorry. I'm sorry she's dead."

She walked back toward the house, and I headed for my car, the rest of the lot currently abandoned. But all I could think was that Parker's car had been parked at the B&B the night Sadie died. He could've left, sneaked back home, and returned.

"Faith," I called just before she disappeared from view. "You said a car pulled in to the lot that night, after Parker was here. Who was it?" I wondered if it was Connor who had parked there.

She shook her head. "I didn't get a good look. There were two people walking to the party. I only know that one of them was in a blue skirt. I could see it in the moonlight."

Faith continued inside, the sound of her footsteps echoing on the wooden steps out of view.

I tried to think who had worn a blue skirt that night. Most people were in jeans, khaki shorts, a few sundresses with jackets over the top. It was impossible to remember what clothing people had worn. I could barely remember my own. There was only one person I knew by heart.

I closed my eyes and saw Sadie spinning in the entrance of my room. *What do we think of this?* Her blue dress, shimmering. *You know you'll freeze, right?* Pulling on my brown sweater over the top.

Goose bumps rose in a rush.

From behind, from where Faith had stood, it would've looked like Sadie was wearing a skirt.

And suddenly, I saw Sadie take out her phone, seeing the message I sent: *Where are you?* And then: *???*

I saw her with the clarity of a memory instead of my imagination. Saw it with a fervor that made it perfectly true. Frowning at her phone, sending me that message—the last one, the one I never received. The dots lighting up my phone:

I'm already here.

275

SUMMER

2017

The Day After the Plus-One Party

I didn't sleep. After I returned to the guesthouse, I sat by the window, numb, waiting for something to make sense. But the world had shifted, and nothing registered. Time kept jolting in fragments. I'd seen, from the window, Grant and Bianca return in the middle of the night. I watched various police cars come and go before daybreak. But my mind kept circling back, picturing Sadie standing in my doorway. Hearing her calling my name, an echo in my memory.

I saw the two men coming before they knocked, saw them quietly speaking to each other as they approached.

The police. Here to question me about the night before. About Sadie.

WE SAT AT MY kitchen table, four chairs pulled around the clean white surface. I took a seat across from Detective Ben Collins and Officer Paul Chambers as they introduced themselves—though I heard the detective call the younger man Pauly when they were taking out their notepads.

"Avery, I know this must feel unnecessary," Detective Collins said. "Cruel, even, given the circumstances." His voice dropped lower, as if someone else might be listening. "But it helps to go over things right away, before people forget. Or before they talk to others and the stories start to mix." He waited for me to respond, and I nodded. "Yesterday, when did you last see Sadie?" he asked.

My eyes drifted to the hallway, to my open bedroom door. I knew the answer, but my thoughts lagged behind, as if they had to travel through some other space first. "Around noon, maybe. She came over when I was still working."

He nodded. "Did she tell you anything about her plans for the rest of the day?"

I pictured her spinning in my doorway. Grabbing my sweater. Her hands fidgeting with the ends of her hair. "She didn't say anything, but she was supposed to meet us there. We go to the party every year." What else could she be getting ready for, if not that?

"So she never said she'd be at the party."

She hadn't, but it was just assumed. Wouldn't she have told me otherwise? "She told Parker not to wait for her." My voice sounded raspy, even to me. "That's what Parker said."

"And you? Did she tell you not to wait, too?"

I shook my head. "She knew I was going early, to open up the house and set things up. But she always came to the Plus-One party. I texted her. See?" I held out my phone so he could see the sent messages—the lack of response. "She was texting me back. I saw the dots." Officer Chambers took down my number, made note of the time and content of my messages.

"How many drinks had you had by then?" Detective Collins asked.

"Two," I said. *Three.*

They shared a quick look. "Okay. We haven't been able to locate her phone yet. It appears it was on her when she . . ." Here, he trailed off, but I leaned closer, trying to understand. *When she fell? Jumped? Was pushed?*

Officer Chambers jotted something down. But the detective was the only one asking questions. "How was she acting, last you saw her?"

I closed my eyes, trying to see. To give them something, anything. As if I could pull her back here with words alone. The way she'd spun on her feet. Rolled her eyes. Pieced through my closet. Shrugged on my sweater, her energy spilling over—"Like Sadie," I said. *Like everything was fine. Like I'd see her again soon.*

He leaned back in my wooden chair, and it creaked. I tried to read his notes, but they were tilted out of my field of vision. The only sound was of our breathing.

"You, Luciana, and Parker each arrived at the party separately," he said. "How did that go again?" Like he'd already heard this from someone and I was just confirming the details.

"I was there first. Luciana arrived next. Parker arrived last."

Here, a pause. "And Connor Harlow? We heard he was at the party."

The feel of my hand trailing down his arm, leading him to the bedroom.

A nod. "Connor was there, too."

Detective Collins tore off a sheet of paper in the silence, jotted down a list of names, asked me to fill in the arrival times: *Avery Greer, Luciana Suarez, Parker Loman, Connor Harlow.*

I estimated as well as I could, then paused at the last name. I frowned at the page, my eyes unfocused and burning with fatigue. "Connor was there before Parker. I'm not sure when," I said.

Detective Collins twisted the paper back his way, eyes skimming the list. "That's a big gap between you and the next person."

"Yes, I was setting up. The first-timers, they always come early." There was something in his eyes I couldn't read, a line I'd just drawn—and we were on opposite sides. I cleared my throat. "I brought over the liquor. Opened up the house. It's my job, overseeing the Lomans' properties."

"So you've said. How did you get there last night?" he asked.

"I took my car," I said. The trunk was full of the box of liquor, the leftovers from the pantry.

"And where is that car now?" He made a show of looking around the house, as if it might be hidden away somewhere.

I let out a shaky breath. "When the police showed up at the party, I left with Parker. I wasn't thinking. I just followed him out. My car was blocked in by that time anyway, at the house across the street." I looked out the front window, toward my empty spot. "I guess it's still there."

He put down his pen, eyes focused intently on mine, as if there were a hole in my story and he was about to pry it open. But then he continued on. "After the officers arrived at the party and you returned here with Parker . . ." He looked down at his notes. "Parker and Luciana went inside the main house. And you?" He peered up, already knowing the answer. He was the one who found me after all.

"I went out back."

"Why?"

Because I was drawn there. Could sense it before I saw it. Her life was my life. "The police at Breaker Beach," I said. I looked to Officer Chambers, wondering if he had been one of the people there waving us past, but he kept his eyes down. "There was a cop blocking us from getting any closer. But there's a way down from above. I wanted to see."

"And did you? Did you see?"

I shook my head. "No."

He leaned closer, dropped his voice, like this part was off the record, just between us. "You looked panicked when I saw you there."

"I was. She's my best friend. I didn't believe it. But . . ."

"But?"

"Her shoes. I saw her shoes. And then I knew." My hands started trembling, and I squeezed them tight, to try to get them to stop.

As he was staring at me, my eyes drifted to the windows to my right. Through the trees to the view of the ocean, the terrifying vastness of it. The converging currents and endless depth; the secrets it held.

"Okay," he said, leaning back. "Let's go through the night again." As he spoke, he looked down at the list I'd given him. "Parker and Luciana were together most of the party." He raised his eyes to me to confirm. There was no point, then, in mentioning the fight upstairs. Or the time I was alone with Parker. They drove over together. They left together. They were together most of the night.

I nodded. "Are you looking at the party?" I asked. I didn't understand why the details mattered. She hadn't been there. The party had been on the other end of town.

"No, we're looking here," the detective said. Officer Chambers peered around my living room as if there might be some clue that he had missed. "The house, to the cliffs, down to Breaker Beach. That's the scene. The reason I'm asking you about the party"—he leaned forward—"is to find out whether anyone was missing." He picked up his pen, raised an eyebrow. "So. Can anyone vouch for you the entire time, Avery?"

I shook my head, confused, desperate. "Parker, Luce, there was a houseful of people. They saw me. I was there."

"You could've left. They can't account for every single moment."

"But I didn't. And I told you, she was messaging me. She was fine."

"What about Connor Harlow?"

"What about him?"

"Would you know his state of mind last night?"

His shirt sliding over his head. Guiding me to the bed—

"I wouldn't know anything. Me and Connor don't speak anymore."

"But you saw him there."

Connor's face, inches from my own. The feel of his hands on my hips.

"Yes," I said. "I saw him."

"Was he there the whole time?"

The power of this moment, constricting the air. No one could be sure, really, who was there and who had gone. A party like that, you could only say the thing you hoped others would say for you. A deep-buried instinct to protect your own. "Yes. None of us left."

———

LATER THAT MORNING, AFTER the police had returned to the main house, I saw a figure standing at the edge of the garage, staring at a phone.

I opened my door, called her name in a voice that was almost a whisper. "Luce?"

She startled, then turned my way, and I walked out to meet her. Up close, her eyes were bloodshot, her face gaunt and makeup-free.

"I have to get out of here," she said, shaking her head. Her hair was pulled back tight, severe. "I don't belong here right now. I'm trying to . . ." She tapped at her phone, exasperated. "I'm trying to find a way to get to the bus station. If I can get to Boston, I can make it home."

It was then I saw that she had a bag in her other hand, her grip tight on the tan leather handles. Her eyes searched mine as if I might have the answers.

"I'd take you myself, but I don't have my car. It's still at the overlook." I swallowed. "Maybe you can take Parker's car. Since Grant and Bianca are here now."

Her eyes widened. "I am not asking him that right now." She looked over her shoulder at the house and shuddered. "I don't belong there. It's not my place. It's—"

"Okay, come in. Luce, come on." A hand at her elbow to get her inside. I led her there, into the living room.

She sat on the couch, her back inches off the cushions, hands folded carefully over her knees, luggage on the floor in front of her. I gave her the number of a car service she could try; she was clearly rattled, unable to focus enough to find this information herself.

"Stay here. I'm going for my car. If you're still here when I'm back, I'll drive you to the bus myself."

She nodded, staring at nothing.

It was the last time I saw her.

I started walking. Down Landing Lane, past Breaker Beach, where there were cop cars blocking the lot, the whole area roped off. I kept walking into the town center, where a solemn, shell-shocked air had settled over everything, like a thick fog.

My throat tightened, and I bent over on the sidewalk, hands on my knees.

"Avery?" A man turned from the back of his SUV at the curb. Faith's father, securing a crate of coffee into the back of his vehicle, trunk open. "You okay, there?"

I stood and wiped my knuckles across my cheeks. "I left my

car," I said, my voice stuck against my windpipe, like I was choking. "At the party last night."

He looked over his shoulder, up the road, in the direction of the party. "Well, come on, I'll take you there."

His car smelled of coffee grinds and fresh laundry, the world continuing on with or without Sadie. We drove up Harbor Drive, past the police station at the top of the hill. "Terrible news, about the Loman girl. I heard you were close."

I could only nod. Couldn't think about Sadie in her blue dress, standing at the edge. Barefoot, listening to the violence of the sea below.

He turned the car toward the Point, then cleared his throat. "Do you have a place to stay?"

"Yes," I said, not understanding the question. Before realizing, without Sadie, the entire foundation of my life was about to shift.

"Well," he continued, "you let us know. End of season, you know we have the room, should you need it."

I turned to take him in—the deep lines of his weatherworn face, the longer, graying hair pushed back like he was facing the wind, and the sharp angle of his nose, like Faith's. "I don't think Faith would like that," I said.

"Well," he said, turning past the bed-and-breakfast, heading for the homes up on the overlook, "that was a long time ago."

"It was an accident," I said.

He didn't respond at first. "You scared us all then. But you came out the other side okay, Avery." He pulled onto Overlook Drive, where the Blue Robin was located.

"This is good," I said as my lone car came into view. I wanted to be alone. Not think too hard about what I had done and what I had meant to do. What I was capable of when the bonds that held me in check were released.

"You sure?"

"Yes. Thank you."

He gestured down the tree-lined road, from here to Sunset Retreat and the Blue Robin. "These all gonna be rentals, then? Every one of them? They're gonna keep building?"

"Not right away. But yes, that's the plan." I stepped out of the car. "Thank you for the ride." He nodded but kept his gaze down the long lane of uncleared lots.

I walked down the street, imagining the stream of people heading toward the party the night before—and then racing out, after the police arrived. I'd missed whatever happened in the aftermath, but it was obvious that people had left in a rush. The tire marks in the place where the grass met the road. The trash and debris left behind on the shoulder. An empty bottle. A pair of broken sunglasses.

My car was in the driveway of Sunset Retreat, facing out. But it looked like someone had driven across the yard: tire tracks revved all the way down to the dirt below. I imagined a bottleneck of vehicles and someone impatient, driving around everyone else.

The front door of the Blue Robin across the way was ajar, a darkness beckoning.

I stepped across the threshold, taking it all in. The air pulsed, like the house was alive.

There were half-empty bottles on the counters, the ticking of a fan set too high, the stench of sweat and spilled liquor. And the candles, burned down to the wick, wax pooling at the base. Most had extinguished themselves, but there was one burning by the back window, set just below the web of cracks. I blew it out, watching as the smoke drifted upward, seeing the night fragmented through the glass.

Upstairs, there were several jackets remaining on the bed in the first room. And a shoe, of all things.

My fingers twitched with misplaced energy. There was too much out of my control. Too much I could never change.

I pulled out my phone and called the cleaning company. Told them to come as soon as they could and to send me the bill directly; I didn't want this to go to the Lomans right now. I didn't want them seeing it, the reckless mess we were making as their daughter was dying.

Downstairs, I threw the bathroom towels into the washer, dark with grime. But that was the benefit of white towels, white sheets—the open, airy feel of a place, the cleanliness. It was an easy illusion to maintain with a half-cup of bleach.

In the bedroom, the chest with extra blankets was open, but nothing seemed missing or used—just a stack of folded quilts—so I eased it shut.

And then, feeling more myself the more I took control, I found the number for the window company and left a message. That we would need a replacement for a damaged window at 3 Overlook Drive, and to call me when they needed access to measure.

After, I pulled the front door shut but didn't lock it—I didn't have the keys. I'd have to come back and check up on things after the cleaning.

I walked across the street to my car, and my eyes burned. Every place I stepped, everything I saw, was a place that Sadie would never be and never see. Even my car felt vaguely unfamiliar to me now. The granules of sand below the driver's seat, which had been there for who knew how long—but all I could see was Sadie, brushing off her legs after a bonfire at Breaker Beach. The papers stuffed into the door compartment, and I pictured her balling up a receipt, stuffing it out of sight. My sunglasses wedged into the visor, and I saw her lowering the shade to check the mirror, saying, *God, could I be any paler?*

I couldn't shake the scent of the house as I drove. The liquor, the sweat, something almost animal about it. So I kept the windows down, let the fresh air of Littleport roll in.

I drove in the opposite direction, toward the winding mountain roads, where the sun cast a pattern through the trees as the wind blew, like an incoming eclipse.

SUMMER

2018

CHAPTER 26

I **was standing outside the** bed-and-breakfast after Faith disappeared inside. I was glued to my spot, trying to process what she'd just told me. Another car had turned up the night of the party—and Sadie had been inside.

Sadie had been *right here* a year earlier, stepping out of a car in the parking lot of the B&B, walking the path to the party. I looked into the trees down the path, imagining her ghost.

———

I DROVE BACK TOWARD the Sea Rose, needing to be alone, to think. Everything I'd believed about that night was wrong. Could everything I'd thought about Sadie be wrong, too?

Over the years, our lives had become so tangled, pieces of each other indecipherable. The details blurring and overlapping. My home was her home, keys on each other's rings, her thumb pressed to the front of my phone, the same tattoos—or was it a brand?

And yet how had I missed that she was *there*. She had arrived at the party. But somehow she'd ended up back on the cliffs behind her house, washing up on Breaker Beach. How?

I edged the car away from downtown, looping around the back roads to avoid the traffic, before cutting back toward the coast and the Sea Rose. All along, the night played over in my mind. The things I had told the police and the things I hadn't.

Faith taking a swing at Parker outside, breaking the window. Connor arguing with Faith in the shadows after, by the time Luce came to find me. The bedroom door had been locked. I'd wanted to find the tape in the bathroom to secure the window, but someone else had been in there. I'd slammed my hand on the bedroom door, but no one answered.

Had Sadie been in that room when I'd pounded on the door? I'd found her phone in the house—in that very room. Maybe no one had moved it there. Maybe it was Sadie all along who had lost it. Placed it. Hidden it.

But that didn't make sense. How had no one seen her leaving? No one had seen her at all, not that they were saying. Someone would've noticed her—how could you not? Greg Randolph, surely. And we would've seen her if she'd left through the back patio, walking down the path, heading toward the B&B parking lot.

But. The lights had gone out, the commotion on the patio. Ellie Arnold falling—or pushed—into the pool. She insisted she was pushed. She was adamant about it, furious that we didn't believe her.

We had all moved to the back of the house then. Had been drawn to the scream, the chaos, like moths to a flame.

Had Sadie sneaked out the front while we were distracted?

I tried to picture it. Someone needing to get her out of the house. Looking frantically for the best option. The back door, no longer a choice. The car at the B&B, too far. What would they do? A faceless person looking through the bathroom cabinets, the dresser drawers—for anything. Looking through her purse, seeing the keys there. Finding mine instead.

The tire tracks in the grass I'd seen the next day when Faith's father dropped me off—because my car had been blocked in.

I sucked in a breath. She had been there. What if she'd been in this very car.

I pulled over abruptly, at the curve of the road heading back into town, staring at the passenger seat. Looking for signs of injury. I ran my hands over the beige upholstery—worn and weary. I jerked up the emergency brake and looked under the seat. There was nothing but dirt, sand, debris—a year of memories.

But I remembered the next morning, when I'd returned for the car. How I'd sat in the seat, feeling a vague unfamiliarity to it. I'd thought, at the time, that it was my entire world, my perspective shifting at the loss of Sadie. But now . . .

My head spun, and I turned the car off. I walked around back, hands trembling, and slipped the key into the trunk lock. A dim light flicked on, and I peered into the empty space.

It smelled faintly of fabric, of gasoline, of the sea.

My hands shook as I ran my fingers across the material. The dark felt was slightly matted, covered with fragments of fibers. It had pulled away from the edges, peeling at the corners, from both time and use.

I took a deep breath to steady myself. Maybe this was just my imagination going three steps too far—forward and back.

I pulled up the flashlight of my phone and shone it into the back corners of the trunk—but it was completely empty. There was a darker spot in the corner, closer to the front, on the right. Just a slight discoloration—I ran my fingers across it but couldn't be sure of what it was. Vodka, beer—half-empty bottles that could've spilled the night of the party. Or a leaking grocery bag in the months that followed. The car was old. It could've been anything.

I set the phone down so I could get a closer look, and the light shone up at the surface, catching on a groove on the underside of the metal roof. At the opposite end, on the left. I ducked my head underneath, ran my fingers over it. A dent, some scratches. Another dent beside it. My knuckle fit in the groove. I ran my hands against the cool underside of the trunk. A web of scratches near the seam.

It could be anything. It could be nothing. My mind, like Sadie's, picturing all the ways death could be so close. My fingers smoothed back the felt peeling away from the corner, and a glint of metal caught in the beam of the flashlight at the corner. I leaned closer, body half tilting into the trunk as I picked it up.

It was a small piece of metal. Probably lost from a bag. Gold, and spiraled, and—

I dropped the metal. Stepped back. Looked again.

Her gold shoes that had been in the box of evidence—missing a piece of the buckle. I'd thought because they'd been worn down, the holes of the strap pulling, the stitching showing, the bottoms scuffed. But the missing piece of her buckle—*here,* in the trunk of my car.

I looked at the indentations and scratches again.

Like she'd kicked her shoes against the roof of the trunk. Over and over again.

Oh God. Oh God oh God. I dropped the light, dropped my hands to the bumper to steady myself.

Sadie had been in this trunk, alive. Sadie had been here, trying to fight. Trying to live.

I slid to the ground. The cool pavement beneath my knees, my hands braced on the bumper, the bile rising in my throat. The only light on the dark road was from the trunk, a sickly yellow, and I couldn't get a full breath. Sadie. Sadie had been there. Inches away at the party. And she had been *here*. In my car, waiting for me to find her. To save her.

The scratches on the trunk—she had wanted to live. All those years courting death, joking about it, and she had fought it. Given it everything she had. Sadie, who I once believed could overcome anything.

I couldn't breathe. Just a wheeze as I struggled for air.

The headlights from another car shone down the road, and I pulled myself up on the bumper to steady myself. The wheels came to a stop behind me, and the car door opened, but the engine continued running, the lights illuminating the empty road.

"You okay there?" A man's voice.

I turned to face him, but I had to raise a hand to shield my face from the blinding light, and my eyes watered, picturing Sadie. Sadie alive and then dead. Somewhere between here and there.

I blinked to focus the image before me, and the tears escaped.

"Whoa, whoa." The shadow in front of the lights grew larger. Broad shoulders, hands held out in front of him. Detective Ben Collins stood in front of me. He placed a hand on my elbow, another on my shoulder, and guided me away from the car to the curb.

The trunk gaped open in front of me, and my stomach heaved again, so I had to rest my head on my arms, folded across my knees. He crouched down so his gaze was level with mine, and I shook my head, trying to focus.

"Have you been drinking?" he asked gently. Close enough to smell the mint on his own breath.

"What? No, no." I took a deep breath, slowly raised my head.

He looked back at the car, then at me. I finally understood how Sadie had gotten from the party to the bluffs that night. The absolute horror of the thing.

Finally, I had a piece of evidence that proved what I had believed, that everyone would take seriously—a place to point the investigation. My car, with the trunk open, where Sadie had been—except everything circled back to me.

I couldn't say anything without implicating myself.

He couldn't search that car without a reason—unless he thought I was drunk or high. I had to get ahold of myself.

"Carsick," I said, hand to my stomach. "And . . ." I waved my hand around uselessly, searching—

"I know, I know," he said, patting my knee. "The dedication tomorrow. Everything coming back. I know you two were close." He let me sit there in silence, looking over his shoulder. "Did you need something from the trunk?" He gestured to the car, the sickly dim light beckoning.

"No. I thought I had some water, something to drink, in there. I don't, though." I didn't want him to look. Didn't want him to see what I had seen, discover what I had just discovered. I sucked in a breath, and it sounded like a sob.

"Sit tight," he said, and I was powerless to stop him. Powerless to prevent him from looking if he wanted to. That piece of metal still in view—how obvious would it be?

But he headed for his own car, parked behind mine. It wasn't his police vehicle, I realized now, but a sedan, blue or gray, hard to tell in the dark. He turned off the engine, so it was just me and him and the crickets and the night.

He came out with a water bottle, half empty. "Sorry, this is all I have, but . . ." He poured the rest of the water onto a hand towel, then placed it on my forehead. The crispness of it helped settle my stomach, focus my thoughts. He moved it to the back of my neck, and when I opened my eyes, he was so close. "Better?" he asked, the lines around his eyes deepening in concern.

I nodded. "Yes. Thank you. Better."

I pushed myself to standing, and he reached a hand down to help me. "All right, I've got you." Compassion, even from him, in this moment. "Listen, I've been looking for you. Hoping to talk to you. Can I follow you back? Or swing by sometime later? There are some things we need to clear up first, before Sadie's dedication tomorrow."

"Is it . . ." I started. Cleared my throat, made sure I sounded lucid, in control. "Is it about the investigation? Is it reopened?"

He frowned, but it was hard to see his face clearly in the dark. "No, it's something we found on her phone. Just wondering who took some of the pictures. Whether it was Sadie or you." He smiled tightly. "Nothing major, but it would help to know."

I couldn't tell, then, whether this was a trap. Whether he was luring me in under false pretenses, ready to strike. But I needed to hold him off. "I can't tonight," I said. Not yet. Not right now, with the car. Not until I had a direction to point him instead. His face hardened, and I said, "Tomorrow morning?"

He nodded slightly. "All right. Where are you staying?" And I knew, right then, he'd heard what had happened with the Lomans. That I wasn't supposed to be living there. That I had been kicked out and abandoned. Every single thing happening right now was telling him to look closely at me.

"With a friend," I said.

He pulled back slightly, like there was someone coming between us. "Does this friend have an address?"

"Can we meet for coffee in the morning? Harbor Bean?"

His mouth was a straight line, his face unreadable in the night. "I was hoping for a bit more privacy. You can come by the station, if you'd prefer . . . or I can pick you up, we can chat on the way to the dedication."

I nodded. "I'll send you the address tonight when I'm back."

"Great," he said. "You sure you're okay to drive?"

"Yes," I said, shutting the trunk as I spoke, swallowing dry air.

His headlights followed me all the way into downtown, until I circled the block and he continued on, up toward the station. I parked one block up from the Sea Rose, walking back. I couldn't shake this feeling that nothing was safe here. Not Sadie and not me. Someone watching in the dark. Something waiting for me still.

That there was something toxic at the core here—a dark underbelly happening in the gap between us all, where no one else was looking.

———

BACK INSIDE THE SEA ROSE, I took the list of arrival times from my purse. Added one final name: *Sadie.*

Had I been talking with Luce and Parker when she sneaked inside? Had she slipped through the front entrance, heading straight down the hall for the bedroom?

I tried to feel her there, place her in my memory. Find the moment when I could turn around and see her, call her name and intervene. Change the course of everything that followed.

Someone had brought her there. Anyone could've hurt her, but someone else knew she had been there, and had kept silent. A house full of faces, both strange and familiar. Luce had summed it up when she stumbled out of that room upstairs: *I have never seen so many liars in one place.*

———

A YEAR AND A half after my grandmother died, Grant Loman bought her house, helped with my finances. He took control when I was barely keeping afloat, and he made sure I stayed upright. But at some point, I remembered how to read a ledger, how to track my finances.

So I knew that by the time my grandmother died, any supposed large regular payment she had once received no longer existed. After her death, I had transferred the small amount left in her account to my own. That old account no longer existed. There was no easy way to find the deposit that Sadie had discovered.

But maybe it existed elsewhere, in another form—maybe evidence of it lived on.

Everything I had left of my grandmother was in the single box that I'd moved with me to the Lomans' guesthouse—with a slanted *K* for *Keep,* which Sadie had labeled herself years ago. Now I pulled it out onto the kitchen counter, emptying the contents: the photo albums, the recipe book, the bound letters, the clipped articles about my parents' deaths, the personal folder with all the paperwork transferring assets.

I couldn't find any receipts, anything extravagant.

The only large asset in her possession was her house.

After I sold that house, I kept all my real estate details, organized every one of them—a paper trail, as Grant had taught me.

It was the first file I had created, data I'd never looked at too closely, because why would I need to? But I had it, our payment history, stored in my computer files.

I scrolled through the mortgage history now on my laptop with a fresh eye. It seemed that in the years before her death, my grandmother had paid a low monthly sum on automatic withdrawal. But earlier, she used to pay more. There was a line in the timing, a before and after, when the mortgage payment had dropped significantly.

When she'd paid it down with one large lump sum.

Here. Here it was. Money going out. A piece of evidence left behind after all.

I traced the date, finger to the screen.

It was the month after my parents had died.

I sat back in the chair, the room turning cold and hollow.

I'd thought we had gotten a life insurance payment—that's what Grant had mentioned when he helped me organize the records. I was in good shape because of that.

But I looked again. An even one hundred thousand dollars. The same amount that Sadie had discovered, sent from the Lomans to my grandmother. Not a life insurance policy at all. Not an inheritance, either. Money, suddenly, where there had been none.

My stomach twisted, pieces connecting in my head.

I pulled up the images from Sadie's phone—the photos she had taken. The picture of the winding, tree-lined mountain road. And I finally understood what Sadie had uncovered. The thing tying me to the Lomans. The cash payment she had found.

It was a payoff for my parents' deaths.

CHAPTER 27

H*ere's a new game:* If I'd known the Lomans were responsible for my parents' accident, what would I have done?

All night I played this game. In the dark of the house, with nothing but shadows and ghosts for company. What I would say, what I would do—how I would corner them into the truth. No: What I would take from them instead.

I felt it as I sat there—not the creeping vines of grief, pulling me down. But that other thing. The burning white-hot rage of a thing I could feel in the marrow of my bones. The surge gathering as I stepped forward and pushed.

I wanted to scream. Wanted to scream the truth to the world and watch them fall because of it. I wanted them to pay for what they had done.

But there was a flip side to that knowledge. Because here was what else that payment provided: a motive. *My* motive. All of the evidence fell back on me. The phone that I had found. Her body, with signs of a struggle, in my trunk. Me, wandering around the back of the Lomans' house that night, looking for any piece of evidence left behind. And the note on the counter. It was my handwriting. My anger. My revenge. It was *mine*.

———

THERE WAS A KNOCK at the front door, and I peered out the gap between the front curtains, expecting that Grant or Parker had somehow found me. Or Bianca, come to tell me to leave again. But it was Connor. I saw his truck at the curb, so obvious on the half-empty street. "Avery? You in there?" he called.

Shit, shit. I unlocked the door and he strode inside as if I'd invited him.

"How did you know where I was?" I asked as he looked around the unfamiliar house. His eyes stopped on the stacks of family albums and letters on the counter.

He paused a moment, staring at the article on top of the pile, a black-and-white photo of the wreckage—*Littleport couple killed in single-car wreck*.

"Connor?"

"She told me what happened," he said, dragging his eyes back to me. "Faith." He was breathing heavy, wound tight with adrenaline.

"How did you know I was here?" I repeated. I thought I'd been so careful, but here he was, unannounced. I didn't like the way his gaze lingered on my things. I didn't like the way he was standing—on edge.

"What?" He shook his head, like he was trying to clear the conversation. "It's not hard to find out if you know what you're looking for." I took a step back, and he frowned, his eyes narrowing. "You told me you weren't living at the Lomans' anymore. But you're not at Faith's, most of the hotels are still full . . . Plenty of people mentioned seeing you around. I checked a couple of the rental properties until I saw your car downtown. This was the closest one." He started pacing the room again, like there was nowhere else for his energy to go. "Faith didn't hurt Sadie, I told you. You believe her, right?"

"Wait." My eyes were closed, my hand out. I couldn't follow both conversations at once. "People told you they'd seen me around?" I'd noticed it recently, hadn't I? The way people looked at me, the way they watched. How they seemed to recognize something about me. I thought it was because of the investigation, new rumors that might be swirling. But maybe it had always been there. And like the Lomans, I'd become desensitized, unaware of the gazes. "Right," I said, hands gripping the counter in front of me, spanning the distance between me and Connor. "The girl fucking around with the Lomans up there. Is that the talk?"

His throat moved as he swallowed, but he didn't deny it. "The girl doing *something* up there."

I looked to the side, to the covered windows and the dark night beyond. I didn't understand why he was here, what he wanted. How many people knew I was hiding out here? Hadn't I learned better than to think I was invisible by now?

"It wasn't Faith," he repeated.

"Yes, I know it wasn't Faith. I know what that money was for now." My hands tightened into fists. My entire adult life built on a lie. On a horrific secret. Molded by people I thought had given me so much but instead had taken everything.

Connor stopped moving, watching me carefully. Maybe this was my downfall—always too trusting in the end; choosing someone else over the solitude. Yet again thinking people had anything but their own interests at heart. We were alone in this house, with no one else around. He had kept things from me already, and we both knew it. But Connor was *here*. And he'd come for me that

305

night, a year ago, when Sadie had texted him from my phone. With him, there was always a push and pull. Logic versus instinct. I didn't know which motive had brought him to my door in the middle of the night, but I'd learned long ago it counted only when you knew someone's flaws and chose them anyway.

"The Lomans, they paid off my grandmother after my parents died."

He blinked, and I watched as his entire demeanor shifted. "What?"

I sucked in air, thought I was going to cry. Then I stopped trying to fight it, because what was the goddamn point? "They killed my parents. They were responsible somehow."

Connor looked over his shoulder at the closed door, and I wondered if someone was walking past. "Who? How?"

I saw it then, back to the start, every moment with them—until it slipped, slowly and horribly, into focus:

The picture of Parker in the living room—his face youthful and unmarked. The way Sadie was teasing him about the scar last summer, not letting it go. The dark look he would give her that Luce had noticed. Shaking and shaking until something broke free.

The double take when Parker saw me sitting in Sadie's room the day we met—he knew who I was. Of course he did. *Avery Greer, survivor.*

"Parker," I said quietly into the night. "It was Parker."

The scar through his eyebrow, his own reminder. Not a fight but an accident—Sadie had just figured it out for herself. An accident that he had caused. But Parker Loman was untouchable. Somehow he had gotten away with it. One hundred thousand dollars—the price of my parents' lives. Given for our continued silence. One of two payments that Sadie had uncovered. I wasn't sure whether the other payment was related—someone else who knew the truth—or whether the Lomans had covered up more than one horrible action.

Parker can get away with literally anything.

They will sacrifice anything for the king.

That was what we were worth to them. Two lives. Everything lost. The entire future of who I was supposed to be—just gone.

I was wrong. This place, it wasn't the thing taking from me. It wasn't the mountain road, the lack of streetlights, the brutal extremes. It was the people up on the bluffs, looking out over everything. Covering up for their own. How old must he have been—fourteen? Fifteen? Too young to be driving. Something he wouldn't be able to talk his way out of, no matter what the excuse. Some laws could not be bent or skirted.

His question that night, as he stood over me at the party in the bathroom—did I think he was a good person. Needing me to absolve him in his own mind. No. *No,* there was nothing good about him. Nothing at his core but the belief that he was worth every little thing he had been given.

Instead of the simple truth, the only thing that mattered: Parker Loman had killed my parents.

"I'm supposed to meet up with Detective Collins tomorrow," I said. "If I tell him, I can't control where the investigation goes from there." I said it like a warning. I said it to see what Connor would do or say. I wouldn't be able to stop the police from looking at Connor or me.

Connor looked at the front door again, and I started to wonder whether there was someone else here with him. Or maybe I was just seeing the danger inside everyone suddenly—all the things we were capable of. "Parker hurt Sadie?" he asked.

"I don't know," I said. I thought back to what Luce had said about the darkness between Sadie and Parker. Sadie had believed

I was a secret, and I was. The reason they took me in, the reason it was *the right thing to do*—the reason Parker did the double take the first time he saw me. He knew exactly who I was. And she finally saw him for the truth.

I didn't know who had hurt Sadie or why. Only that she had uncovered the secret at the heart of both of our families, and now she was dead. Taken from the party back to her home in my car.

All of us were there that night. It could've been anyone.

Suddenly, I needed Connor to leave. I needed to sort out my thoughts, to protect myself. I crossed my arms.

He shifted on his feet. "Are you going to the dedication tomorrow?" he asked.

"Yes. You?"

"Everyone's going," he said, holding my gaze.

I shook my head, looked away. "I'll talk to you then." A set of headlights cut through the front curtains before continuing on. "You need to go," I said.

"You can come with me. It's a one-bedroom apartment, but I can sleep on the couch—"

But I knew exactly what I needed to do. I couldn't take down the Lomans on words alone. You couldn't fight that sort of power with nothing but belief. You needed proof.

"I'll see you tomorrow at the dedication, Connor," I said, opening the front door. Holding my breath. With Connor, I realized, I was always waiting to see what he would do.

He turned at the entrance to say something. Then thought better of it. He peered down the dark road, eyes narrowed. "You're not supposed to be here, are you."

I didn't answer, closing the door slowly as he backed away. Through the gap in the curtains, I watched him walk to his truck, a shadow in the night. And then I watched the brake lights fading into the distance until I was sure he was gone.

WITH MY NEW UNDERSTANDING of my past, Littleport in the dead of night became something else. No longer were these the winding roads of single-car accidents, of a lack of streetlights, of drifting off the road while you slept. But a town where the guilty roamed, unapologetic. It was a place that made killers of men.

I was on edge, continually checking my rearview mirror, trying to remain unseen as I drove back to the Blue Robin.

Here, I believed, was the scene of the crime. Not the Lomans' house, or the bluffs, or the beach, as the police had declared last year. But here, on the other side of town.

After I told the police, they would have to search this place, rope it off, close it to civilians. And I needed proof to back up the story I believed.

I used the light from my phone to illuminate the path in front of me as I walked from the driveway to the front door. Up here, with all the undeveloped land, every gust of wind turned threatening, and I kept casting the beam of light into the trees, down the empty road, until I was safely alone inside the house. And I didn't turn on the lights. In case someone was watching. I could feel them each in a shadow of my memory: Faith, the police, Parker at the edge of the garage. There were so many people who saw things, who knew things. Now Grant and Bianca were here, too, and I knew, just as Luce did—they would do anything to protect the king.

I moved by memory, my hand trailing the couch, the chair, the kitchen counter, as I walked by. The beam kept low and away from the windows. My mother's painting on the wall, her voice in my ear: *Look again. Tell me what you see.*

This was the trick, I understood. Not to change the angle or the story, or to take a step forward or back—but to change yourself.

I remembered that night, standing behind my mother while she took the pictures on the Harlows' boat that would ultimately lead her to this. The piece she tackled over and over, like there was something she was chasing. Now I saw everything out of frame, everything that slipped this painting into context—the boat she was standing on, the fact that Connor and I were playing a game of I Spy behind her. The stark clarity of that moment, while the shadows before us kept fading, disappearing into the night. As if the life she was living and the life she was chasing were one and the same all this time.

I backed away from it now, heading toward the closed door at the end of the hall. Luce and I had tried the handle that night, but it had been locked. I'd slammed my hand on the wood then—hoping it had made whoever was inside jump.

Now the door creaked open, shadows of furniture looming in the darkness. With the curtains pulled closed here, I finally flipped the light switch, illuminating the white bedspread, the dark wooden chest, blankets piled beside it. The lid creaked open and I peered inside—the scent of pine, of old quilts and dusty attics.

This had been open, I remembered, when I came over the day after the party to clean. Had her phone been here even then?

Next the bed, running my hand over the soft material. I walked the wood floors, the hardwood popping, past the closet, to the bathroom.

There was a high window over the toilet to let in light, but it didn't open. A long mirror trimmed in white. A vanity raised off the tile on boxy wooden feet. We'd cleaned the floor of water, Parker and I, after Ellie Arnold came in here with her friends to warm up. The water had been everywhere, grimy towels left behind in the corners.

I ran my fingers across the granite surface of the vanity now, the swirling marble, gray and white. The hard corners. I dropped to my knees, remembering how wet the floor had been that night—the towels heaped in the corner, that I'd put in a plastic bag.

The next day, I'd run them through the wash with bleach, to get them clean.

I peered under the vanity at the darker, untouched grout—harder to clean and see. I stood again, leaning my weight into the side of the vanity until it scratched against the tile, away from the wall. I kept pushing, inch by inch, until it was wedged against the shower, my breath coming too fast. The space left behind was fully exposed, the dirt and debris, and the darker grout, stained from water left sitting.

I dropped to my knees, ran my fingers over the chalky residue.

A corner stained rust brown. A spot missed. I rocked back on my heels, a chill rising, and scrambled out of the room, seeing everything clearly this time.

A fight behind a locked door; the phone knocked from her hand, the surface fracturing. A struggle taking her farther from the door, from the exit. A push in the bathroom. Falling, hitting her head. The blood pooling. Someone else trying to clean, desperately. Taking the spare towels and wiping up the mess. Needing to move her.

Searching through her purse, finding the keys. Peering out the window above the toilet, pressing the buttons on her key—seeing my car light up across the way.

Grabbing a blanket from the chest to cover her. Losing her phone in the process, in the chaos. Where it fell to the base and remained—waiting to be found.

Wrapping her up. God, she was so small. Peeking out into the hall and flipping the power at the circuit breaker. But who?

Had it all been to cause a scene in the dark? A distraction while someone had carried a dying or unconscious Sadie to the car?

If so, I had covered it up, all of it, when I'd come back the next day. Running the evidence through the washer with bleach, ordering a window replacement, closing the wooden chest—and leaving her phone inside. I had erased her, piece by piece, until she became invisible. And I needed to pull her back into focus.

My hand shaking, I used the camera on my phone to take pictures of everything: the spot behind the vanity with the rust-colored stain of blood, the chest of blankets, the hallway circuit breaker, the distance from there to the front door. Gathering proof of it all before I was barred from this place. The story I could see, that only I bore witness to—the ghost of her moving in the gaps between my memories.

I could see it all playing out. Three steps back, three steps forward. A girl in blue, spinning in my room, to a flash of color in the sea, a pale leg caught on the rocks—hanging on until she was found.

———

ON THE WAY BACK, I veered away from the harbor—away from the coast. Toward the mountains instead. Found myself winding down a small back road that I hadn't traversed in years.

It was a long half-paved road, forking off into packed-dirt driveways leading to older homes, surrounded by trees.

I slowed until I was in front of the last house on the street: a ranch home tucked out of sight from the road, the ground covered in pockets of grass and dirt. The Harlows still lived next door, an outside light just visible through the trees. I parked my car at the wide mouth of my old driveway, under the low branches of a knotted tree.

The details weren't visible in the dark, so I could only imagine the colored pottery on the front porch, the hand-painted *Welcome* sign that once hung from the door. The wooden chairs that had been built by my mother, the dull green paint chipping, and a low table between them.

I could picture my mom reading on the front porch. My dad with a drink and her feet in his lap. Both of them peeking up every few moments to check on me.

My own life had forked in the dead of night, right here.

But this—this was the life that should've been mine. My dad catching me around the waist as I ran inside—*You're a mess,* he'd say, laughing. My mom shrugging, *So let her be.*

Memories and imagination. All that remained of the life that was taken from me.

———

I MUST'VE DRIFTED TO sleep in the car—the buzz of my phone jarring me awake in a panic.

I took a moment to reorient myself, curled on my side in the driver's seat. In the daylight, this home was no longer my home. Wind chimes in place of colored pottery, the hand-painted *Welcome* sign replaced with a wreath of woven vines. Bright blue metal chairs on the front porch, pops of color in the mountain landscape.

My phone buzzed again—two texts from Ben Collins.

Pick you up in a half hour.

Still need your address.

A man exited the front door, walking down the porch steps, heading for the car parked at the side of the house—but he stopped when he saw me. Changing directions, heading this way.

I responded to Detective Collins: *Sorry, something came up. Meet you at the ceremony.*

The man walked slowly up the drive, and I lowered the window, a thousand excuses on my tongue.

"We just moved in," he said with a smile. He was maybe the

age of my dad when he died. But he always seemed younger in my memory. "It's not on the market anymore."

I nodded. "I used to live here when I was a kid. Sorry. I just . . . wanted to see how it looked now."

He looked over his shoulder. "Beautiful, isn't it? Lot of history to the place."

"Yes. Sorry to bother you. I was just in the area . . ."

The sun caught off the wind chimes over their porch, and he rocked back on his heels. I rolled up the window, starting the car.

Parker had taken everything from me, and I still couldn't prove it was him. But I knew there was one more place to look, and there would be only one last chance to do it.

My heart pounded against my ribs. It was time to go. Sadie's dedication would be starting soon.

Everyone would be there.

CHAPTER 28

I *was four blocks away* from Breaker Beach and barely able to find a spot. Everyone was here, I was right. The dedication would be starting soon. I took the first spot I found, then stopped inside the Sea Rose to gather everything I had—all the evidence that had led me to this point. Keeping everything in one place so I could present it all to Detective Collins after the dedication.

Slinging my bag across my chest, I headed toward the ceremony.

———

I SAW THEM ALL. People spilling out from Breaker Beach into the parking lot, standing on rocks behind the dunes. Cars double-parked in the street, a bottleneck of vehicles and spectators. It was a Tuesday morning, and people had given up their time, their work, their business for this. It was a show of support for a girl larger than life. It was the only thing left to give.

A crowd had gathered near the entrance to the beach, the bell at the center, words hand-chiseled in brass.

I saw Bianca standing beside Grant on a raised platform, stoic, head down. Grant's hand was at the small of her back, and Parker stood behind them both, scanning the crowd.

The Randolphs, the Arnolds, they were all there, near the front. I kept moving through the sea of people blocking off the road. As I passed, I saw the Sylvas, the Harlows, families I'd known forever, here to pay tribute—another person lost to Littleport. The committee stood in a row behind the makeshift podium, Erica beside Detective Ben Collins, his sunglasses over his eyes, both solemn and still.

The commissioner stepped forward, and the microphone sent her voice crisp and clear. "Thank you for joining us this morning as we celebrate the life of Sadie Janette Loman, who left a mark on this town and all who knew her."

People bowed their heads, the low murmur of voices falling to silence.

Forgive me, Sadie.

I continued on, pushing past the edge of the crowd—rounding the curve and heading up the incline of Landing Lane.

I peered over my shoulder once, but no one was in sight. No one could see where I was going.

Grant and Bianca's car was gone—they must've driven down to Breaker Beach together. It was an easy walk except for the slope of the road, which made it near impossible in dress shoes.

Though I'd seen them all down at the dedication ceremony, I peered in the front windows first, hands cupped around my eyes. The lights were off, and there was no movement inside. I rang the bell, then counted to ten before using the key they'd never demanded back.

But that turned unnecessary—the door was already unlocked.

The biggest lie of Littleport—a safe place, nothing to fear. As if they were saying even now: *No secrets here*.

"Hello?" I called as I stepped inside. My voice carried through the downstairs.

The house was deserted. But there was evidence of life. A pair of shoes at the entrance, a jacket tossed over a kitchen stool, chairs off-center in the dining room. This time I didn't bother with the downstairs, knowing exactly what I was after.

Upstairs, I ignored the closed door of the master, the light shining into Sadie's untouched room, heading instead for Grant's office. The locked closet. The files.

The desk looked different from last week—the surface cleared, everything organized. As if Grant had taken his rightful spot, relegating Parker elsewhere. I opened the top desk drawer, moving the assortment of flash drives around—and panicked.

I couldn't find any key.

Someone must've used it recently or hidden it. I stared out the office window and started tearing open the drawers one by one. Empty, empty, empty.

My pulse raced. In desperation, I ran my hands against the underside of the desk drawers, searching for anything. My heart jumped as my nails snagged on a metal bracket, a tiny compartment. I ran my fingers over the surface until I felt the button, and a small drawer popped forward.

I gripped the key firmly in my palm.

Leave it to Grant to put everything back where it belonged. Cleaning up the mess and disorder of his son.

Now I stood in front of that closet with purpose. Pulling out the bound files, stacking them on Grant's desk.

Faith had never made it this far. She'd sneaked inside, just as we'd done years earlier, but this time with a purpose. She'd told me she was looking for something—anything. Something she could

317

use against the Lomans. But she had not gotten to this. The charity files, the blueprints. The purchase details of the rental properties.

In here were only the things concerning Littleport. I knew what had irked me, had me coming back to this closet once more: a medical file. For things that must've happened here.

I flipped open the bound folder marked *Medical*. Inside were the records from private doctor visits coordinated by people like the Lomans—home visits, so they wouldn't have to wait in the lobby of urgent care. Anything, for a price.

The first thing I saw was the record for Sadie's strep test two summers ago. Behind that, an angry rash from a reaction to her new sunscreen. Then a cough that lingered in Grant until Bianca made the call herself, surprising him when the doctor showed up mid-workday. Courses of treatment, a history for their records.

I moved back in time, years passing, until a word grabbed my attention—*stitches*. It was only one sheet, scarce on details.

Parker's name and date of birth. A diagnosis of laceration. A treatment summary. There was a note about signs to watch out for, a possible concussion. A prescription painkiller. A referral to a plastic surgeon should he need one. My hands started shaking.

And there, at the bottom, beside the doctor's signature, was the date. Two days after my parents' accident. As if the Lomans had tried to keep it hidden, avoid suspicion, before they realized they would have to get their son medical attention.

I wondered if that was why he had the scar—if they had waited too long, making sure the investigation was deemed a single-car accident first.

Maybe the second payment that Sadie had copied on the flash drive had gone to him, this doctor who knew that Parker had been significantly injured, and was paid, in turn, for his silence. Who was rewarded for not asking too many questions.

This was it. As close as I could get to the proof. I looked out the window, but the driveway was empty. I took a picture of this document with Parker's injury, including the date of treatment, and I sent it to Detective Ben Collins's number, with a note: *I need to talk to you about Parker Loman.*

Then I sent Connor a text: *Is the ceremony still going on?*

I checked the window again. Still no car.

I started stacking the files away again, then stopped. I didn't care if they knew. Grant's words in my ear, a cruel whisper—that he had overestimated me. Like Faith, I wanted them to know. Who else would know better where to look than someone they had taken into their home?

My life had diverged because of them. Everything I'd lost, because of them.

My phone dinged with a response. Not from the detective but from Connor: *It's almost over. Where are you?*

I wanted to see Connor, to tell him. He may have kept Faith's secrets, but he'd also kept mine. And after everything, he deserved to know the truth.

But I needed to find Detective Collins first, ask to speak at the police station, present everything I'd found—calmly, clearly. I didn't know for sure who'd killed Sadie. Couldn't prove yet that it was Parker—but I had his motive now. The most important thing was that they believe me.

I had gathered up my things, ready to go, when a door closed somewhere in the house.

I froze, my hands hovering over the desk. I didn't even breathe. Footsteps on the stairs, and I looked frantically for somewhere to hide. The only place hidden from view was the closet, and all of the paperwork was already out. If the footsteps veered the other way down the hall, I could make a run for it—

319

"Avery?" The voice was so close. A man. Not Parker. Not Grant. There was no point in hiding. Whoever it was, he was already looking for me.

And then Detective Ben Collins stood in the open office doorway, his forehead knotted in confusion. His eyes scanned the desk, my hands hovering over the top. He took a step into the room. "What are you doing in this house?"

I swallowed nothing, my throat parched. "Did you get my text?"

"Yes," he said, moving closer to the desk. "And I saw you heading this way earlier. You didn't answer my question. What are you doing in here?"

I was breaking and entering, and he'd found me. He knew what I'd been looking through and where to find me. Cornered me and caught me red-handed.

"Wait," I begged, hands held out in front of me. "Just wait, please." I had to show him right then, before he could change his mind, bring me in, call the Lomans, and I'd never stand a chance. The Lomans could ruin anyone. "I have to show you something." I rifled through my bag, pulled out everything I'd brought with me. Trying to clear some space on the desk. "Here's what I sent you," I said, holding out the medical form for Parker. "See?"

His forehead was scrunched in concentration as he read the document. "I don't know what I'm looking at here."

"This is evidence that Parker was hurt the same time my parents died in a car accident."

He stared at me, green eyes catching the light from the window. I couldn't read his expression, whether he believed me, whether he was putting things together himself.

"Sadie," I said, handing him the flash drive, my throat scratching on her name. "She found evidence that her family paid off my grandmother after my parents' death. One hundred thousand dollars. It's here."

He took it from me, frowning. Turning it over in his hand.

"I have more," I said. I had everything. I tallied the evidence, pushed the folder I'd brought across the desk in his direction. The matching account number from my grandmother's checkbook. It had to be enough. "There's proof that my grandmother paid down her mortgage with this money right after their death. And," I said, taking out my phone, my hand shaking, "proof that Sadie was hurt at the party last year. Detective, she was *there*." I pulled up the photos I'd just taken, handed him my phone, the words tumbling out too fast. Trying to walk him through the course of events—the blood-stain from the bathroom, my belief that someone had taken her from the house, wrapped her in a blanket, lost her phone in the process.

"They used my car. My trunk," I said, a sob caught in my throat. "The crime scene was *there*. Not here. She didn't jump."

The corners of his mouth tipped down, and he shook his head. "Avery, you have to slow down."

But that wasn't right. I had to speed up. Sadie didn't want a fucking bell, a sad quote. She wanted *this*. To be seen. To be avenged. And he wasn't paying attention. What did I need to do to get him to see?

He stared at the photos on my phone, his hand faintly shaking as well, like I'd transferred my fear straight to him. His eyes drifted to the window behind me, and I knew what he was thinking—the Lomans would be back soon.

He had to believe me before they arrived.

"There have to be people in the department who remember the accident," I said. "Who know something. It was a long time ago, but people remember." It was horrific, that was what the first officer on the scene said. I had the article with me in that folder on the desk. "Maybe we can talk to the person who was first on-scene. Maybe there's some evidence that didn't make sense." Another piece of proof to link the cases together.

I opened the folder, pulled out the article—so he would remember. Detective Collins had once told me that he knew who I was, what I'd been through—that it was a shitty hand to draw. He was older than me. He must've remembered this.

"Can I . . ." He cleared his throat, holding up my phone. "Can I hang on to this?"

I nodded, and he tucked my phone into his pocket, then pulled out a pack of cigarettes, sliding one out, a lighter in the other hand. "Bad habit, I know," he said. His hand shook as he flicked the lighter twice before it caught. A slow exhale of smoke, eyes closed. "Sometimes it helps, though."

I imagined the smoke soaking into the Lomans' walls, the ornate carpet beneath our feet. How they'd hate it. I almost spoke, on instinct, and then stopped. Who cared?

In the article, there was a black-and-white picture of the road—how had I not seen it before, the same image Sadie had taken on her phone? The arc of trees, so different in the daylight—but it matched.

The article also had a picture of the wreckage left behind. The metal heap of a car crumpled against a tree. My heart squeezed, and I had to close my eyes, even after all these years.

I skimmed over sentences, paragraphs, until the part I remembered—that had been seared into my mind years earlier.

"The first officer on the scene gave a statement to the reporter," I said. Reading the words that I'd wanted to forget for so long. "Here it is. *'There was nothing I could do. It was just terrible. Horrific. I thought we had lost them all, but when the EMTs arrived, they discovered the woman in the backseat was still alive. Just unconscious.' The loss will be felt by everyone in the community, including the young officer—*"

I stopped reading, the room hollowing out. Couldn't finish. Couldn't say the words. Watched, instead, as everything shifted.

He raised his eyebrows, flicked the lighter again. Held it to the base of Parker's medical paper, letting it catch fire and fall into the stainless-steel trash can.

I stared once more down at the article in my hand. The truth, always inches away, just waiting for me to look again.

The unfinished sentence, our paths crossing over and over, unseen, unknown. *Officer Ben Collins.*

CHAPTER 29

Smoke spilled *from the* top of the garbage can, the air dangerous and alive. "You knew," I said, stepping back.

Detective Ben Collins stood between me and the doorway, not meeting my eye. Systematically dropping page after page
into the trash. Each piece of evidence I'd given him, every piece
of proof. One after another into the burning trash. He had my
phone. My flash drive. The evidence of the payments—

The other payment, the one Sadie had found and copied, stored
on the flash drive alongside the payment to my grandmother. That
had gone to him. "The Lomans paid you off, too," I said.

Finally, he looked at me. A man cut into angles, into negative
space. "It was an accident. If it helps, he didn't mean to do it. Some
kid speeding past me, driving like a bat out of hell in the middle
of the night. I didn't know it was Parker Loman when I took off
after him—he didn't see the other car coming. The lights must've

blinded them to the curve. Both of them ended up off the road, but the other car . . ."

"The other *car*—" I choked out. My *parents*. There were people inside. People who had been taken from me.

How long had he waited to call the EMTs after Parker Loman stepped from the car? Had Parker asked him to wait while he pressed his hand to the cut on his forehead, seeing what he had done? Or had Grant Loman called in, explained things, convinced him to let his son go—that there was nothing to be done now, no use ruining another life in the process—a plea but also a threat?

Had my parents bled out while he waited? Did they fight it, the darkness, while a young Ben Collins weighed his own life and chose?

The garbage can crackled, a heat between us as we stood on opposite ends of the desk.

"Avery, listen, we were all young."

I understood that, didn't I? The terrible choices we made without clarity of thought. On instinct, on emotion, or in a drastic move, just to get things to stop. To change.

"I think about it often," he said. "I think we all do. And now we're doing the best we can, all of us. It was terrible, but the Lomans have supported this town through thick and thin, giving back whenever they can. I made a decision when I was twenty-three, and I've been trying to make peace with it ever since." He held one hand out to the side. "I've given *everything* to this place."

His eyes were wide now, like he was begging me to see it—the person reflected in his eyes. The better person he had become. It was true, if I gave it any thought—he was always the person involved, who volunteered. Who organized the parades, the events. The person people asked to join committees. But all I could see was the lie. It had been built into the very fabric of who he was now.

"They're *dead*!" I was yelling then. Finally, a place to direct my anger. Instead of sinking further into myself. Instead of succumbing to the spiral that caught me and refused to let go.

He flinched. "What do you want, Avery?" Matter-of-fact. Like everything in life was a negotiation.

I shook my head. He was so calm, and the crackle of the flames was eating away at the air, destroying everything again.

I needed to get out of this room, but he was blocking the way.

He stepped to the side, and I instinctively moved back, toward the wall. "We'll talk to Grant, work something out. Okay?" he said.

But he had it wrong. Of course he couldn't do that.

"Sadie," I said, finally understanding. Her flaw was my own—she'd trusted the wrong person. My life was her life. She must've taken this same path, landed at his name—and believed he would tell her the truth. "You killed her," I whispered, hand to my mouth at the truth, at the horror.

He had been the man who had brought her to the party. The man no one had seen.

His eyes drifted shut, and he winced. "No," he said. But it was desperate, a plea.

I could see it playing out, what she would do—three steps back, finding Ben Collins in the article, just like I had done. Asking him to pick her up, directing him to the party. Sadie, empowered by what she'd uncovered, believing she had everyone right where she wanted them—for one final, fatal strike. She'd hidden away the money trail; all she needed was him. The money she had stolen from the company—for this. For him. Never seeing the danger in the places where it truly existed. "All she wanted from you was the truth," I said.

He blinked twice, face stoic, before speaking. "What good would that do now? I'd be burying all of us. And for what? We can't change the past."

For what? How could he ask that? For justice. For my parents. For me.

To say the truth—that Parker had been responsible for the death of my parents. Because inside that family was a perpetual power struggle, and Sadie must've finally seen a way to bring down her brother. A calculated, fatal move.

But something else had happened behind that locked door during the party. She had misjudged him. Had she pled her case, offered the money, believing he was on her side—before he struck? Or had they argued, the danger slowly shifting from words to violence, until it was too late?

"The blood in the bathroom. You *hurt* her," I said in a whisper. Not a car inadvertently driving another off the road. But hands and fists on flesh and bone.

"She slipped," he said. "It was an accident," he repeated. "I didn't know what to do, and I panicked. None of it would bring her back."

But his words were empty, hollow lies. Sadie was breathing. He had to have known she was breathing. Otherwise, why bring her to the cliffs? The water in her lungs, the fact that it could look like a suicide, the placement of her shoes—the last step of his cover-up. His cool, crisp mind, planning to end one life in order to save what was left of his.

Had the Lomans turned him into a killer years ago? Making him complicit, shifting the line of his own morality until he could justify even this?

He flipped the flash drive into his palm again, tucked it in his pocket. "She told me there was someone else who had the proof. I always thought it was you."

Only it hadn't been me. It was Connor, though he didn't know it. That must've been why Sadie had wanted him at the party, had brought them both there. Safety in knowledge, in numbers. In a crowd.

There was nothing left on the desk but the article about my parents' accident. Like he was erasing all traces of Sadie once more.

"She was awake," I said. "She tried to get out of the trunk. I have proof." Something he could not destroy in this room.

Everything changed then. His face, the smoke, the crackle of flames.

"Your trunk," he said, monotone. "The phone *you* found, the person *you* were fighting with, evidence in *your* trunk. The daughter of the family who just *fired* you. You do not want to do this, trust me." As if I were a nothing. Powerless, then and now. The person he would blame. The person who would pay.

Now I understood why he kept questioning us about the party. Looking for who might've seen him or Sadie. Who might've seen him bringing her limp body out front. Who could've seen him throwing her from the bluffs, or returning my car after, or walking back for his own in the lot of the B&B.

And then I was there. He saw me on the cliffs while he was "finding" her shoes. His prints would be on them if he was the one who found them. He'd said the same thing about me when I'd brought him Sadie's phone.

That was why he had asked me, over and over, about that night. Why he'd watched me so closely during the interview, looking for what I was hiding. He was terrified that I knew more than I was saying.

The last piece of the puzzle. The unspoken question he was asking that night: Had I seen *him*?

"Just tell me what you want," he said, reaching for the article on the desk.

"Stop," I said, and I grasped for it myself—such a stupid thing to cling to. I could find another one in print or in records. But it was the fact that something was being taken from me again, without my permission.

I had the paper in my grip, but he lunged in my direction, grabbing my arm.

Crystal-clear.

This man had killed Sadie for knowing the truth. I would not get a chance to prove my innocence, to present my side of the case. He had killed to protect himself—nothing more. And now I was the threat.

I jerked back, his fingers slipping away, and raced around the desk for the door. He lunged in my direction again, knocking the garbage can, the papers tumbling out in a trail of embers and flame. Catching on the ornate rug. His eyes widened.

I ran. Stumbling out of the room with Ben Collins steps behind me. He called my name, and the smell of smoke followed. He'd catch me too easily on the stairs—the open, airy spiral. I dove into the nearest room, slammed the door behind me.

Sadie's room.

There were no locks. And nowhere to hide, everything designed to show the clean lines of the place. The bare wood floor under the bed. The open space. No place for secrets here.

The fire alarm started blaring, an even, high-pitched cry.

Maybe the fire department would come. But not soon enough.

I pulled open her glass balcony doors, let the fabric billow in. It was too far to jump. The only room you could jump from safely was the master bedroom, with the slope of grass beneath their balcony—which Connor, Faith, and I had climbed through years ago.

It was all I could do to flatten myself against the wall by her bedroom door before it flew open again. Ben Collins walked straight for the open doors to the patio, leaning over—peering out. And I took that moment to dart down the hall in the other direction.

He must've heard my steps—everything echoed here—because

he called my name again, his voice booming over the sound of the fire alarm.

But I was at the other end of the hall, smoke spilling out of the office between us.

Slamming the door to the master bedroom, I raced for the balcony. One leg over the railing, hanging from my fingertips, imagining Connor below, my feet on his shoulders. A six-foot drop. I could do it.

I heard the door open as I let go, the impact from the ground jarring me. I stumbled, then righted myself and ran for the cliff path. I was already calling for help, but my pleas were swallowed up by the crash of the waves.

"Stop!" he called, too close—close enough to hear not only his words but his footsteps. "Do not run from me!"

Witnesses. All I could think was *witnesses*. Sadie had been behind a locked door, inside a locked trunk. No one had been there to see her go.

I was not a criminal running from the cops. I was not what his story would make me.

The outline of a man emerged near the edge of the cliff path, and I almost collided with him before he came into focus. Parker. "What's going—"

I reeled back, and Detective Collins froze, mere steps away from the both of us. The water crashed against the rocks behind us. The steps down to Breaker Beach were so close, within sight—

"He killed her!" I yelled. I wanted someone else to hear, someone else to see us.

"What?" Parker was looking from me to the detective, back to the house—where the blare of the fire alarm just barely reached us.

"She knows about the crash," Detective Collins said, breathing heavily. Deflecting, refocusing. I looked between the two of them, wondering if I had only doubled the danger. What each would do to keep his secrets. The detective's hands were on his hips as he strained to catch his breath, his arms pushing his coat aside, revealing a gun.

Parker turned to me, his dark eyes searching. "An accident," he said, the words barely formed. Barely falling from his lips. The same thing Detective Collins had said, that Parker's parents must've said—the lines Parker clung to. Still, I noticed, the thing he didn't say. Neither he nor his sister ever capable of an apology.

Parker looked at the detective. "You told her?"

"Sadie knew," I said before he could answer. No one had told me. Sadie had led me there. My steps in her steps. But now it was just the three of us here, and the violent sea below, all the terrible secrets it kept. "She found out the truth, and he killed her."

The detective shook his head, stepping closer. "No, listen . . ."

Parker blinked as a wave crashed below. "What did you say, Avery?"

But I never got the chance to respond.

The detective must've seen it in Parker's eyes, the same as me. The sudden burst of rage, the anger gathering, until something else was surging through his blood. Detective Collins reached for his gun just as Parker lunged.

I couldn't say who moved first. Which was the action and which the reaction. Only that Parker was on him in the moment his gun was in his hand—but he never got a grip on it, never pointed it wherever it was intended to go.

The surge in the marrow of his bones, the fulcrum on which his life balanced, as he pushed Ben Collins backward and the gun fell from his grip, hitting the rock.

A shot, ricocheting up. A sound that split the silence, that gave us all pause. A flock of birds rising at the same time as all our lives shifted—the tipping point. I saw it first in the widening of Ben Collins's eyes. The desperate reach of his empty hands toward me. His feet stumbling once, twice, as the momentum carried him backward, into the air.

I watched. The color of his shirt disappearing over the edge. And then nothing, nothing, nothing more. Just the sound of the water colliding with the rocks below.

And that was when I heard the scream.

And saw all the people of Littleport, gathered below on the beach, turn our way, to bear witness.

CHAPTER 30

n the distance, a buoy bell tolled. A hawk cried, circling above. The water crashed in a surge against the rocks. Time kept moving.

"It was an accident," Parker said, sliding to the ground as the people came running.

All these accidents.

The first officer arrived on the bluffs, racing from the road, calling for others to get back.

There were shouts from below, people wading into the water from the beach. But it was too late, and we all knew that.

"No one move," the policeman said as he took in the scene. I recognized him then—Officer Paul Chambers, the other man who had interviewed us last year.

Officer Chambers looked at the house in the distance, the smoke rising. Then at Parker, heaving on the ground, holding his arm.

"He killed Sadie," Parker said. "He was going to hurt Avery." Looking at me, pleading. A negotiation, even then. "He had a gun. I had to do it. I had to stop him."

Never had I felt such power, in the moments he held his breath, and everyone was watching. I did not confirm, I did not deny.

I felt Parker's gaze on the side of my face. Heard his desperate whisper. *Please.*

"No more talking, Parker." That was Grant, his voice cutting through the spectators' in warning.

There were faces I knew in the crowd. The Sylvas, the Harlows, the Lomans—Grant was on his phone as Parker sat there, holding his arm. Connor pushed his way to the front of the group, but another officer had arrived, keeping everyone back. There were sirens. More shouts from below. A directive to move the cars, move the people—that emergency vehicles could not get through. Behind us, the smoke had reached the open balcony doors of the second floor, billowing out.

The Loman house was burning, someone was dead, and we were still on the ledge.

"You killed my parents," I said. Loud enough that others could hear. Not only Officer Chambers but the people who had gathered, watching. Connor, Faith, Grant and Bianca.

Parker winced, shaking his head, though we both knew the truth.

"I know you did. And Sadie is dead because she found out, too." All these people I'd lost could be traced back to him, and I wanted him to pay.

Parker kept shaking his head. He remained silent, as his father had instructed. Even as he was told to stand. Even as the handcuffs clinched behind his back. Parker's eyes drifted side to side as he was led through the crowd, as if desperate for someone to fix this.

He went quietly, head lowered. A man, just like any other.

———

AT THE STATION, I gave them everything. But I had lost so much to both the fire and the sea.

The evidence had burned. My phone. The flash drive. It was all gone. But I'd copied the file of the flash drive to my laptop. And I'd transferred Sadie's photos from her phone as well. Officer Chambers looked surprised at the mention of Sadie's phone—it seemed that Ben Collins had kept this information to himself, never mentioning the discovery of the phone to anyone else.

I didn't know whether it was enough, the things we had left.

———

AFTER, I STOOD IN the lobby of the police station with nothing. My car and my laptop would have to stay with them as evidence. I asked the receptionist to use the phone, but I couldn't think of a single number by heart.

"Avery." I turned at the sound of Connor's voice. Saw the truck behind him through the glass windows, parked haphazardly, like he'd been waiting.

I didn't ask where we were going as I buckled myself in— didn't know where *to* go right then. But when Connor turned up the overlook, I knew.

He parked in the gravel lot of the B&B, turned off the engine. A box of my things was already on the front porch. Connor pushed his door open but paused before stepping out.

"End of the season, there's always room."

335

SUMMER
2019

First Day of Summer

Through the open windows, I could hear the waves crashing against the rocks. The wind blowing in off the coast, the leaves rustling overhead.

Sunlight flickered through the open curtains as the branches swayed above.

I took down the glasses, pulled out the bottles and the plates of food from the fridge. Shook out the cushions, dragged a few extra chairs around back. Getting everything ready.

They'd be arriving soon, up the drive of Landing Lane.

—

THE HOUSE COULD NOT be salvaged. It shouldn't have been built in the first place. Sadie had hinted at this years ago: It wasn't safe. Not something this size, that stretched beyond the easements. They'd paid around the permits the first time. It would not happen again.

There's still a footprint if you know where to look. Where the grass is a finer, paler green. A slight dip in the dirt where the pool used to be.

But from the guesthouse, it's just a quirk of nature, a clearing of trees before the rocks. A stunning, unobstructed view that greets me each morning.

A reward, for a risk.

———

I HEARD, THROUGH OTHERS in town, that Parker had worked out a deal. Heard he was confined to house arrest. Heard he wore an ankle monitor. Heard he was removed from the company.

Most of these were probably rumors. All I cared was that he was gone. And that they would not be coming back.

In the winter, after I sold the plots on the overlook, I offered a low but fair price for this property. It's not like anyone could rebuild up here. Only the guesthouse was set back per the guidelines. But that was all I needed.

I took this property for the view itself, looking out over all of Littleport and everything I'd ever known.

My one regret is I didn't get to see Grant's face when he realized what I had done.

———

IN THE WINTER OF last year, I'd sold everything I had to the Sylvas. A strip of plots up on the overlook that I'd been holding on to for myself. All hidden under the name of an LLC.

I'd started investing years earlier with the money from the sale of my grandmother's house. Cash from the Lomans themselves when they bought my grandmother's place. Bianca was the only one who ever asked where my money had gone. Grant, it seemed, wasn't paying attention.

There was nothing in my contract with the Lomans that

prevented me from setting out on my own. Making my own investments. So I took that first sum and invested it with a small group in a plot of land a few towns up the coast.

We'd flipped it, each took our share of the proceeds, kept moving.

I had an eye for it and the guts to do it. And apparently, those were the two main ingredients of success. To risk everything for a chance.

It was the start of a new season in Littleport, and we were here today to toast the beginning of something—a joint venture with Faith, renting out their new properties.

Greg Randolph had once called me Sadie's monster, but he was wrong. If I were anyone's monster, I supposed, I was Grant's.

Taking everything he'd taught me, investing that initial money with no fallback. Risking everything, over and over, on investment properties in towns up and down the coast. Believing there was something that would keep people coming—the power of the ocean, the vastness of it, the secrets it promised—and they did.

It was reckless, maybe, with no fallback, and no promises.

But Littleport has always been the type of place that favors the bold.

ACKNOWLEDGMENTS

Thank you to everyone who helped see this project from its earliest idea to the final book:

My agent, Sarah Davies, for all of the wonderful support, on this and every book.

My editors, Karyn Marcus and Marysue Rucci, for the sharp insight, guidance, and encouragement at every step along the way, from first idea to finished product. And to the entire team at Simon & Schuster, including Richard Rhorer, Jonathan Karp, Zack Knoll, Amanda Lang, Elizabeth Breeden, and Marie Florio. I'm so fortunate to get to work with you all!

Thank you also to my critique partners, Megan Shepherd, Ashley Elston, and Elle Cosimano, for all of your feedback and support.

And lastly, as always, to my family.

Read on for an extract from…

THE GIRL FROM WIDOW HILLS

PROLOGUE

I WAS THE GIRL WHO survived.

The girl who held on. The girl you prayed for, or at least pretended to pray for—thankful most of all that it wasn't your own child lost down there, in the dark.

And after: I was the miracle. The sensation. The story.

The story was what people wanted, and oh, it was a good one. Proof of humanity, and hope, and the power of the human spirit. After coming so close to tragedy, the public reaction bordered on rapturous, when it wasn't. Whether from joy or pure shock, the result was the same.

I was famous for a little while. The subject of articles, interviews, a book. It became a news story revisited after a year, then five, then ten.

I knew, now, what happened when you turned your story over to someone else. How you became something different, twisted to fit the confines of the page. Something to be consumed instead.

That girl is frozen in time, with her beginning, middle, and end: victim, endurance, triumph.

It was a good story. A good feeling. A good ending.

Fade to black.

As if, when the daily news moved on, and the articles ended, and the conversations turned, it was all over. As if it weren't just beginning.

THERE WAS A TIME when I knew what they were after. Reaching back to that cultural touchpoint, whenever someone would say: *The girl from Widow Hills, remember?*

That sudden rush of fear and hope and relief, all at once.

A good feeling.

I HAVEN'T BEEN THAT girl in a long time.

CHAPTER 1

Wednesday, 7 p.m.

THE BOX SAT AT the foot of the porch step, in a small clearing of dirt where grass still refused to grow. Cardboard sides left exposed to the elements, my full name written in black marker, the edge of my address just starting to bleed. It fit on my hip, like a child.

I knew she was gone before I woke.

The first line of my mother's book, the same thing she allegedly told the police when they first arrived. A sentiment repeated in every media interview in the months after the accident, her words transmitted directly into millions of living rooms across the country.

Nearly twenty years later, and this was the refrain now echoing in my head as I carried the box up the wooden porch stairs. The catch in her voice. That familiar cadence.

I shut and locked the front door behind me, took the delivery down the arched hall to the kitchen table. The contents shifted inside, nearly weightless.

It clattered against the table when I set it down, more noise than substance. I went straight for the drawer beside the sink, didn't prolong the moment to let it gather any more significance.

Box cutter through the triple-layer tape. Corners softened from the moisture still clinging to the ground from yesterday's rain. The lid wedged tight over the top. A chilled darkness within.

I knew she was gone—

Her words were cliché at best, an untruth at worst—a story crafted in hindsight.

Maybe she truly believed it. I rarely did, unless I was feeling generous—which, at the moment, staring into the sad contents of this half-empty box, I was. Right then, I wanted to believe—believe that, at one point, there had been a tether between my soul and hers, and she could feel something in the absence: a prickle at her neck, her call down the dim hallway that always felt humid, even in winter; my name—*Arden?*—echoing off the walls, even though she knew—*she just knew*—there would be no answer; the front door already ajar—the first true sign—and the screen door banging shut behind her as she ran barefoot into the wet grass, still in flannel pajama pants and a fraying, faded T-shirt, screaming my name until her throat went raw. Until the neighbors came. The police. The media.

It was pure intuition. The second line of her book. She knew I was gone. Of course she knew.

Now I wish I could've said the same.

Instead of the truth: that my mother had been gone for seven months before I knew it. Knew that she hadn't just disappeared on a binge, or had her phone disconnected for nonpayment, or found some guy and slipped into his life instead, shedding the skin of her previous one, while I'd just been grateful I hadn't heard from her in so long.

There was always this lingering fear that, no matter how far I went, no matter how many layers I put between us, she would appear one day like an apparition: that I'd step outside on my way to work one morning, and there she would be, looming on the front porch despite her size, with a too-wide smile and too-skinny arms. Throwing her bony arms around my neck and laughing as if I'd summoned her.

In reality, it took seven months for the truth to reach me, a slow grind of paperwork, and her, always, slipping to the bottom of the pile. An overdose in a county overrun with overdoses, in a state in the middle of flyover country, buried under a growing epidemic. No license in her possession, no address. Unidentified, until somehow they uncovered her name.

Maybe someone came looking for her—a man, face interchangeable with any other man's. Maybe her prints hit on something new in the system. I didn't know, and it didn't matter.

However it happened, they eventually matched her name: Laurel Maynor. And then she waited some more. Until someone looked twice, dug deeper. Maybe she'd been at a hospital sometime in the preceding years; maybe she'd written my name as a contact.

Or perhaps there was no tangible connection at all but a tug at their memory: *Wasn't she that girl's mother? The girl from Widow Hills?* Remembering the story, the headlines. Pulling out my name, tracing it across time and distance through the faintest trail of paperwork.

When the phone rang and they asked for me by my previous name, the one I never used anymore and hadn't since high school, it still hadn't sunk in. I hadn't even had the foresight in the moment before they said it. *Is this Arden Maynor, daughter of Laurel Maynor?*

Ms. Maynor, I'm afraid we have some bad news.

Even then I thought of something else. My mother, locked up inside a cell, asking me to come bail her out. I had been preparing myself for the wrong emotion, gritting my jaw, steeling my conviction—

5

She had been dead for seven months, they said. The logistics already taken care of on the county's dime, after remaining unclaimed for so long. She would no longer need me for anything. There was just the small matter of her personal effects left behind, to collect. It was a relief, I was sure, for them to be able to cross her off their list when they scrawled my address over the top of all that was left, triple-sealing it with packing tape, and shipping it halfway across the country, to me.

There was an envelope resting inside the box, an impersonal tally of the contents held within: *Clothing; canvas bag; phone; jewelry*. But the only item of clothing inside was a green sweater, tattered, with holes at the ends of the sleeves, which I assumed she must've been wearing. I didn't want to imagine how bad a state the rest of her clothes must have been in, if this was the only thing worth sending. Then: an empty bag that was more like a tote, the teeth of the zipper in place but missing the clasp. There once were words printed on the outside, but everything was a gray-blue smudge now, faded and illegible. Under that, the phone. I turned it over in my hand: a flip phone, old and scratched. Probably from ten years earlier, a pay-as-you-go setup.

And at the bottom, inside a plastic bag, a bracelet. I held it in my palm, let the charm fall over the side of my hand, so that it swung from its chain that once had been gold but had since oxidized in sections to a greenish-black. The charm, a tiny ballet slipper, was dotted with the smallest glimmer of stone at the center of the bow.

I held my breath, the charm swinging like a metronome, keeping time even as the world went still. A piece of our past that somehow remained, that she'd never sold.

Even the dead could surprise you.

In that moment, holding the fine bracelet, I felt something snap tight in my chest, bridging the gap, the divide. Something between this world and the next.

The bracelet slipped from my palm onto the table, coiling up like a snake. I reached my hands into the bottom of the box again, stretched my fingers into the corners, searching for more.

There was nothing left. The light in the room shifted, as if the curtains had moved. Maybe it was just the trees outside, casting shadows. My own field of vision darkening in a spell of dizziness. I tried to focus, grabbing the edge of the table to hold myself steady. But I heard a rushing sound, as if the room were hollowing itself out.

And I felt it then, just like she said—an emptiness, an absence. The darkness, opening up.

All that remained inside the box was a scent, like earth. I pictured cold rocks and stagnant water—four walls closing in—and took an unconscious step toward the door.

Twenty years ago, I was the girl who had been swept away in the middle of the night during a storm: into the system of pipes under the wooded terrain of Widow Hills. But I'd survived, against all odds, enduring the violence of the surge, keeping my head above water until the flooding mercilessly receded, eventually making my way toward the daylight, grabbing on to a grate—where I was ultimately found. It had taken nearly three days to find me, but the memory of that time was long gone. Lost to youth, or to trauma, or to self-preservation. My mind protecting me, until I couldn't pull the memory to the surface, even if I wanted to. All that remained was the fear. Of closed walls, of an endless dark, of no way out. An instinct in place of a memory.

My mother used to call us both survivors. For a long time, I believed her.

The scent was probably nothing but the cardboard itself, left exposed to the damp earth and chilled evening. The outside of my own home, brought in.

But for a second, I remembered, like I hadn't back then or

7

ever since. I remembered the darkness and the cold and my small hand gripped tight on a rusted metal grate. I remembered my own ragged breathing in the silence, and something else, far away. An almost sound. Like I could hear the echo of a yell, my name carried on the wind into the unfathomable darkness—across the miles, under the earth, where I waited to be found.